The Lister Legacy

THE LISTER LEGACY

Jan Drabek

Beaufort Books, Inc.

NEW YORK   TORONTO

Cataloging in Publication Data

Drabek, Jan, 1935-
  The Lister Legacy

ISBN 0-8253-0015-0

1. World War, 1939-1945 - Fiction. I. Title.

PS8557.R32L58 813'.54 C80-094015-6

Cover design
  Maher and Murtagh

Photo
  Paterson Photographic Works

First published in 1980 in the United States by Beaufort Books Inc., New York

Printed in Canada   First Printing

ISBN 0-8253-0015-0

To the memory of those who have died
and to those who are ready to die
in their efforts to bring democracy
back to my native country.

Part One:
The Mission

1

Kriminalinspektor Ernst Kamm of the Zamberk detachment of the Geheime Staatspolizei, commonly referred to as the Gestapo, didn't expect too much of the man. A peasant girl had come in the night before to say that her employer had hidden at least 200 kilograms of flour. According to her story, he had had it ground and then had hidden it somewhere. But they had spent a good three hours ransacking the farm on the outskirts of Lisnice and found nothing. Now the farmer (Kamm had some time ago forgotten his unpronounceable name) lay on the floor in front of him in the basement room they used for interrogations. He was unconscious. The last blow to his solar plexus by Corporal Röhmer had been a bit too strong.

Inspector Kamm gazed at the limp body without much interest. It had happened so many times before that it had become tedious. Obviously the farmer had said or done something to the girl and she took vengeance on him. Could even have been a lovers' quarrel; who knows about these Czechs? There was also a small chance that the farmer was a good actor and that the flour was safely stashed away. They should get the girl and ask her a few questions, but even that would probably be a waste of time. But there was value in reminding the

Czechs of the Gestapo's presence. The farmer with his black and blue marks would serve that purpose.

The drudgery of the process and its crudity were beginning to get on Kamm's nerves. The food-hoarding populace, the use of the Gestapo to settle their peasant feuds, their hateful stares, the poverty-stricken region with its stone-filled fields and emaciated cattle — it was all filled with a dreariness he had never come across in the Rhineland. He longed to get away from it.

"Röhmer," he said, touching the body of the unconscious farmer with the tip of his boot, "pour some water over him and get him cleaned up. Then get him out of here."

"Release him, sir?" the corporal's eyes widened in surprise.

"Yes," Kamm repeated impatiently. "Get rid of him."

On his way up the steps Kamm turned around.

"Tell the men they can have the evening off, but one of you stay on duty. Tell him where the rest of you will be so I can get you together on a moment's notice."

He gave the instructions although he knew they were unnecessary. The German soldiers would be at the pub across the square; that's how far their imaginations extended. They would be at the same old table, re-telling the same lies about their sexual prowess to each other because no one else would sit with them. Even the tables near them would be empty.

Upstairs Kamm poured himself a glass of wine and rested his foot on a stool which he pulled closer to his armchair. It was time to get out of Zamberk. Time to leave it all behind and to head west, back to the Rhineland. Soon things wouldn't be so pleasant for Germans outside the Reich. The phone rang and Kamm let it ring a couple of times before he moved.

It was Leimer in Prague.

"Kamm? Listen carefully," he shouted into the receiver, knowing well the unreliability of long distance telephone connections.

"There'll be all sorts of trucks arriving in your area in the next few days. I want you take care of the trucks *and* their drivers. Understand?"

"Where will they be arriving from, sir?" Kamm asked. Aside from being wildly indiscreet over the phone, Leimer felt that Kamm was disturbing his train of thought.

"From all over. It's not important. Spread them out across the countryside, not too many at one place. And keep the drivers near their trucks. Put them up at farmhouses and places like that, understand?"

"Yes sir."

"In a few days they'll contact you and then you will know where to direct the trucks."

"Yes sir. Pardon me, sir, but *who* will contact me?"

There was a pause.

"Probably someone from the Reich."

"Yes sir," replied Kamm. And, astonished at his boldness, he heard himself asking:

"Sir, does this have anything to do with Adam Hill?"

"No!" Leimer shouted into the phone. Then he paused a moment. "That's none of your damn business. Make sure that the drivers are put up somewhere near your headquarters so you can reach them quickly. And Kamm, make damn sure that no one unauthorized gets anywhere near the trucks, understand?"

"Yes sir."

"If there are any questions, or if you have anything to report, call me immediately, is that clear? Even if it's in the middle of the night."

"Yes sir."

There was a click and Leimer was off the line. Kamm put down his receiver, full of thought. The trucks were bad news. They must be connected with Adam Hill and whatever it was that was going on there. The hill had been in Sudetenland and now was part of the Reich. The fact that its access roads led through the Czech Protectorate did not make any difference. It was the Reich's affair and up until now it had been mostly handled from there. The trucks constituted a radical departure from that policy. Also a headache for Kamm.

Rumors abounded throughout the region as to what was actually going on at Adam Hill. Maybe it was one of those weapons that the Führer had promised. The war's tide certainly needed turning right now. Leimer was connected with the trucks and was in charge of the antiparachutist and antisabotage section of Prague's Gestapo. That meant someone was worried there could be attempted sabotage. Why? By whom? Kamm doubted that even Leimer knew but the activity on Adam Hill was important enough to take all possible precautions.

He lit a cigarette and settled back into his favorite armchair. He had made a mistake in waiting this long. He should have already been on his way to the Rhineland.

Kriminalinspektor of the Gestapo Ernst Kamm took a sip from his wineglass. He didn't like what was happening. He didn't like it at all.

2

Lieutenant Commander Douglas R. Howard of the Royal Canadian Navy parked his car some distance from the center of town so he could walk the rest of the way. In spite of the occasional sign pointing to an air raid shelter and the strategically placed sandbags, there was an air of serene calmness about the ancient university city, as if Cambridge wanted to say that it had survived worse times through the centuries.

He passed the famous landmarks of Round Church and King's College Chapel, thinking about his own alma mater, Queen's University in Kingston, Canada, built in style somewhat reminiscent of this one. At least half of all those who passed him wore a uniform. The university was being used for military training. Now, in January 1944, only months before the summer which, according to persistent rumors, would be the season for the invasion of the European continent, it was full to capacity.

He made his way to Professor Andrew Summerville's basement laboratory where a white-haired man detached himself from a group of students near a window and started toward the commander.

"Professor Summerville?" The commander

looked into his deeply lined face, "I'm Douglas Howard ..."

"I know," the professor replied quickly while exchanging his white smock for an overcoat. "Maybe we had better go for a walk."

Summerville silently led the way toward a nearby park. Once there, he decreased his pace and looked at the Canadian.

"You want to know if I received the memorandum and if I read it, don't you, commander? The answer to both questions is yes. The arrival of a special courier from the Supreme Allied Headquarters caused quite a stir in the lab. In the future I would advise a less spectacular approach."

Commander Howard smiled.

"I'm sorry professor, but the matter is urgent. By far the most urgent I have been associated with during my entire military career."

"How long has your military career been, commander?"

"Four and a half years."

"Hmm, I was wrong then. I thought you must be relatively new. Your writing seems strangely devoid of all the military jargon which I unfortunately meet so often."

They walked a few steps, Howard waiting for the professor to offer his comments without being coaxed.

"About your memorandum," Summerville finally obliged. "Your extremely frightening proposition is, of course, entirely based on surmise. You have no definite proof, do you?"

"It's called circumstantial evidence, professor. In war we can't always take time to prove things beyond a reasonable doubt. Usually we must act much quicker than that."

"Yes, yes, I am quite aware of that," Summerville agreed absentmindedly. "Before committing myself I merely wished to know if you have come across any other evidence since the memorandum was written."

"No, we haven't. Frankly, I don't think we will. Not unless we have the opportunity to examine the containers thoroughly. And I'm afraid there isn't much chance of that, is there?"

"I suppose not. It is merely that I am not used to venturing opinions with so little evidence.

"Commander Howard," the professor continued, "largely because of this terrible war, science has been able to make progress most of us never dreamt of a few years ago. Bacteriology is no exception. We have made giant strides in our understanding of the behavior of germs. Unfortunately, this understanding can also be used for nefarious purposes, such as those which you describe in your memorandum."

"Then we were right. It would be possible to infest a coastline with bacteria, wouldn't it?"

"Yes, it would. Of course, it would be much easier in warm waters."

"How about the English Channel? Would it be possible there?"

The professor thought a moment again before committing himself. But in the end he decided to plunge in.

"Yes, it would be possible even in the English Channel. Probably for a limited amount of time, nevertheless possible. An incredible amount of technical and scientific expertise would be needed and, of course, almost unlimited funds."

"Do you think the Germans are capable of it? I mean do they have enough of both — money and technical expertise?"

"The acquisition of research funds for human

destruction seems to be no problem anywhere these days, commander."

Howard had hoped for a resoundingly negative answer. The professor noted his disappointment.

"You must understand that while my opinion of the German scientific ability is high I still would not think them capable of succeeding without Robert Tiesenhausen on their side. And they definitely *do* have him on their side. I met him once at a conference in Zurich. He left no doubt in my mind that he is a dedicated, fanatical Nazi. Some suspect that he was to have received the Nobel Prize in 1935 for his work in bacteriology, but the committee was afraid he would insist on appearing at the ceremony in his Nazi uniform. They finally settled for a countryman of his, Hans Spemann ... But you knew all that, didn't you?"

"Knew what, professor?" the commander asked innocently.

"That I knew Tiesenhausen, that I had met him in Zurich."

"We had an inkling," smiled Howard. "You don't think there is anyone else in Germany capable of putting the biological warfare plan into operation?" asked the commander, subtly changing his subject.

"In seven or eight months? Because that is what we are concerned with, isn't it? I should say not."

The commander smiled. Nowhere in the memorandum was there a mention of a time limit. But it was general knowledge that the invasion had to take place during the next summer, if only because to hold the rapidly assembling troops in readiness for another year would be impossible. The professor was right. They were concerned with the next eight months at the most.

The professor had something else on his mind.

"Commander," he started slowly, "while I can see how the Germans could go about starting a biological war, I am not quite sure why. After all, Hitler could have used gas and germs before. He has been at this dreary business almost five years now."

"If Hitler hasn't used gas or germs until now, professor, it certainly wasn't because of any moral scruples. When he was on the offensive and fighting on land, it simply didn't suit his purposes. But now the situation is different. He is fighting a defensive war. In northwestern Europe his main defense is the sea for which biological weapons, as you yourself seem to think, are eminently suitable."

The professor nodded.

"With Dr. Tiesenhausen in charge, how long do you think it would take to produce enough germ cultures to infest the beaches?" asked the commander.

"I would say three months. But here I may be quite wrong. You see, commander, I am totally unqualified to measure one highly important factor."

"Which factor?"

"The psychological one. We are dealing with scientists and technicians many of whom are fanatics. We simply aren't familiar with that type over here. At least I'm not. Tell you the truth, commander, I hope I never will be."

It started to rain on the way back to London. Darkness fell quickly on the wet, depressed winter countryside and it was not pleasant in the unheated

Austin. Howard's thoughts went back to the beginning.

The beginning had come shortly after he had been reassigned from his position as a Canadian Navy liaison officer aboard the HMS *Queen Emma*, headquarters of the Royal Regiment during the Dieppe Raid. He was now on the staff of General Frederick Morgan, which was entrusted with the preparation of a plan for an Allied reentry into northwest Europe. Since General Morgan's staff was only a field office of the Combined Chiefs of Staff, it was eventually destined to be swallowed up by the Supreme Allied Commander in Europe. Initially there had been some confusion about its proper function. As a result, there was more freedom than expected for the various officers on Morgan's staff to define their own jobs.

There followed several months of paper shuffling for the newly promoted Canadian Lieutenant Commander. None of it had anything to do with his previous training, a BSc degree in biology at Queen's, then a year of medical studies at McGill. When war broke out, as a naval reservist Howard volunteered for active duty. He spent a couple of years aboard troop ships, shuttling between Halifax and Liverpool. Then came the Dieppe assignment aboard H.M.S. *Emma*, finally the paper shuffling on General Morgan's staff. The deadly routine was finally interrupted when he was called into the office of an earthy American Colonel named Barrie, Howard's superior. He was handed a one-page typewritten report, now several weeks old, on the interrogation of a German prisoner. It was a form with which Howard was by now thoroughly familiar. In his southern drawl, with which Howard was now equally familiar, Barrie asked:

"Hey, will you look into this stuff, Doug? Probably another Kraut POW wanting to increase his rations by telling stories, but there could be something to it."

The report concerned the statement of an Afrika Korps corporal, captured by the British at Cape Bon. By way of background the interrogator explained that the German corporal had been wounded in the Ukraine in the summer of 1941. While convalescing, the corporal served as a clerk at the OKW, the Wehrmacht's headquarters in Berlin. There he occasionally came across documents with the heading BVFE. The German corporal had no idea what the initials meant, although he did suspect that they had something to do with western defenses since he had been assigned to the command of Colonel Finckh, Quartermaster West.

The interrogator, a British intelligence officer, added a note that the German was quite rational and that consequently there seemed little reason to doubt what he said.

Of course, he had not said very much. Given the German penchant for abbreviations, the letters might have identified nothing more sinister than the organization for routing of woolen underwear for the German units in France. But the initials were completely unknown to anyone on the Allied side and Howard decided to include them among the questions interrogators were required to ask all German prisoners.

It wasn't until late in 1943 that a Wehrmacht Captain named Joachim Beck was taken prisoner near Salerno and without much coaxing betrayed the meaning of the initials BVFE: *Biologische Verteidigung der Festung Europa* — Biological Defense of Fortress Europe.

The commander immediately requested that Beck — who too had served under Colonel Finckh — be flown to London. Two days later Beck explained to Commander Howard personally that there was a whole section in Finckh's office with the name BVFE, but that Finckh himself seemed to have little authority over it. It seemed as if it were purposely hidden in several departments concerned chiefly with supply, away from prying eyes. Beck was the first to link Professor Robert Tiesenhausen with the operation, saying that the scientist was a frequent visitor at the BVFE offices. Late in the summer of 1943 the staff of BVFE moved to some new, secret location. Beck himself was transferred to the Italian Front shortly afterwards.

At that point all paper shuffling had ended for Commander Howard. The job of tracking down information concerning BVFE now occupied him night and day. First, all exiled governments in London were asked to instruct the underground in their countries to be on the lookout for the relocated BVFE staff. At the same time Allied air forces were requested to step up their reconnaissance, although no one knew precisely what it was they were supposed to be looking for. The results were almost immediate. Via a Swiss businessman on a trip to Prague, the Czech underground managed to let the Allies know that there was something going on at the Adam Hill fortress in the Orlice Mountains. Adam Hill, built by the Czechs in the 1930s, was a series of fortifications, consisting of a large main bunker, connected by underground passages to pillboxes and auxiliary bunkers located in places as much as three kilometers away. The hill was part of Sudetenland and consequently now within the Reich, but it was still only a few kilometers away from the Reichsprotectorate Bohemia-

Moravia — the German name for what was left of prewar Czechoslovakia.

A member of the Czech underground had delivered milk to the main bunker on Adam Hill. He reported seeing strange-looking containers stacked under a camouflaged cover nearby. He did not get farther than the entrance to the main bunker, according to the Swiss businessman's message, but he did see people in white smocks about. Most importantly, at the nearby Czech village of Pastviny, a German family had recently moved into a lakeshore villa which had formerly belonged to a Jewish banker. The head of the German family answered the description of Professor Robert Tiesenhausen.

3

Lieutenant Stephen R. Cummings of the U.S. Air Force saw the dark blue expanse of the Channel in the distance and automatically looked at the fuel gauge of his P-38. A moment later he banked sharply to the left. He had enough left for a ten-minute hop along the beach.

At least there would be some excitement. Except for the coastal areas the Germans weren't wasting ammunition on single fighters any more. He had been scouring the northern French countryside most of the sunny afternoon, his cameras ready to photograph any suspicious movements, but this time he drew a complete bank. Aside from countless horse-drawn carts and a couple of trucks near Lille which looked to him French enough to be left alone, there had been nothing. Disappointed, he was on his way back to his field at Lympne when he recalled his instructions to take a fresh look at German defenses along the coast whenever possible.

He knew the area below him well. To the right, partially obscured by the haze produced by the smokestacks, lay Calais; to the left, guarded by the Wehrmacht's crack 47th Division, were the winding beaches of Cap Gris Nez. He started to descend from his 8,000 feet, the flak clouds around him becoming more numerous, occasionally even lightly buffeting his plane. He was low enough now to distinguish the long fringe of white foam of the breakers, the scattered tetrahedrons on the beach, and, farther inland, the camouflaged bunkers. There were also people, he realized with surprise, several hundred of them on the beach, some in the water, others on the sand, all gathered around what seemed to be an enormously long piece of pipe, leading from one of the bunkers. Some, with shovels in their hand, were obviously attempting to bury it.

But by the time he took all of that in he was already over the sea. For a minute or two he headed north, then he executed a wide turn to the left. The idea was to return to the French coast a few miles to the west, then hop over the dunes and take a picture of the surprised Germans as they were laying their pipe.

The first part of the maneuver went well. To the west of Cap Gris Nez the beach was quiet. The noise of his engines probably brought the Germans out of their holes, but by the time they managed to man their guns he was already beyond the dunes, out of their sight.

At the Cape they were waiting for him though. There were moments when the flak around him was so thick that it provided him with an effective smokescreen and at one point he was certain that he felt several bullets slap into the port side of his fuselage. Then he was directly over the pipe-laying scene, his fingers pushing the red camera button over and over again until it was time to pull his nose up. He then pointed it directly northward — toward England.

And that's when he was hit. It was as if some gigantic hand had suddenly grabbed the Lightning and pushed it some twenty feet to the side. He looked back at his twin rudder. All seemed in order there. The controls were a bit sluggish, but still operational. He flew straight for a while, noting that he was at 900 feet, then tried gently to pull on the stick. The aircraft didn't respond. And neither was there a response when he pushed the lever which would ordinarily bring his wheels down.

A few minutes later he spotted the English coast but by that time his plane had dropped to 500 feet the port engine was emitting black smoke and his fuel gauge registered zero. He lined up the P-38 with the length of the reddish beach, then cut power. At the last moment before he touched ground he buried his face into the crook of his elbow resting on the instrument board.

Although he had had no more than two or three glasses of wine, it seemed enough to relax him. Perhaps a bit too much. Howard was sitting in a smoke-filled club off Shaftesbury Avenue with Roger Stillwell, his distant cousin and a captain in the U.S. Air Force, and Roger's date, Sybil something. Sybil was a perky nurse in a meticulously ironed blue uniform and with her hair done high up in a roll. At first she said little.

Roger, a bomber pilot, was quietly sipping on a glass of harmless ginger ale because next morning he would take his B-25 into the air from his field south of London to drop his terrible load on Düsseldorf from a sky filled with deadly flak clouds. Howard envied Roger. Soon it would be two years since he had last seen action aboard the *Emma* off Dieppe. And here was Roger Stillwell, sipping on a soft drink and adding missions over Düsseldorf, while he himself was carrying voluminous files to the upstairs offices.

"The fact is that all of us — every last one of us here, Roger — would give their right arm to be where you are. I mean in the thick of things, right in there where it's noisy and dusty and where people get killed."

"Just speak for yourself, commander, if you don't mind," Sybil interrupted him angrily. "I don't have the slightest desire to be in the thick of things. I feel that I am doing a perfectly adequate job here, putting back together those fools who wanted to be in the thick of things and those unfortunate young men who simply had to be there. Believe you me, there is nothing very glorious and heroic about a limbless body or a head without a face."

Roger Stillwell seemed accustomed to the radical views of his lady friend, but Howard looked up in surprise. He had to admit that what she was saying sounded sensible, but it also was totally out of tune with the attitudes one usually encountered. Most important of all, it was also completely out of tune with his own thoughts. He reacted angrily.

"You mean one shouldn't volunteer for anything, is that right? We should sit here and wait until it all blows over?"

But that wasn't what he meant to say at all. It was too imprecise, almost petulant. Sybil leaned across the table toward him so she could be better heard above the din of the place.

"You haven't been listening, commander. I said that certain unfortunate young men had to be there and to them I shall be eternally grateful for getting the job done on behalf of all of us. But it's the fools who actually *want* to be there that usually manage to get wars started in the first place."

"Do you have any idea what it would be like if everyone felt the way you do?"

She leaned tiredly back in her chair.

"I've heard that argument before. Many times. And it simply doesn't hold water. If everyone felt the way I do we would have a lot less mock heroics and mercifully fewer of those ridiculous American war movies. Maybe it wouldn't be as much fun, but it sure would make a lot more sense. To me anyway."

When Stillwell and Sybil got up to dance, Howard's thoughts quickly meandered back to Adam Hill. It was quite likely that things would start happening soon; that there would be no more time for evenings like this. Not that he would miss them, but his frustrations were bound to grow. Although he would probably be in on the planning stage of any operation against Adam Hill, he would certainly not be part of any operational one. The land-locked Protectorate of Bohemia-Moravia was not a likely destination for a Canadian Navy officer.

He watched the crowd mill rhythmically around the postage-stamp-sized dance floor, thinking about what Sybil had said. It could not have been very pleasant for her to watch the steady flow of the wounded and maimed through her ward. But that was mainly because in a hospital there wasn't a chance to measure their sacrifice against what had been accomplished. It must have all seemed so useless to her.

Later on he walked with them through the dark, now silent London. On his way back to his room near Marble Arch he was caught in an air raid. He quickly found his way into a sandbagged shelter and tried to doze off in a remote corner. But the explosions became louder until the tiled walls trembled, the air became heavy with dust, and small pieces fell from the ceiling. In the darkness Howard felt himself seized by rising panic and he started to shake uncontrollably. Between explosions came calmer moments though, when he sensed that his fear was mainly due to the confined space in which he found himself imprisoned. Also, to the fact that he was so obviously without any control of his own destiny.

One by one, Howard carefully examined the pictures drying on the line in front of him. Finally he turned to the American Air Force lieutenant.

"Can I speak to the pilot?"

"He is unconscious, commander. Not expected to live."

"I'm sorry. The man has done an incredible job."

"Yes. He would probably have come out of it with just a few scratches had he bailed out. But that would have ruled out any chance of saving the film."

Howard thought for a moment.

"May I use your phone?" he asked, and when the American pointed to his desk, the commander dialed a number.

"It's Howard. Will you get me an appointment with General Bedell Smith? Now. In about two hours. Something's come up."

4

When Howard entered, Eisenhower's Chief of
Staff, General Walter Bedell Smith, was seated
behind a large oak desk which almost filled his
office. On the general's left was a youngish-looking
British captain who smiled and rose first.

"Nice to meet you, commander," Bedell Smith
greeted him, rising. "This is Captain Blackwell of
the 2nd British Commandos." Howard nodded to
both men and took a seat that had been offered to
him on the general's right.

"Well, let's get right to it. General Eisenhower
has read your memorandum and I don't need to tell
you that ..."

"There is something else now, general," Howard interrupted him, reaching into his briefcase.
"These pictures were taken by an American reconnaissance pilot yesterday afternoon. We don't know
exactly where because he's unconscious, but I don't
think that there can be any doubt that the Germans
have started putting the machinery in place."

Bedell Smith took the pictures from Howard's
hand, his face tightening as he examined them.
Finally he looked up.

"Commander, this is the biggest threat to our
reentry into northwestern Europe we have come

across so far. What would be your next suggestion?
What should be done?"

For the first time since he came in, the commander smiled.

"I think it would be pretty similar to yours,
general. That is, if the presence of commando Captain Blackwell here indicates anything at all."

Bedell Smith became noticeably more relaxed.

"Then you'd agree that the biological warfare
threat cannot be destroyed on the site. And even at
its source on Adam Hill it cannot be eliminated
from the air."

Commander Howard nodded.

"Captain Blackwell here will join you in devising a plan of action. I understand you have a
degree in biology and some medical studies in your
background."

"Yes sir."

"And some excellent personnel reports from
your former commanding officers. You'll be in
charge of planning the operation, commander. It
will have top priority and your plan will include all
phases of the operation — personnel selection and
training, strategy and recovery of the participants
after the objective has been achieved. Also, find a
code name for it. How soon can you report?"

"Within a week, sir. We have begun with the
preliminary stuff already."

"From here on the entire operation will be
classified top secret. In fact, the whole subject of
the possibility of biological warfare being waged
by the Germans cannot even be hinted at. Not
under any circumstances. You can well imagine
what it would mean to the morale of our troops.
The planning and the actual liquidation of the
BVFE must be achieved in absolute secrecy. And
it must stay secret when it's over."

"Yes sir."

"Then it is understood that you have been entrusted with the planning of a commando action behind enemy lines, designed to destroy the Germans' ability to wage biological warfare on French beaches for at least six months."

Commander Howard looked up in surprise and the general smiled.

"The last part is for your ears only. Well ..." the general rose from his chair and extended his hand to the commander and Captain Blackwell. Just before they left, Bedell Smith seemed to have thought of something else.

"I know what I am asking is probably impossible without at least fifty percent casualties. That is, if we're lucky. But without it, General Eisenhower's task of landing 150,000 men on French beaches becomes absolutely impossible," he said.

Howard and Blackwell nodded silently.

5

"Let me get this whole weird thing together," an obese American Brigadier General with a cigar and airborne insignia on his uniform bellowed at Commander Howard only moments after the naval officer had been introduced. "You see, I may not be very bright, but the way I read this proposal of yours is that you want to drop three highly qualified guys deep into Kraut controlled territory, and you want them to blow up a bunker — a whole hill or something — in a country where they have never been before, where their local contacts are nonexistent or at best highly doubtful. And also where thousands of people have been executed and two villages razed to the ground because of the last batch of paratroopers that have been dropped there. Is that right?"

Howard studied the fat general for a moment but for the life of him he couldn't think of his name. Others seated around the large table he recognized from their pictures. There was Eisenhower himself at the head, Bedell Smith and the sharp-nosed Montgomery flanking him. The commander's former boss, Sir Frederick Morgan, was also seated at the table, as well as General Omar Bradley and the round-faced Patton. Among them the airborne general was more of an exception than the rule. He certainly is not typical of the generals I've met, thought Howard. More like a caricature.

"Yes, that's right, general," he finally replied softly.

"Then I'm pretty sorry that for once I do understand the plan. It's the goddamndest thing I've ever come across in all my thirty-two years of soldiering," the general roared.

"And that ridiculous name for the thing — Operation Lister — what the hell is that supposed to mean? Is it some sort of a gargling thing — you know, like Listerine Antiseptic?" The fat general roared with laughter but stopped abruptly when he realized he was laughing alone.

"Joseph Lister, sir, was an Englishman and a pioneer in fighting bacterial infection. We thought his name appropriate for the operation. The mouthwash, by the way, was named after him."

The fat general looked around him as if searching for help. A colonel in a white turtleneck cut through the embarrassing silence.

"My name is Lovatt, commander. I've had some experience with commando raids. I think that, particularly when one considers the circumstances, your plan is quite remarkable. There is one thing, however, that bothers me a little: the vagueness of the escape route. We've found that it can be a serious stumbling block in any operation when the way to get out is not clearly defined. As far as morale is concerned, men don't really mind facing death while achieving the objective. But the extreme danger can only last so long and then it becomes unbearable. Are you certain there isn't a better method here for the team's recovery?"

Commander Howard sighed.

"I'm afraid there isn't, colonel. We have examined the various possibilities and Poland is by far the best of them."

The commander rose and walked to a large wall map of Europe hanging on the wall opposite the big windows.

"At present the Russian lines are about here, a bit southwest of Kiev. That's about 600 miles from Adam Hill. But it is assumed that if the Red Army continues its present rate of advance, by the summer it should have cut the distance in half. If, in addition, the parachutists keep moving eastward, there is a good chance they will reach Red Army lines before next winter. An attempt to reach Allied lines in Italy or even to reach Switzerland would mean crossing not only German-occupied territory but large areas of Germany itself. That, of course, would be suicide."

Eisenhower looked at Air Marshall Leigh-Mallory who was seated across from him.

"There is no hope of recovering the men from the air?"

Leigh-Mallory shook his head.

"Not too much, sir."

"What do the Czechs do? They have dropped quite a few parachutists into the area, haven't they?" asked Montgomery.

"Yes sir," replied the commander, "but none have had an escape route. They were all expected to remain there until liberated."

"Has it worked?" asked Patton. "I mean have they at least survived?"

"Colonel Moravec, the Czechoslovak Chief of Intelligence here in London, doubts that any of their men dropped from England are still alive."

A gloomy silence fell over the crowded room. As soon as he realized how depressing the mood had become, Bedell Smith entered the conversation.

"I don't think there is any doubt that this would be one of the most hazardous missions that we have undertaken in this war. No doubt about it at all. As a matter of fact you can read in Commander Howard's report that we can expect at least a fifty percent casualty rate. Without it however, we are now quite convinced, there can be no successful invasion of northern France. It's as simple as that."

"Are there any questions or points to be brought up?" asked General Eisenhower after a moment of silence. Howard put his paper in his briefcase, shut it and rose.

"Will you please wait outside, commander?" Eisenhower smiled. "We will have our decision for you in a few minutes at the most."

The commander walked out, feeling quite exhausted by the ordeal. In the hall he was met by George Blackwell.

"How did it go? Have they approved the plan?" the young officer asked excitedly.

"Not yet. Do you have the personnel files I asked for?"

Blackwell looked at him in surprise.

"But you said the plan has not been approved!" Howard didn't bother to explain.

"Could I look at them please?"

Blackwell handed him four large envelopes. Howard seated himself on a bench nearby to study them. Ten minutes later General Bedell Smith came out of the conference room, smiling.

"You have a green light, commander. Full speed ahead I think you say, don't you?"

The commander shook his hand. Then he started down the long row of marble steps, taking

them two at a time and at such a pace that Blackwell found it difficult to keep up.

6

At a camp near East Grinstead in southeast England, Sergeant Tom Evans of the U.S. 101st Airborne Division leaned against a beam in the back of the mess hall and for the umpteenth time watched Fred Astaire and Bing Crosby effortlessly team up in song and dance in *Holiday Inn*. It was a marvelous antidote for the drizzle which had been falling for days. The music periodically managed to make Tom forget what was ahead and, even more important, what was behind.

Totally unbearable were Tom's thoughts of Nebraska, of the Omaha suburb of Papillon, where he had with his own hands built a small house near the Union Stockyards and where he had moved with his young wife in 1935. During the height of the Depression, he managed to get himself a job as a drug salesman. A boy was born to the Evanses early in 1940, but Tom never heard him talk. On the day the curly-headed child first said "daddy" his father had completed basic training in New Jersey. Before Tom was to be shipped overseas his wife came to New York where they spent what were to be their last moments together.

Two weeks later, while Tom was still aboard a troop ship in the Atlantic, she and her curly-haired

Stephen on the seat beside her were killed in a head-on collision with a fruit-laden truck on Highway 30 — the same road that Tom used to travel on so often in his Ford, the back filled with drug samples. Anne had been driving to visit her mother to show her Stephen's new tooth.

The tumult, the carnage of Monte Cassino left Tom Evans with little opportunity for thoughts about his family's tragedy. Back in England he went through parachute and advanced hand-to-hand combat training and finally he was transferred to the 101st as part of a program to increase the number of combat veterans among the members of the airborne division.

Several times he had been offered leave, first as his ship docked in North Africa, then after his unit had been pulled out of Italy, and again after his arrival in England. He refused each time. He also had no plans to return to Nebraska after the war. He would stay somewhere in the East and start anew. At the age of thirty not all could be lost.

Tom noticed a messenger with a flashlight entering the mess hall. He spoke with the projectionist for a moment then the lights came on and the corporal-messenger called out Tom's name.

"I haven't got the slightest idea what they want, sergeant," the young Lieutenant on duty at the office answered his question with a smirk. "General Eisenhower stopped confiding in me right after the German commandos rescued Il Duce from that goddam castle in northern Italy. You, know, I think he blames all of us Wops for that."

Tom glanced at the name — Lt. Giorgio Grappa — on the desk in front of the officer and he grinned.

"And now for the subject at hand," the lieutenant continued. "About half an hour ago I got a phone call from SHAPE that you're wanted by some Lieutenant Commander Douglas R. Howard and that you're to report to him as soon as possible. That means tonight." The officer's finger ran down a well-worn train schedule on the wall beside him. "Let's see, there's a train at five past midnight. Be on it. We're typing your orders right now."

Tom nodded, saluted and started toward the door.

"Oh sergeant, come to think of it I do have a pretty good idea what it's all about. It's them Navy bastards. Lately they have been raiding our ranks with promises of three hot meals a day and a dry hammock every night. Don't let them talk you into it. What they don't tell you is that the goddam German U-boat captains are getting more and more accurate and — what's even worse — that there is no liquor allowed aboard Uncle Sam's ships. Not even a drop."

"I'll try and remember that, sir," Tom smiled as he turned to walk out into the damp cold. There was a three-mile walk ahead of him through the unfriendly night to get to the station.

Lieutenant Stanislaw Jaroscynski of the Polish Free Forces was drinking at the Princess Street Railway Station, still a bit dazed by the sudden turn of events. Not that by now he hadn't learned to adapt quickly to new surroundings. God knows there had been enough of them since September 1939. After the fall of Poland he had made his way south, passed from friend to friend until he had reached Turkey. With the Carpathian Division he had taken part in the defense of Tobruk (where he received a piece of shrapnel in the hip for his trouble), then was transferred to England where he received his commission. But he also had to fight incredible bouts with boredom there. The deadly inactivity of camp life in the Midlands soon made him volunteer for commando training in Scotland.

At lunchtime Jaroscynski had been called to the administrative office, handed a travel chit and orders to report to an address in London.

It was an annoyance. Even if he turned around in London and went right back to Scotland he would miss a couple of days of training. That meant he would probably miss a whole week in the end while waiting for the next batch of trainees to arrive so he could make up the lost instructional hours with them. And a week now in 1944 was invaluable. He knew that the big operations were just around the corner — the push toward Rome and the collapse of Italy, the landings in France and, above all, the liberation of his native Poland.

He finished his tea and looked at his watch. In ten minutes the express for London would leave. He gathered his things and walked downstairs to the platform where the long train stood already filled with people, mostly soldiers. A burst of steam periodically came from underneath the cars.

He got on the first car behind the engine, miraculously found an empty seat, and wrapped himself up in his heavy overcoat. Moments later he was fast asleep.

7

With giant strides the two officers crossed the living room of the old red brick house at Barham in Kent. Then one of them, Captain George Blackwell, knocked on the closed double doors leading into what was once the kitchen. When an invitation to enter came, Blackwell pushed the doors apart with both hands, bidding the other, taller officer to enter. Inside Commander Howard rose from his paper-covered desk. He came around to greet the arrivals.

"Captain Mindon? That certainly was fast work, I didn't expect you until tomorrow at the earliest."

"We were lucky. There was an American hospital plane flying in from Catania. The high priority of my orders helped. They managed to squeeze me aboard."

The commander put two chairs in front of the desk and beckoned Blackwell and Mindon to sit down.

"I've been reading about you captain. Compared to you all of us here sound like novices. The Vaago Raid in Norway, Rommel Raid in North Africa, clearing the Naples approaches — you seem to have done them all."

"And what is it this time, commander?" asked

Mindon without the slightest attempt at easing
into it. The abruptness surprised both the commander and George Blackwell.

"We're up against German coastal defenses of
France which could prevent us from ever landing
on those beaches," started the commander.

"Well I have no frogman training but if ..."

"We have to destroy the defenses *before* they
are installed on the beaches."

With Blackwell's occasional help the commander then explained the BVFE threat. Mindon
sat in his seat throughout the whole thing, seem-
ingly without making the slightest move or batting
an eye. When the commander was finished he
asked quietly,

"Where do I fit in, commander?"

"You are to be the leader of a three-man team.
Because of your language training and commando
experience you are pretty close to invaluable."

"Do the others speak Czech?"

"One is a Pole. The other an American whose
widowed mother married a Czech farmer in
Nebraska. He is probably the most fluent and col-
loquial Czech speaker of you all."

"Do I still have a choice?" Mindon smiled and
both Blackwell and Howard knew he had
accepted.

"Only theoretically," Howard shot back.

"Then I accept the assignment — both in theory and practice."

He slapped his thighs and started to rise.
"When do we begin training?"

"Your team has already begun. They're out for
a jog right now. But it's expected that you will
utilize mostly the training you received elsewhere.
You see, we only have a month at the most before
the drop."

In the evening, after all the introductions and the get-acquainted dinner, a stocky officer in a foreign army uniform arrived at Barham with a bulging briefcase. Introduced by Commander Howard as Colonel Moravec, the Chief of Intelligence of the exiled Czech government in London, he took a seat among them next to the blazing fire. Then he opened his briefcase and in fairly good English sketched in the current situation on occupied Czechoslovakia. He thereby managed to shatter instantly the illusion of well-being which had developed in the comfortable living room of the old house.

"The picture I have painted of my country is not pretty. It's absolutely ugly, but I don't want you to start your journey with false ideas. As parachutists you will be pursued by the Gestapo with all the stubborn perseverance of a crazed hunter of wild animals. The idea, of course, is not to have them even suspect your presence, to methodically erase every trace you may have left behind from the very moment you land. An abandoned parachute or even a parachute strap can mean the difference between life and death. Because that's what we suspect Hitler ordered two years ago as punishment for any Allied parachutists found in Czechoslovakia. We are told by our informants that under no circumstances are they to be treated as prisoners of war — even if they are wearing a uniform. I assume, commander, that every member of the team will carry the brown pills?"

The commander nodded.

"Wait a minute, what brown pills? What're you talking about?" asked the aroused Evans.

"Cyanide pills, sergeant," Moravec explained. "They are mercifully quick. A capture by the Gestapo means several weeks of torment before death.

The pills deny them that pleasure as well as any possible information."

"Are we under orders to use them?"

"No, Tom," the commander answered after a few moments of thought. "I don't know what others do but I cannot order a man to commit suicide. Though I would certainly urge him to do so."

A silence full of thought pervaded the room, disturbed only by the occasional crackle of the fire. Finally the Czech officer continued.

"But you also have an advantage that not even our last parachute team, Group Antimony, had. They were dropped in October 1942; you will be dropped in February 1944. You have the Russians on the offensive and the Allies in Italy. The Germans are on the run and Russian lines are within reach on the Polish border. That is a luxury about which our thirty-odd parachutists never even dreamt."

Mindon had let the fire in his pipe die out as he watched the Czech officer with increased interest. Moravec went into the detailed description of the documents they would carry and the clothing they would be wearing, manufactured in prewar Czechoslovakia. Then he unraveled a map of the Orlice Mountains region before them. Still later, when he produced a plan of the Adam Hill interior, Mindon became even more impressed with Moravec. Finally the Czech concluded his lecture, stating that they would go much more thoroughly into most of the subjects he had introduced that evening during the oncoming weeks. He started to gather his material to catch the midnight train back to London.

"Colonel Moravec," Mindon asked just before Commander Howard escorted the Czech officer to his car for the ride to Canterbury, "what do you think of his mission — of the commander's plan for the assault of Adam Hill?"

The Czech thought for a moment.

"I think that it must be attempted. I also think that under the pressure of time and circumstances Commander Howard has come up with a remarkably thorough and yet flexible modus operandi."

"But?"

"Pardon me?"

"There *is* a but, isn't there?" Mindon pressed on.

Moravec looked at Howard questioningly. The commander finally nodded.

"Go ahead. He has the right to know."

"Captain Mindon," the Czech officer took a deep breath and straightened up proudly. "I believe that a mission such as this to be conducted on Czechoslovak territory should be entrusted to the Czechs. I have protested the present arrangement several times already."

After his departure Mindon turned to Howard, his face one gigantic question mark. But the commander was not about to volunteer anything.

"Just why is that commander? Why are you opposed to the job being done by Czech exiles?"

"Because," Howard started reluctantly, "because experience has shown that natives tend to be subject to waves of emotion which at times may entirely obscure their rational judgement."

8

Jiri Palka stood on the side of Pastviny lake
directly opposite the promontory with Hana Dykova's house. He was absolutely motionless. He had
been like that for the past five minutes, listening to
the frozen countryside the way an animal does
before venturing out in the open. Hidden by the
forest and heavy underbrush, he scanned not only
the lonely house in front of him, but all the
approaches to it. Before arriving at his spot he had
watched the house from another angle, where the
long, winding road leading up to it was readily
recognizable in spite of the snow which covered it.
Nothing seemed to be moving. Except for an occasional gust of wind there was no sound.

The downstairs windows of Hana's house were
lighted. Through his binoculars Jiri Palka could
see her seated at a rustic table, occasionally turning the pages of a book. Again he marveled at her
beauty. Having seen her many times on the screens
of Prague movie theatres, she was no stranger, but
black and white film did not do her justice. It could
not reproduce the dramatic contrast of her flaming
red hair and soft, snow-white skin. But for almost
five years now Hana had not appeared in a film. It
was an absence which had been explained by
tuberculosis, but Palka knew better. Had Hana

Dykova simply announced her retirement from films at the age of twenty-five the Nazis, who had just occupied the country, would have regarded it as a provocation. They would have been certain to take vengeance on her. Goebbels regarded film as one of the mightiest German propaganda means available: he intended to find an important role for prominent artists in the occupied lands.

So Hana Dykova was chosen to co-star in an ambitious production of *Frederick the Great* in which she was to portray Catherine of Russia. The first scenes had already been shot in the Berlin studios when Hana, through skillful use of glass particles in her mouth, started to cough and spit blood. She was eventually replaced by a gladly collaborating Austrian actress and returned home to Prague. There a sympathetic doctor substituted a consumptive's X rays for hers and Hana retired to the Orlice Mountains with the full sympathy of the Germans. They had no inkling of the prominent role she played in the Czech underground.

Satisfied that the coast was clear, Palka effortlessly slid down on his skis until he reached the frozen surface of the lake. Across the lake his tracks would be most noticeable, but he took the necessary precautions. Before reaching its surface he took off his long, heavy overcoat and tied it to his waist. That way his tracks would be smeared into a single wide band — quite a common indication that someone from the village had been to the forest to gather firewood which he then dragged across the lake. To keep any suspicion from falling on Hana he took the route far to the right to some hedges below a copse of trees. There he put his coat back on and started to climb toward the house. Only then was he satisfied she was alone and he quickly proceeded toward the door. He knocked softly twice and, after a few moments, a third time. Hana turned on the lights and soon appeared at the door, looking at him through the small window with a wrought-iron grill over it. There was the rattle of a chain being removed before the door opened.

"Jiri! Come in! Here, let me help you with the skis," she said with genuine happiness in her face.

She pulled shut the long curtains inside her roomy kitchen. They seated themselves behind a table with large cups of chicory coffee in front of them. They talked about the news of the latest Allied advances which had come over the BBC in Czech the night before. They chuckled at the thought of the once-proud German Army running back home across the frozen Russian plains. Suddenly Palka grew serious.

"Hana, the London people are interested in what's going on at Adam Hill."

"Do you know what it is?"

He succeeded in loosening the last small icicle from his mighty moustache and he placed it neatly on the saucer alongside his cup.

"We have an idea. We have already let London know about it. I won't tell you what is the idea or how we got the message to them. The less you know the better. But if they decide in London to do anything about what we have told them we may need your help."

Hana sipped on her chicory coffee for a moment before replying.

"Before Colonel Moravec left for London in 1939 we met one afternoon in Prague at the Cafe Slavia. I told him I would help but that I would want to stay here in Orlice Mountains where I grew up. He understood. In the summer of 1939 this place was very conveniently located for the Czech Army officers on their way to Poland to fight the Germans. With the fall of Poland there hasn't really been that much to do ... Of course I am ready to help."

Palka smiled.

"You underestimate what you have done already, Hana."

"I hope it will be remembered after the war," she smiled. "And remembered quickly, because I wouldn't want the people in the village to hang me on that oak out there in front."

"It will be remembered. I assure you."

There was a lull in their conversation. Palka listened to the fire inside the stove and watched the rising hot and turbulent air distorting the designs on the tile wall behind it.

"Hana," he said after a while, "I think they may send someone. Someone to sabotage Adam Hill. They'll need headquarters somewhere in the region."

"They're welcome here," said Hana quickly, without hesitation.

Palka anxiously stroked his moustache. "I don't have to tell you that ..."

"No, you don't, Jiri. I know exactly what would happen if the Gestapo ... I have no illusions."

Later, with his skis in his hand and his coat already on, he turned around.

"You've lived in England," he asked. "What sort of people are the British?"

"Hmmm ... Fair. Very fair ... Nice, pleasant. Sometimes a bit dull, though."

"And the Americans?"

"The few I've met were impulsive, unpredictable. Quite exciting actually. Why do you ask?"

"Because once this war is over we will have a lot to do with the Allies who won it. And I already know the Russians, I've served there."

"Would you prefer to be liberated by the Russians or from the West?"

Palka's answer was something Hana would have expected from King Solomon.

"One thing at a time, Hana. Let's get the Germans first."

He retraced his steps to the lake, then took off his coat again to cross.

A more than two-hour trek home was ahead of him.

9

At first, Howard doubted Mindon had been a good choice for leader of the team. There was a certain arrogance about him, a readily apparent feeling of superiority. Visiting instructors in judo and hand-to-hand combat arrived from London each morning and invariably they returned there at night, having met not only their equal but frequently their superior in Harry Mindon.

Jaroscynski and Evans were not in such top physical shape. What's more, neither of them had ever seen a man killed or had to defend himself at close range. That is why when it came to the choice of weapons for the team it was Mindon's choice which prevailed. Howard would have favored the Navy's Lanchester, arguing that it was an almost exact replica of the Germans' MP 28 and therefore most sensible as far as the acquisition of extra ammunition was concerned. Jaroscynski wanted the Mark II Sten with which he had fought in North Africa and which, being British made, would have been favored by Mindon as well. But Mindon had sent away to London for the newest version of the U.S. "grease gun," the M 3A1 Model. Mindon showed the versatility of the gun at the firing range on a nearby moor and he neatly demonstrated how the Sten's feeding mechanism frequently jammed and how the cocking mechanism of the new American model had been simplified. When he, in addition, demonstrated the silencer and the flash hider which could be attached to it in a matter of seconds, there was no longer any doubt in anyone's mind. The grease gun had won.

But it did not endear Mindon to the rest of the team, nor did his occasional sarcasm nor his mile carrying full equipment through the English February mud in a little over five minutes, (leaving Evans and Jaroscynski far behind), nor his negotiating the obstacle course in much less than the required three minutes on his very first try.

The truth was that initially Mindon was bored. Because of his extensive experience, the first week of training at Barham consisted for him of unnecessary repetition. But then came subjects completely new to him and his behavior changed. When a Czech Captain came to Barham to talk about Adam Hill and conditions in occupied Czechoslovakia, Mindon was all ears. Suddenly he worked well both with the other two solving hypothetical prolems of the kind they might encounter in the field.

Watching the trio operate together, Howard grew more optimistic about the outcome of the mission. The men started to complement each other. Jaroscynski's mechanical know-how and his ability to improvise quickly on details fitted in well with Mindon's talent for altering the entire approach to a strategic problem at a moment's notice. Evans betrayed an uncanny ability to spot faulty elements in what seemed at first glance a sound scheme. It was he who pinpointed the unreliability of a hypothetical twenty-year-old Czech youth who was to have supplied the trio with information about German movements to and from Adam Hill. Why would the youth still be around when most young men his age had long ago been sent to work in the Reich? Did his father have valuable contacts with Germans in high places? Would it not help such contacts if he informed the Gestapo about the hiding place of the parachutists from England? It was, of course, only a possibility, but enough to make them wary of all helpful Czech youths. Evans realized this and almost every other pitfall which was thrown their way.

On the way to Wilmslow for three days of intense parachute training with the trio, Commander Howard parked his Austin in front of the SHAPE building in London. He went in to report about the group's progress.

A sombre-faced General Bedell Smith handed him an intelligence report which had come across his desk that morning. It was based on observations of the French underground at the coastal town of Ambleteuse, just south of the Cap Gris Nez area. A convoy of trucks had passed through the town with what was thought to be containers from Adam Hill.

"We have discontinued aerial reconnaissance of the Cap Gris Nez defenses because low flying aircraft could tip off the Germans and make them tighten security at Adam Hill. That's the last thing we would want. But the French underground's report indicates the Germans are getting dangerously close to the operational, stage of BVFE. We can't wait any longer with Lister."

"Our drop is scheduled for the first week in March, general. We'll be ready."

"That isn't good enough, commander. Not any more. The men will have to be on the ground in the Adam Hill area by next Friday."

10

Inspektor Kamm finished with relish his portion of roast pork surrounded by sauerkraut and dumplings. He leaned back and relaxed in his padded armchair, lighting a cigarette.

The old hag Zahorelova sure can cook, he thought. His housekeeper's job was not only to prepare his meals but also to clean his office and the apartment on the main floor. The house on Zamberk's town square had been commandeered when the Germans entered the country in March 1939. It was a good choice, made even better by the fact that the owner of the house had been arrested shortly afterward and sent to a camp somewhere for distributing leaflets unfriendly to the Third Reich.

But all that had happened long before Kriminalinspektor Ernst Kamm had been placed in charge of the Gestapo in the region, with a permanent contingent of four men. They occupied the downstairs of an adjacent house and never neglected to express their gratitude for being spared the vicissitudes of the Eastern Front. They were not the only ones.

During Operation Barbarossa — the German invasion of Russia — Kamm mistakenly thought the greatest advantage lay in being transferred from the front lines to an Action Group. Its specific job was to carry out Hitler's so called *Komissarbefehl,* an order which called for the murder of all political commissars attached to the Red Army. The resulting slaughter eventually became too much even for Ernst Kamm's iron-walled stomach. As he traveled with his Action Group across the Ukraine, Kamm began to realize to his great horror that this time Hitler had bitten off much more than he could possibly chew.

The partisans were becoming increasingly bold even in areas where there had been none before. In January 1943, Ernst Kamm was part of an antipartisan sweep near Kiev. He had heard about the surrender at Stalingrad and realized there was only one thing he could do if he wanted to leave the eastern front alive.

The old man was called Nikolai something, that much Kamm still remembered. He had been picked up near Dymer because his name came up as a dying gasp on the lips of a tortured partisan. Kamm was taking Nikolai to the car, hidden by a barn, when he put his plan into operation. First of all, he had purposely failed to bind Nikolai's hands (he later explained that due to the peasant's age he did not consider him dangerous). Once behind the barn, Kamm's hand emerged from his wide pocket with a Tokarev pistol he had taken off a dead partisan. The peasant Nikolai stared at him dumbly as Kamm pointed the pistol to his own hip bone at a carefully rehearsed forty-five-degree angle. Then Kamm calmly pulled the trigger.

The pain was excrutiating but he knew what his next move had to be if he was to avoid military prison for self-mutilation. Profusely bleeding, he nevertheless leaned against the side of the barn and he laboriously pulled his own Walther service pistol from the holster. The peasant Nikolai was beginning to sense danger. He had already turned around, taking his first quick step away from the German, when Kamm's bullet caught him squarely in the nape of his neck. Nikolai fell, first on his knees, then toppled over to the side. Marshalling the last remainder of his strength, Kamm kicked the Tokarev closer to the dead peasant. Then he lost consciousness.

The plan had worked. The soldier who had arrested Nikolai a few minutes before was reassigned to a penal battalion for his failure to properly search the prisoner for weapons, while Kamm was evacuated to a hospital in Kiev. After two operations he was sent to convalesce in Prague. The angle of the bullet's trajectory, which a medical friend had advised, was perfect. Six months later Kamm had fully recovered — except for the expected limp which the doctors assured him would be permanent and which, of course, made him unsuitable for further military service.

In Prague Kamm made the proper contacts. Instead of a mere discharge to his home in the Rhineland he managed to get himself transferred to the Gestapo. The appointment to the Zamberk post with the rank of a Kriminalinspektor couldn't have been more ideal. The Orlice region was wonderfully bucolic — too remote for any serious encounter with sabotage or any other Czech underground activity. Except, of course, for black marketeering. And even that he had manipulated to ensure his comfort. There were butchers who regularly supplied him with the choicest cuts, cloth merchants who managed to find enough prewar English fabric to make elegant suits for him, shoemakers who produced stylish boots of soft leather and the felt *valenky* for the harsh winters. Automechanics overnight mysteriously came up with spare parts for his Praga Lady eliminating the long, cumbersome, and often unsuccessful bureaucratic procedures for requesting the parts through official channels. There were some who brought him jewelry and other valuables in return for small favors. In time Kamm could consider himself a moderately rich man.

Occasionally, however, he had to make arrests and some of these people had even been guillotined in Prague. But by and large the Orlice Moutains appointment had been a delight, with the charming Pastviny lake just kilometers away for a refreshing swim in the summer. There was also the warm house in Zamberk for the winter with the old hag Zahorelova who made such excellent roast pork with caraway seed.

Above all, though, there was the almost heavenly beauteous Hana Dykova. Perhaps she was not yet in love with him, but she was, nevertheless, very fond of him. Unlike the strong-legged, animal-like peasant girls who visited Kamm sometimes for a half a kilo of sugar or an orange or two, Hana was untouchable as befitted a goddess. His visits to her house were something special. He wouldn't dream of besmirching them with the thought of more than polite conversation, only now and then enlivened by an innocent flirt.

All that, however, would sadly have to come to an end soon. There were already people in Zamberk who claimed that in the still of the night they could hear the artillery on the eastern front. It was, of course, nonsense. The Russians were hundreds of kilometers away. Still, it was time to move on. In two months, when it got a bit warmer, he would be on his way to Cologne, where a boyhood friend, now head of an orthopedic clinic, would fill out the necessary forms and operate again — the hip would have worsened through Kamm's faithful service to the Gestapo while pursuing enemies of the Reich. That would keep Ernst Kamm nicely out of harm's way and away from Orlice Mountains which would be invaded by the same Red Army whose political commissars he had systematically butchered on the Ukraine and whose memory was likely to be long.

And even had the Czechs decided not to hold a grudge and had the Red Army forgotten him in the melee, there was still Adam Hill. Whatever was going on there was top secret. With such a classification the Wehrmacht was likely to put up quite a fight in defending it, transforming the whole region into a fiery hell. It was time to be leaving this pleasant, forgotten neck of the woods.

Ernst Kamm took a sip on his cup of mocha. He lit a cigar, pushing a half-finished piece of pineapple cake away from him. The room was pleasantly warm and he closed his eyes in anticipation of a short, relaxing nap.

11

All four of them had gone to bed early after a busy day. Commander Howard still had some doubts whether the men had been sufficiently prepared for the drop only three days away now, but he had also become quite adept at pushing such worries to the back of his mind. They merely wore him down when there was nothing that could be done.

He opened a book of Wordsworth's poems and read the lines:

> Oft have I looked round
> With joy in Kent's green vales;
> but never found
> Myself so satisfied in heart before.
> Europe is yet in bonds;
> but let that pass,
> Thought for another moment.
> Thou art free,
> My Country!

With his night light still on and the book on the floor beside it, the commander slept so heavily that he did not hear the first two knocks. The third not only awakened but startled him as well. He jumped out of his bed, mechanically putting on his robe.

"Yes? Who is it?"

"It's Jaroscynski. I'm sorry to bother you but —"

But at that point Howard had already opened the door. He stared at the Pole.

"What time is it?"

"About three. It's about Captain Mindon. He's really sick."

"Sick? Come on in. What's the matter with him?"

Jaroscynski reluctantly entered the room to explain.

"I went to bed at ten but I woke up at midnight and I heard him moan next door. He claimed it was something he ate, but just now he actually screamed. He is half delirious, commander. He must have a very high fever."

Howard already had his trousers on. On his way to Mindon's room he was tucking in his shirt. One look at Mindon bathed in sweat and curled up in a ball on his bed left no doubt that they had an emergency on their hands. Evans and Jaroscynski carried Mindon down the stairs while Howard hurried to his room to finish dressing. Ten minutes later the Austin was making its way south through the teeming rain.

In Dover, two hospital attendants helped Mindon out and put him on a stretcher. A few moments later a white-haired doctor on duty came out into the semi-dark waiting room to tell Howard it looked like a case of acute appendicitis. Mindon was being prepared for surgery.

After another hour in the waiting room the doctor reappeared to say that the appendix had burst. It wasn't at all certain that the captain would pull through.

The commander already knew the answer.

Still, he thought that the question had to be asked pro forma.

"Doctor, Captain Mindon was training for a mission. A very important one. He was to go abroad this week."

"Someone else will have to fight his battles for a while commander," the doctor said. "He'll be out of circulation for three to four months at the very least. That is if we succeed in getting him back on his feet at all."

Howard remained seated in the stark, tile-covered waiting room. He began to tremble. It would have been easy to blame it on the cold damp-ness but he knew better. His concern for Mindon had been replaced by a shivering realization of the full consequence of what had just happened. He was not in control any more. As he lit one of his rare cigarettes he watched his trembling hand and he knew that it was fear.

That stealthy invader of his senses with whom he had yet to learn how to come to terms.

Howard stopped in Barham just long enough to shave and to give the bad news to the other two members of the team. Then he pointed his Austin northward for London.

There he had to wait most of the morning because Bedell Smith was watching a demonstra-tion of a new landing craft, which was followed by yet another high-level strategy conference. But the general broke a luncheon engagement when told of Commander Howard's visit. He listened to the news, occasionally nodding in sympathy or simply to show understanding. Then the room became still with both men deep in thought.

"How long before we can train another man, commander?"

"Two weeks minimum, sir. Once we find him, that is. I think Sergeant Evans and Lieutenant Jaroscynski are now eminently qualified to be on the team. But they need a third — an administrator and coordinator type. You see, most of the real detailed information about Adam Hill is still unknown. The final plan will have to be hammered out right there on the spot. On the ground in Orlice Mountains."

"I know, I know ... What a mess!" commented Bedell Smith.

"There is only one way out as I see it, sir."

"Yes?" the general reacted hopefully.

"Well, I've been with the group from the start. I have attended all the briefings, put together the basic plan and I —"

Bedell Smith understood instantly.

"How good is your Czech, commander?"

"I don't know any, sir, but my German is perfect."

"Oh? How come?"

"My father came from Lower Saxony. The family name used to be Horwatz."

"Are you married?"

"No sir."

"Hmmm ..."

The general leaned back in his chair.

"Ever made a parachute jump?"

"No sir. But we do have two days before the drop."

Bedell Smith looked helplessly in front of him, evaluating the arguments. Slowly he was coming to the inevitable conclusion.

"In how good a physical shape are you commander?"

"I'm fine. Not the hot specimen that Mindon was, but fine. The physical conditioning is more

likely to play a part later, after the Adam Hill
objective has been achieved. During the escape."

Bedell Smith had to admit this was true. He
also realized he was inadvertently being brought
closer to the commander's thinking. If the danger
emanating from Adam Hill was as great as supposed, there was no alternative. At the same time,
the last-minute substitution of Commander Howard for an almost ideally trained and experienced
commando captain was preposterous. The idea of a
Navy Officer without any commando experience
placed in charge of a mission which would decide
the fate of the most ambitious military operation in
the history of warfare was so absurd that it defied
reason.

"When is your plane scheduled to take off?" the
general asked.

Howard didn't fail to notice that it already was
"your" plane.

"Thursday night."

"From where?"

By now Howard knew that the general had
made up his mind. Answers to all these questions
had been available in a report the commander had
submitted three days before.

"From Hendon Airfield sir, north of here. It's a
Halifax, which will join a bombing run on the German military training field at Pardubice, less than
fifty miles from Adam Hill. The bomber will then
rejoin the rest of the squadron."

"Hmmm ... Can it be done, commander? Can
you pull it off?"

"That we won't know until we're on the
ground, general." Howard's face broke into a broad
smile. "But we'll take a hell of a stab at it, I can
promise you that."

Bedell Smith rose to indicate the interview

was over. He came around his giant desk to shake
Howard's hand.

"Of course, we'll have to get Ike's okay for the
change of plans. But I want to be the first one to
wish you God speed."

The commander sat in the canteen with mug of
coffee in front of him. As he half expected, fear had
slowly descended over him and at times played
havoc with his thinking. The moist hands and his
forehead breaking out with cold sweat were largely the result of the sudden, totally unexpected,
burden placed on his survival instinct. Sybil Hawthorne, Roger Stillwell's girlfriend, should see the
big hero now, he thought. Jaroscynski and Evans
had already adjusted to it but he hadn't. The place
was almost deserted except for a young British air-
man who sat nearby, across a table from a WREN,
held her hand and gazed into her eyes lovingly over
a pot of tea. More than just fear swept over the
commander at that moment. It was irrepressible
anger that took hold of him, anger at no one in
particular. There was so much destruction and
death around that the world had once again descended to the standards of the jungle. He took a
couple of sips on his coffee, then rose to get quickly
out of the canteen. There was lots to be done.

12

With one ear covered by an earphone and alert for instructions, Flying Officer Janacek carried on a heavily-accented conversation with Howard.

"Welcome aboard. You're lucky, commander. The weather is pretty good. In France anyway."

"And farther on?"

"Aah, we must pray," smiled the chubby-faced pilot and then his attention was diverted by something he heard over the earphones. The commander returned to the cabin and found himself a seat toward the back of the fuselage, where Jaroscynski was already eating with great gusto a piece of bread covered with smoked meat. He offered some to the commander, without attempting to outshout the engines, as they revved up in the final preparation for takeoff. Howard shook his head, then settled himself as comfortably as possible on the rough canvas seat, pulling a parachute alongside him to act as an armrest. At that moment he felt the aircraft starting to move. He looked at his watch, now an elderly Swiss model with a cracked and yellowing crystal and a faded leather band which could have been purchased in central Europe a long time ago. It was thirteen minutes past six.

The laboring Halifax left the English coast shortly before seven. Over the Channel it joined the rest of the bomb force. Commander Howard got up from his seat to better see the receding strip of land until, in the dark night, it became indistinguishable from the sea.

He felt a wave of panic engulf him. It was all a terrible mistake, he wanted to shout. Looking around him in the darkened cabin he saw that Jaroscynski was asleep. He had been since shortly after takeoff. Evans was sitting up, unscrewing the top of a large flask of steaming coffee. I have no right to lead these men to their death, the commander felt like screaming. They had depended on Mindon until three days ago. They had the right to because Mindon was every inch a leader, down to the point of being slightly arrogant. But who was he? A naval commander without experience in any sort of land action.

He was standing slightly apart from the other two, staring into the darkened body of the aircraft and supporting himself with one of his hands extended against the bulkhead.

"Would you like some coffee?" he heard over the roar of the engines. Evans stood behind him with the steaming stuff. But there was something strange about the way he held it: his hand was shaking far more than could have been caused by the plane's vibration and he had to support his wrist with his other hand. It still wasn't enough. Now and then some of the coffee splashed over the top of the flask.

Howard looked up in his face. In the dim light he saw an ashen Evans with droplets of sweat on his forehead.

"What's the matter? You look terrible," the commander asked. He took the coffee from the sergeant's hand and sat him down again next to the sleeping Jaroscynski.

"I'll be all right, Doug," he said. "A bit of the shakes. It was bound to come."

Howard sat down beside him, sipping on the coffee, not saying anything.

"Really, I'll be all right in a little while," Evans said. "Exactly the same thing I went through at Salerno. But once out of the landing barge I was all right."

Howard nodded. The sweat on Evans forehead had disappeared. Even in the darkened cabin Howard could see that at least some of the color had come back to his cheeks. Talking about it had done both of them a world of good. The panic which a moment ago had been on the edge of all of the commander's thoughts was now largely gone.

"Are you having a pleasant crossing?" asked Evans with such a good imitation of a posh British accent that the commander burst out laughing.

"Yes, it's actually quite nice, thank you. The coffee is exceptional."

"Well, I'm certainly glad to hear that," Evans continued clowning, "because there's a project of sorts ahead of us which may prove to be a bit of sticky wicket, if you know what I mean, suh."

"I know exactly what you mean," the commander suddenly grew serious, "but we'll come through all right. Just fine."

Jaroscynski stirred and his nostrils widened. He smelled coffee. He reached for the thermos and began unscrewing its top. The commander handed him his cup.

"Where are we?" asked Jaroscynski sleepily. At that moment several shells exploded in their vicinity and searchlights began madly to crisscross the sky around them.

"We're over Nazi-occupied Europe," announced Tom Evans calmly.

A few more times flak appeared around them, but nowhere was it as bad as over what looked like some large city. The trouble was that they suddenly emerged into a break in what up until then had been fairly heavy cloud cover. Immediately beams of light criss-crossed the sky again, accompanied by deafening explosions all around. The commander saw a bomber off their starboard wing burst into flames and begin a corkscrew. It seemed as if one of its wings had been torn off.

Janacek pushed the throttles forward and pulled on the steering mechanism. The Halifax creaked under the strain, engines whining as they began a steep climb. Howard looked at his watch's luminous dial. It was almost ten o'clock. He stirred in his seat, trying to make himself more comfortable in the woolly and bulky prewar European clothes. On his left Jaroscynski was fast asleep again, totally undisturbed by the explosions and by the aircraft's violent maneuvering. But Evans beside him was awake, although he gave no sign of being overly disturbed by it all.

"Where are we Doug, do you know?" he asked the way a passenger would ask who had just woken up aboard the Supercontinental nearing Chicago.

"I haven't got the slightest idea," the commander replied truthfully. The importance of the question waned as the guns grew still again and the spotlights more distant. The commander waited a few moments, then walked up to the pilot's cabin. There, everything seemed calm.

"Hello commander! How are things back there in the darkness? Believe me, just a moment ago I'd have preferred not to see too clearly myself."

"Where were we?"

"Over Stuttgart," said Janacek. "I think that plane that went down was Harry Oberfeld's. Did you see any parachutes?"

"No," the commander said, "I didn't. I'm sorry."

There was a moment of silence with only the drone of the engines in the background. Janacek and the copilot stared into the darkness ahead of them.

When Howard came back, Jaroscynski and Evans were asleep. For lack of better things to do he checked the luggage with the help of a flashlight. LIS-1, 2 and 3 were their parachutes, wrapped in beige cloth. Evans was in charge of a bag marked MK III, containing chemicals and the bomb for Adam Hill. LISA was a bag with the guns and ammunition, assigned to Jaroscynski. LISB was Howard's concern. It contained their provisions, wrapped in Czech newspapers, with maps and some 50,000 Reichsmarks. It was all there. Once on the ground each man would assume responsibility for the supplies assigned to him. Howard sat down against the bulkhead.

He reached into his pocket and pulled out an identity card with the arrogant eagle resting on top of a swastika. According to it, he was Heinz Schenkel, inspector of German railways, traveling in Czechoslovakia for the purpose of better incorporating the facilities into the Reich's system. The card stated he was from Ulm. The cover story and his name had been concocted very carefully, but it was unlikely it would ever be used. Perhaps it would impress overly zealous Czech officials, but certainly not the Germans who could easily verify the facts. According to his cover, Jaroscynski was a Polish subject of the Reich named Jerzy Slowotski, on his way to the Ostrava Steel

Works. Evans was Roman Ostapchuk, a Ukrainian engineer from Belgorod Dnestrovski near Odessa, also on his way to Ostrava to help with the war effort.

There was something else in the commander's pocket — two brown pills in a small box. One was in a glass vial, the other coated with gelatine. Either way it meant a sudden end. A painless one, as the medical officer who came to Barham one evening assured them.

Just a big void, thought the commander as he contemplated the pills. He felt a hand touching him on his shoulder. When he turned around he saw the flight sergeant.

"The pilot would like to see you, sir," he said into Howard's ear with just the right volume to outdo the engines. Howard nodded and proceeded forward. As he entered the cockpit Janacek looked back at him, then pointed to a black mass ahead that looked like mountains.

"That's home, commander.".

Howard didn't quite understand.

"Pardon me?" he asked.

"Home. Czechoslovakia. The Böhmerwald. We call it Sumava, though. A much prettier name, don't you think?"

The commander nodded. He looked at his watch. It was a quarter to ten.

Fifteen minutes later the flight sergeant woke up Jaroscynski and Evans and told them to get ready. The commander returned to the cockpit.

"How long before we jump?" he asked.

"Fifteen minutes at the most. Nervous? I don't blame you. It's important to make a good first impression. The Czechs aren't too used to Canadians, you know. Remember, they'll be judging your whole country by your behavior. You don't mind a few pointers, do you? First of all, use your fork to pick your teeth, never your fingernails. The Slavic people are very particular about that ..."

Howard smiled and waved his hand in mock disgust as he left the cockpit. But he was grateful for Janacek's easy going humor during these last few moments of comparative safety. Back in the cabin Howard felt the pilot starting a wide turn. Jaroscynski was up on his feet for the first time since he had coffee over the English Channel. The flight sergeant was helping him on with his parachute.

"How long?" he asked.

"Ten, fifteen minutes."

Jaroscynski nodded and continued buckling up.

"How is the weather?" Evans shouted from another part of the fuselage.

"Fine. Just fine."

As Howard started getting his own things together, the door of the cockpit opened and Janacek came out. Without a word he shook the hand of each man, then stopped in front of the commander. His face was much more serious than the commander had seen it so far. He stared at Howard for a few moments, then extended his hand toward him.

"Take care of yourself, commander," he said finally. "Don't let them get you." He shook the commander's hand and in spite of the darkness Howard could feel his eyes burning through him.

"The sergeant will tell you when to get out," he said brusquely, immediately turning on his heel and disappearing into the cockpit. Howard looked out the window and saw that the ground below was now covered with snow. It made visibility much better. The Halifax was slowly losing altitude, descending in a wide turn.

"Some coffee, sir?" asked the flight sergeant who suddenly appeared alongside him with another thermos. The commander felt a shiver and took the steaming cup of coffee from the sergeant's hands. After a couple of sips he passed it on to Jaroscynski. He looked at his watch. It was exactly 10:15 P.M.

The red light came on over the cockpit entrance and harshly interrupted the darkness of the fuselage. The flight sergeant put aside his thermos and with Evans' help, after a couple of tries, they finally succeeded in opening the side door. An icy gust tore into the plane. Below, the ground was coming up more clearly. At one point Howard was sure he had seen a portion of the white, frozen Pastviny lake pass by the open door as Janacek continued circling. Their baggage was now alongside the door attached to an auxiliary parachute and they were all hooked to the line above their heads, staring through the darkness at the red light.

Someone touched the commander gently on his back as he stood by the open door. He turned around and looked into Jaroscynski's grinning face. The Pole raised his arm to Howard's eye level, then pointed his thumb upward. It was exactly what the shivering commander could use while making the second parachute jump of his life into a snowy, perilous void.

"Good luck," he shouted at Jaroscynski. Their attention was diverted by the green light which suddenly came on above the cockpit. At the same time Howard noticed that the plane had stopped circling. It was flying in what seemed to be a perfectly horizontal position.

"All right, sir!" screamed the flight sergeant at the top of his lungs. "Go!"

Howard threw himself out of the dark hatch in a downward and outward direction. When, in the next instant, his eyes opened again, he saw the giant rudder of the machine slip by effortlessly above him. He had no sensation of falling while he was still carried by the slipstream. His legs had been thrust upward, but in the next moment as he looked at them, he already saw the parachute's rigging. A moment afterward he felt a jolt as the bulging silk above him swallowed air and the rigging stiffened. His legs were now pointing downward. He looked at the ground below and a bit to his right he was certain he saw the uninterrupted smooth white surface of Pastviny lake.

The commander smiled. No more than 300 yards to the right of him were floating Jaroscynski and Evans, clearly outlined against the white countryside below. A bit farther away the auxiliary parachute with their supplies hung suspended from the sky. In the distance, now invisible, droned the departing Halifax.

Janacek, thought the commander happily, you're a miracle worker, that's what you are. The night couldn't possibly be more perfect for the drop and I don't see how you could be any closer to the target.

13

The men had been repairing a road near Klasterec. During the last thaw a week ago it had become clear it could not possibly withstand the spring onrush of the turbulent arm of the river called the Wild Orlice. A horse-drawn sleigh had made use of the slush that was still on the road to bring several wagonfuls of medium sized gravel. But then the increasing strength of the midday sun melted the remaining snow and the gang set to work, buttressing the road on the side of the river. It was backbreaking work but it paid well.

Shortly after sunset Jindrich Kekl put down his shovel, mounted his bicycle, and started toward Nekor. The thought of a cold, almost two-hour bicycle ride back with frequent dismounting on steep hills did not appeal to him. When he had covered about two kilometers a much better idea came to him: he would visit his daughter who lived in a house nearby with two boisterous kids and a husband who was a farmer and who made an excellent *koralka*, distilled from prunes.

Kekl arrived at his daughter's house just in time for dinner, a thick potato soup followed by an even thicker stew. But to the great displeasure of his daughter, her husband took him away from the stew and into the hayloft above them, where he

stored his *koralka*. They each had a drink, then
came down to say goodnight to the kids. There followed a few more glasses until Kekl looked at his
pocket watch and decided it was time to go. But he
was not allowed to leave yet. It was his daughter's
turn. He had to listen to her tirade against the Germans, against the harsh mountain life, and finally
against himself for not having provided her with
the proper training to be a salesgirl or even a hair-
dresser in Prague.

There was nothing to be said in reply that
would not fan her fire further. And since her own
husband had long ago refused to be on the receiv-
ing end of her complaints, Kekl felt that he owed it
to her to lend an ear. After all, the dinner wasn't
bad at all.

After about an hour of her complaints he
mounted his bicycle in front of the house. He let out
a curse when he realized that his light was not
working again, then he set out through the night.

Howard was first on the ground, quickly followed
by Jaroscynski on his right. A moment later a dull
thud somewhere behind them indicated that their
supplies had also landed. The impact had been
harder than expected, but nothing seemed to be
broken. Jaroscynski was already out of the har-
ness, pulling the parachute toward him by the rigging, being partially successful in collapsing it.
Howard followed suit, anxiously scanning the
countryside around them for some sign of Evans.
In a few moments he had enveloped the parachute
with its rigging, tied a couple of haphazard knots,
then dropped it on the ground. He moved toward
Jaroscynski.

"Where is he? Have you seen him?" he asked in
a loud whisper.

Jaroscynski, too, was now finished. He stood in his place without knowing what to do, alternately shrugging his shoulders and shaking his head.

"Go get the supplies Stan, they're somewhere among those trees," the commander whispered. "I'll take a look around for Tom."

Jaroscynski dropped his parachute near the commander's and disappeared.

Howard examined the terrain. Only now he realized they must be in a quarry. On three sides they were surrounded by at least a ten-foot embankment. On the fourth was an opening along with a clump of trees through which Jaroscynski had disappeared a moment ago. Now he understood why they could not see Tom Evans. If he had landed more than fifty yards from them in any direction he was on top of the embankment and consequently effectively hidden from them.

Whatever it was that had been extracted from the quarry, it had not been during the last day or two. The place was covered by what seemed to be a fairly thin layer of ice — probably water from thawed snow that had refrozen.

"Command ... I mean Douglas, come here," Jaroscynski hissed from the trees. Howard came closer.

"That's the road, right behind those trees. A little bit farther are the houses. I think we are right next to Pastviny. Did you see the lake on the way down?"

A slight noise on top of the embankment made both men scamper for cover. Howard reached in his pocket and got a firm grip on his automatic. But the figure was unmistakably that of Tom Evans. He stood on the edge of the embankment, staring into the quarry, trying to decide if the two lumps in the white field at the bottom of it were parachutes or not. Howard breathed more easily. He stepped forward, away from the trees and waved. The relieved Evans waved back and continued along the embankment toward them.

In spite of the cold, sweat was pouring down the commander's brow. For the third time already he had taken over the small shovel from Jaroscynski, again and again attacking the frozen ground but they had barely scraped the surface. According to instructions they had a maximum of two and a half hours to bury the parachutes, no more. Howard wiped his forehead and looked around helplessly, feeling miserable in his ill-fitting clothes.

"How is it going?" hissed Evans from his lookout position on top of the embankment.

"Not so good," answered Howard. "See anything?"

"Noth ... Jesus, get down ... *get down!*"

Howard dropped his shovel picked up his gun nearby and together with Jaroscynski dived into the bushes. A moment later they heard the faint sound and their fingers tightly gripped the grease guns. Then they saw the lone cyclist pass across the opening to the road, totally in the dark except for a lantern on his handlebars.

A bit later the commander reluctantly returned to his shovel. After a few more attempts to break the ground he realized it was hopeless. He walked to a pile of gravel covered by snow.

"We'll have to bury the parachutes underneath this. It isn't as safe as the ground itself, but we have no choice. We have to get out of here in a hurry now."

Without a word Jaroscynski knelt down beside the commander and with his bare hands began to remove the gravel.

Before midnight the clouds increased and a wind picked up. To those who knew the Orlice Mountains it indicated only one thing — snow.

Jindrich Kekl had left his bicyle near the main road and was making his way up the steep slope with great difficulty. Up until a few moments before he had been watching Hana Dykova's house from a nearby patch of woods, waiting for the delicious moment he knew so well by now, when she would turn out the downstairs lights. A little while later the lights would go on upstairs in her bedroom and if he was lucky — during one evening in about every ten he watched — she would be careless about drawing her curtains. But even with the curtains drawn there would be the shadows, those tantalizing movements as she slipped her dress over her head, unhooked her brassiere, and put on her nightgown.

Maybe it was even better with the curtains drawn, thought Kekl, hurrying up the slope toward the oak behind which he took refuge as he watched Hana. It was then that his imagination was able to fly off unbounded.

At forty-five, Kekl was still convinced that great things awaited him, that the road repair job was only temporary. There were unusual times, when it was advisable to keep a low profile and thereby survive. Just a few more months and the Germans would be gone forever, leaving behind them chaos and a situation full of possibilities in which anyone with a brain in his head could get ahead fast.

He reached the oak. Leaning against the large trunk, he buttoned his overcoat as a gust of wind reached inside his clothing and instantly cooled his perspiration. This may be one of his lucky nights, though. The light suddenly went on in Hana's bedroom and she turned away from the window to uncover her bed without bothering with the curtains. Kekl's breath was taken away as she suddenly looked up and lazily ran her hand through her sparkling red hair. She was incredibly beautiful at that moment, a lonely goddess who deserved two strong arms around her, the warmth and protection of someone who cared, who would do anything to be near her.

Just a few more months, that's all, thought Kekl. Just a few more months and the Germans will be gone with the field wide open to those of us who will dare to take it. Then Kekl will march to Hana Dykova's house in the uniform of a revolutionary officer, the uniform of somebody who automatically commands respect. He will sip tea with her, talk about literature, film, fashion and world affairs. One thing would lead to another, first just a caress or two, then a kiss, an embrace ...

Hana stopped in the middle of the bedroom and began to unfasten her necklace at the back of her head. Kekl knew that this came moments before she would begin to slip off her sweater. He grew rigid in expectation and one of his hands ventured inside his coat, methodically unbuttoning his pants, then entering, firmly holding his organ before starting the gentle strokes. The pace increased when Hana stood only in her brassiere, then the strokes became frantic as her breasts were revealed momentarily, just before her flannel night gown covered them again and she turned away from the window.

Damn! Damn! Jindrich Kekl banged his fists against the oak's bark in the throes of his orgasm. I must have her! I must have her now, on that wide bed in her bedroom, I must have her spreadeagled there so I can enter her and with long thrusts make love to her, atop those magnificent breasts, against her thighs, kissing her full lips over and over again, making love, being in ecstacy. I must have her, I must ...

It had begun to snow lightly. That's why Kekl for a moment thought that his eyes were playing tricks on him. A little distance away, at the two stone pillars which formed the entrance to Hana's property, stood three figures.

He rubbed his eyes. The figures were standing there still, watching the house. What are they doing here, who are they? thought Kekl in panic. Are they after me? He crouched behind the tree, suddenly trembling with cold. For a moment he was about to start down toward the frozen lake but then thought better of it. It could only attract attention.

Who were they? If they were the dreaded partisans what did they have to do with Hana, who was so friendly with the Germans? Did they come to kill her?

The men reached the front door. Two of them stood some distance away from it, well hidden by the bushes. They put down their backpacks and cocked their submachine guns, pointing them at the entrance. Then the figure in front of the house pushed the electric bell twice, urgently. Afterward the man at the door retreated a bit as well, dropping his backpack into the snow.

The light came on in Hana's bedroom instantly. A moment later the downstairs was lit up as well. Finally there was a sound which came from behind the front door.

"Who is it?" she was asking.

The man in front of the door remained silent but he motioned to one of his companions. It was the companion who answered in what seemed to Kekl as strangely-accented Czech.

"Friends. We would like to speak with you."

Now the small window behind the iron grill opened.

"Friends don't usually come in the middle of the night and unannounced. Who are you?"

The man who had been speaking with Hana now conferred with his friend in a foreign language. Finally he spoke.

"I have a message for you from General Moravec in London. He said to tell you that we are part of the big assignment he spoke to you about at the Cafe Slavia in Prague five years ago."

With his mouth agape Kekl heard the rattle of a chain. The door quickly opened and the three men entered.

My God, they're parachutists, thought the astonished Kekl. Parachutists from England!

14

Jindrich Kekl's mind raced back to the time when the parachutists who came from London to assassinate Heydrich were trapped in the Karl Borromaeus church in Prague. Not only they but also anyone who had anything to do with them died. That whole village near Kladno — Lidice — was destroyed because of them. Men died by a firing squad there, but others had been hanged or had their heads cut off in that room in Pankrac prison where even poor Mrs. Suchomel, the butcher's wife from Klasterec, ended her life. Parachutists? They meant terrible death, that's what they meant. Kekl's knees began to shake. What will happen to Pastviny, Klasterec, to everyone at Orlice Mountains?

Then, slowly, he began to see what had to be done. Near the road he picked up his bicycle again and pedaled past the first houses near the crossroads. There he turned right onto the road which descended steeply toward the lake. The first building across the bridge was the well-lit Vitek's pub. Leaving his bicycle in front of it, he rushed inside, reaching the wall telephone in two steps. He took the receiver off and twice rang the bell with his other hand. The operator came on almost instantly.

"Hello? Get me the Gestapo in Zamberk. Quickly, it's an emergency."

While waiting, he became aware of voices next door. He recognized some of them, but did not pay much attention, impatiently listening for a sound which would indicate that a connection has been made.

That's why he hadn't heard the door opening in the darkness behind him when one of the card players left his friends. On his way to the toilet he heard Kekl tell the operator he wanted to speak with the Gestapo. From behind two empty beer barrels the man heard every word.

"Gestapo. Kriminalinspektor Kamm," the telephone suddenly crackled with life.

But Kekl knew no German.

"Three parachutists ... near the lake right now. I saw them," the frightened Kekl shouted into the phone.

"What? What are you saying? Who are you?" yelled back the aroused Kamm. He thought he heard the word "parachute" but he wasn't sure.

"Don't speak German ... I no speak German," Kekl kept repeating helplessly. Suddenly he stopped. He thought he heard something in the darkness behind him. He held the receiver full of Kamm's shouts away from his ear.

"Put the phone down ... Right now," came over in the form of a short hiss. Kekl obeyed. Then he slowly, very slowly, started turning in the direction of the sound.

Inspector Kamm was seated in his armchair, his fingers drumming on the small table beside him. He was far from relaxed. The operator had told him the call came from Vitek's pub. He even spoke with Vitek, who readily identified the man making the call as Jindrich Kekl, adding casually that he seemed to have had quite a bit to drink somewhere before he arrived at the pub. No, Kekl wasn't there any more. He left immediately after completing the call.

"But he has not completed the call!" Kamm shouted.

A veteran of the Austro-Hungarian army in World War I, Vitek spoke excellent German. "He hasn't?" asked the surprised-sounding Czech. "I'm sorry. You see, he is a drunk and I told him to hang up. It wouldn't be the first time that someone made a phone call and I was stuck with the bill. And Kekl was drunk, terribly drunk, he ..."

"Did you see anything strange tonight?" snapped Kamm who had been at Vitek's pub before and knew where the phone was. He also knew what Vitek's answer would be. He is like the rest, very good at playing dumb whenever it suits him.

"Strange? No sir. But I haven't been outside at all."

Kamm did not want the Czechs to know that the Gestapo was on to anything, that he had understood anything Kekl had said over the phone. Keep them guessing, always. Kamm recalled one of his most cherished principles in dealing with the Czechs. He hung up without a word.

Did Kekl say anything about parachutists or not?

Kamm's hip had started to hurt again. He turned over on the side away from his wound to favor it. Damn it all, damn it all to hell — the hip, the treacherous Czechs and the war. He felt as if a cage was slowly being lowered around him, what with the advancing Russians, the trucks for Adam Hill and now the mysterious phone call.

And what about the phone call? What should he do? He could give out a general alarm. That would mean the immediate arrival of the special antiparachutist unit from Königgratz, possibly even more men from Prague. All the Czech policemen in the area would be alerted and through them the population as well. An extensive search would follow, possibly sealing off Pastviny and Nekor. If the parachutists were found, however, it would not be Kamm who got credit for it, but one of the high-ranking officers arriving with the reinforcements. Probably Leimer from Prague who is so worried about his stupid trucks for Adam Hill. A lot of strange people would fan out across the countryside, asking questions and most likely finding out an awful lot about the way Kamm operated. In the end, someone would probably even try to blackmail him.

The other alternative was simply to downplay the whole thing. He would make a thorough investigation but on the local level. He would lock up Kekl and maybe send him to Prague for special handling. In any case, thought Kamm, laboriously raising himself from the chair and picking up his rubber tipped cane at the same time, he had to start doing something.

"Röhmer" he yelled down the steps into the office.

"Corporal Röhmer isn't here sir," replied the man on duty and Kamm could hear his boots as the soldier was double-timing it upstairs.

"Should I get him, sir?" the soldier asked as he reached, breathless, Kamm's apartment.

"Yes, yes. Get them all from their stupid beer. We're going to Pastviny. Hurry up!"

Kamm was not taking any chances. As he sat next to Röhmer, as well as the standard issue

Walther pistol strapped deep inside his fur-collared coat underneath his arm, there rested on his lap a black MP 40 submachine gun. Three spare magazines were in his pocket.

15

This is not good for my digestion; not good at all, thought Kamm. The Praga bounced around on the rough country road, made even rougher by the fact that in places it was covered by a crust of ice. Whenever Röhmer saw such a crust he strained against the brake pedal to approach gingerly. The jolts and incessant gear changing produced a sour feeling coupled with bloating gas inside the Gestapo man's stomach. He recognized that he was paying his price for Zahorelova's excellent sauerbraten.

The Praga was laboring up a hill the Czechs called Sedivec. The Gray One. It matched Kamm's thoughts exactly. The car had slowed down almost to walking speed and its entire dashboard was shaking with the strain on the motor. The motorcycle ahead of them had to slow down as well in order to stay within two car's lengths in front, while the other machine, behind them, at times touched the trunk.

Kamm was restless, at times actually smelling the change of mood that was taking place around him. He disliked night raids, preferring early morning ones, just as the sun was about to rise and one was at the peak of his reactions. Even if the prey had managed to stay awake all night, chances were he would take a nap about this time. It was then too dark to clearly recognize one's assailants, but light enought for the assailants to scout the countryside, to know exactly what they were doing, at whom they were firing.

They were now beyond Sedivec, slowly descending toward the lake alongside dark woods and gently rolling hills. Kamm stared dumbly at the motorcycle light ahead of them. Suddenly the red light seemed to be traveling sideways. He sat up in his seat, moving closer to the windshield to better see what was happening. At the same time his fingers gripped the gun across his lap more tightly. The motorcycle swerved in the darkness, obviously to avoid something. Once the machine was out of the way, Röhmer saw the object on the road as well. He slammed on the brakes of the Praga. On their right were the two motorcycle riders, staring at the object which more and more seemed to be taking on the shape of a human body through the darkness. Röhmer reached to the back seat for his weapon and scampered out.

Thank God we have the Czech policemen with us, flashed through Kamm's mind. Not much of a chance of it being an ambush — the partisans would hardly shoot at their own. But still Kamm wasn't so sure. He slumped farther down in his seat, gripping his gun until his fingers became white, his eyes nervously scanning the nearby forest for any sign of trouble.

One of the Czech policemen approached the body. He knelt down next to it, then turned it over. Only when he came alongside the Praga did Kamm reluctantly roll down the window.

"It's one of the people from Nekor. Works on a road repair gang," the policeman explained in passable German.

"Well, what's he doing here? Is he drunk?"

"No sir. He was drunk, but now he is dead. He must have hit that rock over there with his head coming down. There is a big gash on his forehead. That's his bicycle over there. His name is Kekl."

"Jindrich Kekl?"

"That's right, sir."

Kamm opened the door with considerable violence. Leaving his weapon on the seat he limped toward the body as quickly as he could without the help of his cane. He knelt down and in the meagre light of a flashlight examined the man's bloodied temple. At the same time he became aware of the strong odor of alcohol.

"There is a bottle of the stuff in his rucksack," the Czech policeman announced. Kamm limped to the protruding rock and ran his fingers over its sharp edges. It could have been an accident, but it's also one hell of a coincidence, he thought. He called out to his men as he got back in the car. They were going to see Vitek.

The pub was already dark when they arrived. The Czech policemen knocked on the door. The lights came on in the apartment behind the pub where Vitek lived with his wife. The innkeeper came to the door in his bathrobe and Kamm's men pushed their way in past the Czechs, turning on all the lights as they entered. Only then did Kamm get out of the car and follow them in.

Vitek's wife stood by the entrance to the apartment, her hair up in curlers, apprehensively watching the noisy entrance of the Germans. Kamm ordered Vitek and his wife to sit down at one of the tables, while his men went inside the apartment to search it, their search consisting mostly of throwing each article they found in a closet or a dresser on the floor in the middle of the living room. The Czech policemen stood by the entrance of the pub itself at a loss what to do, obviously embarrassed by it all.

"Who was here when Kekl called?"

"No one," Vitek answered without any sign of fear.

"How come?" fired Kamm.

"I don't know. There just wasn't anyone here."

"Aren't there usually some men playing cards?" It was a shot in the dark. One night Kamm had stopped at Vitek's place and there had been some men playing cards.

"Yes, earlier. They were long gone when Kekl arrived."

"Really? But I heard some voices in the background."

I could hardly hear Kekl himself, thought Kamm, but it's another stab in the dark and it could come up with something. Let's see how Vitek reacts.

"Probably the radio ... Or perhaps my wife was singing. She sings a lot you know, Herr Kriminalinspektor."

And you're a highly skilled liar, it would seem, thought Kamm. He turned on his heel and waved to his men. In a few moments they were all gone. With the release from tension Mrs. Vitek suddenly burst into tears. Her husband gently put his arm around her and led her back to the apartment.

The Czech policemen had left on their bicycles again shortly after Kamm and his men emerged from Vitek's pub empty handed. Kamm had sent them home. Röhmer then started the car and they were on their way back to Zamberk, flanked by the two motorcycles.

Kamm was in a foul mood. His stomach now felt even worse. Was it true that Kekl had been drinking and had hallucinations? Who could tell? Certainly most of the Czechs around could. They knew the exact truth. But that was the Czechs, who were becoming more cocky and downright arrogant with the news of each German military withdrawal. The only thing that still frightened them was blood and pain. And, more than anything, death frightened them because they had been waiting for the end for so long. It was almost within sight now and the thought of dying without seeing the Germans on the run absolutely terrified them.

Kekl spoke only Czech and Kamm had never taken the trouble to learn the language. For what? In a few years there would be no one around here to speak the language any more, he had thought when he first came to Zamberk. For a Czech to call the Gestapo was certainly unusual. Kekl was either afraid of what might happen to the whole region if parachutists were found here, or dead drunk and, as a result, without the usual restraints.

In the morning the Czech police should be split up into search parties to comb the countryside between Pastviny and Nekor. It will be a hell of a job though, thought Kamm, because the Czech police were not particularly ambitious. And now it was beginning to snow to boot, so that by morning all possible tracks would be safely covered.

All of that, plus Leimer's trucks, which had already started arriving, meant that what had once been basically a very pleasant vacation spot would soon turn into something entirely different. There was also the gnawing doubt that Kamm had not done everything that should have been done to get to the bottom of Kekl's phone call. Sure the men would start searching the countryside in the morning, but was that enough? Wasn't there something that could be done right now?

"Stop the car," Kamm suddenly mumbled in Röhmer's direction.

The Praga skidded with its brakes locked so that the motorcycle behind it barely missed it. Kamm rolled down his window and through the large snowflakes gazed at the four men with red, frozen faces who had gathered around him.

"You," he motioned to one of the soldiers, "Get in. The rest of you go on to Zamberk. We're going back to pick up Vitek."

16

Commander Howard had not expected Hana Dykova to be so beautiful. The three men followed her
through the hall, shaking the snow off their boots
on the tiled floor. Hana handed them a small whisk
broom with which they brushed the snow from
their clothing. They took off their coats and she led
them into the roomy kitchen with a ceiling-high
stove in one corner. They settled themselves behind
the heavy rustic table and Hana plugged in a hot
plate on which she placed a kettle of water.

"I suppose we should introduce ourselves,"
Commander Howard began in German, ending up
in English. "And would you mind if we spoke English? I understand you speak it quite well."

Hana smiled.

"My English may be a bit rusty but if you don't
mind," she shrugged her shoulders, "I actually love
speaking it."

"Good. This is Lieutenant Stanislaw Jaroscynski of the Polish Free Forces and Sergeant Tom
Evans of the U.S. Army."

"You really are an international group," commented Hana.

"Yes. My name is Douglas Howard and I am
afraid that I don't belong here at all. I am a commander in the Royal Canadian Navy."

"Well, we will try to make you happy in land-locked, Nazi-ruled Czechoslovakia. But I don't think any of you will like it very much here. My name is Hana Dykova and I used to be a movie star," she said, shaking each man's hand.

"*Tesi mne*," said Evans and Hana's eyes widened in surprise.

"You are Czech? But your name ..."

"I'm from Nebraska. On the farm where I grew up ..."

"Miss Dykova," Howard began, "I think first of all we should explain that we all know what would happen to you if we were found here and we are deeply grateful to you."

"It would happen to all of us, commander," Hana said.

"Except that we are soldiers. On a military assignment."

"Well, we're all involved now. How can I help?" Hana asked.

"Do you know a man who uses the cover name Patek?"

Hana smiled and corrected the pronounciation. The name was the Czech word for Friday.

"Yes, I know him."

"He is our contact. Can you get us in touch with him?"

"I'll try but with all this now ... Are you here because of Adam Hill, commander? Patek mentioned that someone may be coming because of it."

In spite of the fatigue, Howard was immediately on his guard.

"Adam Hill? No, I don't think I know the place ... We're here to establish contact with whatever resistance forces may be operating in the area. The Allies are about to enter Europe and there has been a group like us dropped into every occupied country ... But, of course, the less you know about us the better off you are, Miss Dykova."

"Yes, that's right," she replied, getting up to prepare the tea. Howard noticed that both Tom and Stan were beginning to relax in the warm kitchen, that their eyes were beginning to close.

"Perhaps before you serve the tea you could show us around the house. Is there another entrance to it?" he asked.

"Down in the cellar, through the laundry room. There is a door in the hall which leads to it. Would you like to see it?"

The commander nodded and the three men followed Hana who was using a dynamo-powered flashlight activated by the continual squeezing of her hand. The cellar floor was packed earth and the metal door at the end of it led to an outside area covered by the porch. In front of the porch was a clear area, now covered by undisturbed snow, which gently sloped toward the lake. Halfway down there was a row of bushes. Howard noticed that Hana was trembling as they stood beneath the porch. Without a word he placed his heavy overcoat over her shoulders. She smiled at him in gratitude.

"Is there an attic?" the commander asked on their way back up.

"Yes, there is a small place right above the guest bedroom. It used to be a hayloft when this house was a farm."

"Good. We'll have one man on watch there all the time. It should be possible to see anyone approaching the house from there?"

"On a good day you can see all the way to the main road. And that's about a kilometer away," said Hana.

"Just what we need," Howard nodded. "I'll

take the first watch. Let's have two-hour shifts. I'll wake you up next, Tom."

Vitek was seated in the basement of the Zamberk Gestapo headquarters, in a place to which Kamm jokingly referred to as his "workroom." The innkeeper was in his shirtsleeves, tied to a chair. Twice Kamm had one of his men pour cold water over his head to revive him after a particularly powerful blow. Vitek's hair was hanging in wet strands and chills occasionally made his body tremble. He found it difficult to keep his head from falling to one side.

Opposite him sat a pensive Ernst Kamm, smoking one cigarette after another. The first part of Kamm's interrogation program was over. Vitek had been physically softened. He was now far from the recalcitrant, proud Slav that had been brought in an hour earlier. He had been kicked and beaten at his place, in front of his wife who could not resist running in to help as he lay on the floor. Vitek was still fully conscious then. It was a good thing, thought Kamm, because he could see the rough pushing his wife got from Röhmer, strong enough so that it almost toppled her over. She sure as hell didn't feel like singing then, thought Kamm with a smile. There followed a few more kicks for Vitek while he was on the floor with his wife's frantic screams mixing in. Finally Vitek's near-limp body was dragged out. In the car they left him alone so he could revive in the cold and enter the Zamberk headquarters as a proud, recalcitrant Slav once more. Kamm liked it better that way at the beginning of his interrogations.

He warmed his hands on a coffee mug while in his mind once more he went over the events of the night, painstakingly reexamining each one for pos-

sible clues. Of course there must have been some,
but it was getting late, or rather early, and he
could feel his deductive powers starting to wane.
Vitek here could help him. He could tell him what
he knew, what was behind the phone call and
behind Kekl's mysterious death.

Soundlessly Kamm left his chair and advanced
toward the innkeeper's limp body. Vitek was not
unconscious. Kamm had been through enough of
these affairs to know that he was only resting, taking full advantage of the lull in the proceedings.

An animal-like scream pierced the basement.
Covered with black and blue marks as well as
patches of dried blood, the innkeeper stared at
Kamm with a mixture of hatred and surprise. In
his right nostril was lodged half of Kamm's
cigarette. Vitek's whole body shook in spasms in a
desperate effort to dislodge the burning object
when he finally succeeded and the cigarette fell to
the stone floor, Kamm was already back in his seat.

"Stay awake you swine," the Gestapo man
advised calmly. "We have work to do."

Kamm regarded Vitek's hate-filled look as a
sign of progress.

"Let's go over it again. When Kekl arrived at
the pub what did you do?"

"Nothing. I don't pay attention to drunks."

"Did he have a drink at your place?"

"Yes. Several."

"And then?"

"Then he left ... or so I thought."

"When you found him at the telephone, what
did you think?"

"I was angry. Quite mad. I knew that he was
drunk. That he was probably making some stupid
phone call somewhere for which I would have to
pay. It wouldn't be the first time that I've been left

with a bill."

"What did you do?"

"I told him to hang up and I threatened to hit him if he did not do it immediately."

Kamm lit another cigarette and allowed a few moments to pass before asking the next question. He did not like the way Vitek kept recovering his senses. His answers were perfectly lucid and exact replicas of his previous ones.

"Did you know to whom he was talking?"

"I did not even know that he had made the connection. I would have asked the operator how much money he owed me."

Nodding along with the rhythm of Vitek's speech, Kamm kept staring at the floor in front of him. He kept nodding long after the innkeeper had stopped talking, successfully lulling him into a false sense of security. Then he shot out of his chair and, balancing himself on his good leg, he slapped Vitek across his left cheek with the full force of his palm. The innkeeper's face flew to the right with furious force and Kamm slapped it there again with the back of his hand. Simultaneously his heavy shoe caught the innkeeper in the stomach with such impact that the chair he was tied into toppled over and Kamm had to grab the wall for support. Vitek remained on his side, still in his chair, panting. Favoring his bad hip, Kamm limped over so that now he leaned over him, just a few inches away from the innkeeper's face.

"Now let me tell you how it really was. You have a bad memory, because there was a group of your regular cronies, sitting around your dirty, greasy pub and there were playing with dirty, greasy cards your stupid *maryas* game. And in comes Jindrich Kekl, frightened to death because he has seen the parachutists coming down and he

knows what happens to villages harboring enemies
of the Reich. And because he doesn't want his house
razed and because he doesn't want to end up standing in front of a wall with a mattress propped up
against it to keep the bullets from bouncing off, he
does what is expected of him. He is smart, much
smarter than you realize, Vitek. All that you and
your card-playing cronies can think of is to kill
Kekl as soon as you hear him speaking with the
Gestapo. But that wasn't a very good idea because
here you are, black and blue and half frozen to
death and we have not even begun with the real
questioning."

Abruptly Kamm turned around on his heel
and started up the steps. When halfway up, he
yelled back: "Keep him awake with the water dous-
ings. Don't let him sleep!"

17

Douglas Howard sat by the window in the attic, gazing at the white plain ahead of him. The snowfall had dwindled down to a few small flakes now, which was a perfect situation: there had been enough of it to cover any tracks, but not enough to prevent all communications.

The scene relaxed him. By a slight depression through what must have been fields he could follow the narrow country path through the small group of pine trees immediately in front of the entrance to Hana's house. He was anxious for morning to finally arrive so he could at least see the scenery of the country in which his life would probably end.

Although the attic was not heated, it was well insulated. In addition, his clothes were very heavy and warm but there was a danger he might doze off. He had brought up with him a pot half-filled with freezing water. Periodically he reached into it and washed his face. He also smoked frequently although he had not yet acquired a taste for the dark, roughly shredded tobacco of Czech cigarettes.

He heard noise at the entrance to the attic and turned around to see who it was. Even through the darkness he recognized Hana, now fully dressed in trousers, a turtleneck sweater and a heavy overcoat. She was carrying a blanket as she crawled toward the gable in which he was ensconced with his gun resting on his knees.

"I thought you might need this."

"Thank you, I'm fine. It's cool and that keeps me awake."

Hana settled herself alongside him. "I would like to stay here for a moment with you. Do you mind?"

Howard looked at her and wondered how anyone could possibly mind. He shook his head without a word.

"You see, for me you really represent the end of the war," she explained. "I can see it in you. I guess it's hard for you to understand, but the arrival of Americans here at Pastviny cannot really mean anything else."

"And Canadians," the commander smilingly corrected her.

"Sorry. Canadians too, of course," Hana returned the smile.

"I guess we have a lot to learn about how things are here. Has it been bad for you?"

"No. I've been lucky. Very lucky, compared to some."

Howard nodded without a word.

"Where is your home in Canada?"

"The last one was in Montreal. But it wasn't much of home. A rented room."

"Is your mother language French or English?"

"Neither. I first learned how to speak in German."

Hana's eyes widened.

"You are German? And you fight against them?"

"Oh, I was offered service in the Pacific. But here I am more useful. I only *speak* German. My heart is definitely Canadian, Hana."

She relaxed at the sound of her name.

"Will you be going to Pastviny tomorrow?" asked Howard, abruptly changing the subject.

"Yes, I will try to contact the man you call Patek."

"I wish I could be along. It's not easy to be in the country I've heard so much about and not being able to go out of the house."

"You'll see it, I promise. Some day I'd like to be able to show you Prague."

A broad grin spread across Douglas Howard's face.

"I wish the Americans would hurry with the invasion," he said.

When it stopped snowing shortly before sunrise, no more than half a foot had fallen. Hana got up early. She came downstairs, made a cup of chicory coffee and some porridge for Jaroscynski who was on watch in the attic and then ate some herself. As she was putting on her felt boots, Tom Evans came down with the commander.

"You should be getting some sleep," Hana reprimanded them after a greeting.

"We can sleep all day. Am I right in thinking that Patek won't be coming before tonight?" asked Howard.

"That's right," replied Hana. "He works during the day. And he would probably wait until tonight even if he didn't. He prefers to move only after dark."

The commander nodded.

"He sounds like a sensible man."

"Very sensible. That's part of the reason why he has survived until now."

Hana had finished dressing. Even in her

heavy, shapeless coat and babushka she was attractive, Howard thought. *Very* attractive.

"Where will you meet him?" he asked.

"I won't see him. I'll simply leave word. He'll know by noon. I'll be back in about two hours."

She grabbed the bag beside her on the bench, quickly unlocking the door.

"Good luck," Howard said. Hana turned around and looked at him. Then she nodded in reply before closing the door behind her.

Over his porridge, Tom suddenly stopped eating and looked at Howard. "Now that we are on the ground, what would you say are our chances of doing the job and getting out alive?"

The commander thought for a moment. The Christmas card scene outside the window made him feel slightly ridiculous talking about any danger. So far it had been more like a winter holiday.

"Hard to say. We have landed all right and found shelter without much of a problem. But we haven't established contact with the underground yet. So far our moves have been strictly defensive. Maybe we have proved that left alone we can take care of ourselves, but nothing more. And that's not what we're all about, is it? We're not supposed to be a Boy Scout expedition."

Tom shook his head, thinking about it.

"What about Hana? How does she strike you?"

"Car coming ... with a motorcycle. They're Germans!" Jaroscynski yelled from the attic. In the next moment Howard roughly pushed the table away and with two long strides reached the hallway, closely followed by Tom Evans.

"How far are they?" yelled Howard, taking the steps up two at a time.

"Just turned off the main road. We have maybe five minutes."

Near the top of the stairs Howard turned to Tom.

"Go into Hana's bedroom and see if there's anyone coming from the back!" Without a word Tom turned left at the top, while Howard continued up the ladder into the attic. Once there, he sat down, panting, next to Jaroscynski and took the binoculars out of his hands. The car was a military one. So was the motorcycle which was following it. Both were painted khaki. The motorcycle had a driver and a man in the sidecar — both in uniform and with submachine guns slung across their backs. He thought he could see three men in the car but he wasn't sure. In any case they had to follow the path toward the house in a wide arc and that gave those in the house some time. Stan was right. They probably still had five minutes before the Germans reached the house.

The commander's mind raced. Hana! She had alerted the Gestapo, she was with them!

"Anyone coming from the rear, Tom?" he yelled in Evans' direction.

"I don't see anything ... I don't think so."

The commander was now climbing back from the attic. "Come on with me," he called to Tom. Without stopping he continued into the cellar where all their equipment had been stored.

"Go out the cellar door and cover the back of the house. You won't be able to hear us, but we'll hear you. If you see anyone coming, start shooting."

They had grabbed their guns and were filling their pockets with extra ammunition. Tom put on his overcoat and started to go out.

"Tom, if it looks like we've had it up front — if the firing has stopped there — do your best to get away. You have your pills?"

Tom nodded. A moment later he was out. On his way back up it flashed through Howard's mind that he had just instructed Evans not to die needlessly and in the next breath asked him if he had his cyanide pills. He must think I've cracked under the strain, he thought.

He was again crouching beside Jaroscynski at the attic window, gazing at the slowly approaching car. The two vehicles had reached the bend in the path. They were about halfway between the main road and the house.

"Chances are they will not try to drive all the way to the house," he said. "With the snowdrifts in front they're bound to get stuck."

Stan nodded, not taking his eyes off the approaching vehicles.

"There *must* be another group of them coming from the back ... they can't hope to ... with just five men ..."

Howard thought for a moment.

"I'll take another look from downstairs," he said starting down the ladder.

But there was nothing. The white surface of Pastviny lake was undisturbed. Even a careful examination of the shore area showed no fresh tracks. It doesn't make sense, thought the commander. Hana must have told them there are three of us. Why would they send so few men and arrive over the most exposed approach to the house?

"Stan! Where are they?"

"Almost at the gate now."

"Listen! No shooting until they start, all right? They have no idea where we are. Don't tell them."

"Okay ... They've stopped at the gate. Now they're getting out."

"How many are there?"

"Three in the car, two on the motorcycle ... Wait a minute! They're not coming down to the house. Only one is, the civilian, the rest are ..."

The whole thing was becoming absolutely insane. Unless, of course, the man in the civilian clothes was coming to negotiate. But negotiate what? They were already dead and the limping German with a fur-collared coat coming down the path could only offer lies.

With difficulty the German made his way through the snow to the front door. Then he stopped, waited a few moments, knocked. Softly, politely. It was certainly not the act of an arrogant Nazi who held all the top cards.

Slowly, ever so slowly, Howard drew aside a corner of the curtain in the living room. He watched the back of the German at close range now, and still his manner seemed no more than that of a man making a social call. There was no impatience, no gruff gestures. He let the curtain drop into place again just as the German started to turn. Howard stood there beside the window, more sensing than actually seeing the man with the fur collar returning to his car. Then he heard the car door slam and the engine start.

As the commander took a deep breath, he noticed that the other end of the curtain was obscuring most of a picture which hung on the wall right next to it.

He drew that part of the curtain away and instantly came face to face with a near life-size portrait of a frowning Adolf Hitler.

18

They were seated in a semicircle around the attic window with two photo albums they had found in the living room beside them. One of them was opened to a page which showed Hana Dykova in a lively conversation with Hermann Göring.

"Why should she do it? It doesn't make sense, does it?" asked Tom, eager for an explanation.

There was no explanation. Gone was the Christmas card atmosphere of the place, with its benign, snow-covered hills and placid lake which a few moments ago had reminded Howard of Lac Tremblant in the mountains near Montreal. Now it seemed to hide threats all the more frightening because they were irrational; they made no sense.

"Someone's coming," mumbled Stan Jaroscynski from underneath the binoculars. Howard lifted his eyes from the pictures.

"It's her," Stan said after a moment. "And she is alone ..."

I'll go down," Howard said, raising himself off Hana's blanket.

"Should I come?" asked Stan.

Howard thought a moment.

"No," he said finally. "I think I'd better do this alone."

As Hana entered he stepped out from behind

the door, quickly placing his arm around her neck from behind. Unable to make a sound, her frightened eyes watched as he coarsely searched underneath her half-buttoned overcoat. Satisfied that there were no weapons he spun her around. Although she was staring into the barrel of his gun, she nevertheless relaxed when she recognized Howard.

"Thank God, I was afraid that ..."

"Undress ... Everything."

"What? But I ..."

"Take all your clothes off and spread them in front of you."

"But commander I ..."

She was stopped by the blaze in his eyes. Something had happened while she was gone that had changed everything. Whatever it was there was need for an explanation. But the commander's face didn't give the impression he could be placated by talk. She took off her coat and bulky sweater, then her boots. She started to unbutton her dress but he stopped her with a motion of his hand, studying her face intently.

"What is the matter? Commander, I would like to help."

He motioned with his gun for her to enter the living room. Without a word he positioned himself in front of the portrait.

"Hmmm, Adolf. I thought that might be it. You didn't see him last night, did you?"

"Neither did we see your photo albums," the commander noted dryly.

"Sit down," Hana pleaded. Howard reluctantly complied. She lighted a cigarette and offered him one, which he refused. But he lowered his pistol and allowed it to rest on his lap.

"What you have seen are props, commander.

In my closet I even have a series of framed photographs of the Führer and me at the Eagle's Nest with Bormann and Goebbels. But I only bring them out when important Nazis come to visit. I have to have them out if I am to keep up a front, if I am to be regarded as a friend of the Germans. Very few villagers still speak to me, but it makes my house fairly safe when it's needed to hide parachutists from Britain."

"What about the army?"

"Which army?"

"A motorcycle and a military car arrived this morning while you were gone. A man in civilian clothes and several soldiers came to visit you."

"Did he limp?"

Howard nodded.

"Ernst Kamm, the Gestapo inspector from Zamberk."

"And?"

Hana was showing irritation.

"For God's sake commander, do you have any idea what the resistance is like? It isn't the charge of the Light Brigade. After Heydrich was assassinated anyone who ever had been heard to utter a word against the Germans was shot within hours. There was a man not far from here. Three years ago he took out German citizenship and joined the Nazi Party. He was shot too. Do you know why? Because he had the same name as one of the assassins. Try to understand things a little bit. My friendship with Kamm is of great value." There was no proof that what she was saying was true, but certainly the force of her argument could not be dismissed.

"What about Patek, will he come?"

Hana nodded. "Tonight," she said.

Patek was prompt. Exactly at eight there was a soft knock on the door. Hana opened it with the grim-faced Howard in the darkness a few feet away. The lights in the hallway came on suddenly and the newcomer was facing two men with guns. He was searched, then ordered into the living room. Howard went in and closed the door behind the two of them. Stan led Hana into the kitchen.

"I'm glad to see you're so cautious," commented Patek in German. "Are you satisfied now?"

Howard looked at him sharply.

"You served as an officer before the war. Where?"

"In Pilsen."

"Division?"

"The Second."

"Regiment?"

"Thirty-fifth."

Howard relaxed. He extended his hand to the newcomer.

"I am Lieutenant Commander Douglas Howard of the Royal Canadian Navy. This is Lieutenant Jaroscynski of the Polish Free Forces and upstairs is Tom Evans. He is an American."

"And I'm Jiri Palka, otherwise known as Patek."

Howard examined Palka's bewhiskered, weatherbeaten face with lines that seemed too deep for his age. There was deadly determination all over it.

"Glad to know you," the commander said.

Palka leaned closer to him.

"Look, we have to move on. We have quite a job ahead of us," he said.

Howard called in Jaroscynski and Hana.

"The third man is upstairs. He will have to stay to watch, we don't want to be surprised by the

Gestapo."

"Call him down. There is a man watching outside," said Palka. Moments later they were all assembled in the living room, right under the unfriendly portrait of Adolf Hitler.

"About Adam Hill," the commander started. "I thought if one or two of us hid in your milk wagon we could get inside then ..."

"That could have been possible last week," Palka interrupted. "Now they don't let me in any more. I have to leave the wagon at the first bunker. *They* take it up."

"But we could still hide in it, couldn't we?"

"No. They search it now. You couldn't get past the first bunker that way. How about false papers as repairmen or something? We could get them for you."

"It would take too long. We must be in the fortress before noon Monday. Because of the air raid."

"What air raid?" asked Jaroscynski.

"You weren't told because we might have been captured right after landing," explained Howard. "The inside sabotage at Adam Hill and the air raid must come within moments of each other, otherwise the Germans would have time to move the containers which are stacked outside."

Palka nodded in agreement.

"But if we can't get inside with the wagon, what can we do?" asked Jaroscynski.

Palka paused a moment, drawing in his breath.

"Kidnap Tiesenhausen. He lives less than a kilometer from here in a house as isolated as this. We could force him to go up to Adam Hill with us, leaving his wife behind as a hostage."

"He has two bodyguards. With submachine guns," Hana warned.

"Are they ever outside?" asked Palka.

"No. At least I've never seen them outside the house. They ride with him in the car though."

"That's our information too. They can be overpowered. They *can* be surprised," said Palka.

"Why do you think Tiesenhausen would cooperate?" asked Howard. "Aren't the fanatical Nazis usually ready to sacrifice their own grandmother?"

"I don't think Tiesenhausen would be. As a matter of fact I wonder how many of them would sacrifice anything if faced with this situation. Not now, when they're running on all fronts."

"But it's still a risk, isn't it?" asked Jaroscynski in his bad German.

"Yes," Palka replied simply. "There is a considerable amount of risk." He turned to the commander. "Particularly since you were seen coming down."

"By whom?"

"By a local man. He even managed to call the Gestapo but we don't think he told them so much before we got to him. He didn't speak much German and he was also a well-known drunk. We made sure that when he was found there was plenty of liquor around and inside him."

"*Was* found?" asked Howard.

"Yes, commander, he is dead now," Palka explained.

"Aren't the Germans suspicious, though?"

"Oh, they're always that. Always. They even arrested the innkeeper at the place from where the phone call was made to the Gestapo."

"Vitek? Does he know anything?" asked Hana.

"Everything. He was in on everything," said Palka gloomily.

"Then we don't have much of a chance, do we?"

asked Jaroscynski. "What would happen if the Gestapo started searching the area?"

"If they really searched then not even my dog would get through. But they won't go to all the trouble unless they have more proof. And that won't happen unless they break Vitek down."

"Do you think they will ... break him down?" asked Howard.

Palka thought for a moment. "No. But I have been wrong before. The thing that's in our favor is that they have nothing on Vitek. If they don't get anything out of him he is likely to go free. And if they do, it will mean the end of him as well. Besides, the Gestapo has to work fast. He has to be broken before Monday morning — about thirty-six hours from now — in order for it to mean anything. I think Vitek will hold out that long."

Palka took a piece of paper from his pocket and unfolded it. "Now this is Adam Hill as it looks today ..."

19

Shortly after midnight Howard completed a wide circle around the Tiesenhausen villa. Hidden by the bushes, trees, and even snowdrifts most of the time, he now had an adequate idea of the place, its blind spots and of nearby hiding areas. On the whole he was satisfied. There were no other buildings nearby. On the other hand there was a road which connected with the main one and it had been cleared of snow. In front of the Tiesenhausen house stood an Opel with military markings.

Hana was still reading in the living room when he returned. Jaroscynski was sleeping and Evans was at the lookout in the attic. The commander planned not to disturb her but she called to him as soon as he came in. He came into the living room. She was wearing her night clothes with a polka dot housecoat over them which Howard found very appealing.

"I've stayed up because I thought you might have some questions about the Tiesenhausen house. That is ... if I am to be trusted again."

Howard looked at the floor.

"Of course you are. I am sorry about this morning, but I think you understand ... How well do you know the house inside?"

"I know it quite well. I was good friends with

the Abeleses, the previous owners. Some people say
they have ended up in Dachau, others that they are
in New York. I sincerely hope it's New York."

Howard sat down at the coffee table, gazing
embarrassingly at the large spots where his heavy
socks had been mended. He had left his boots at the
entrance.

"There is actually something I'd like to know
Miss Dykova. I ..."

"Hana."

"What? Oh, yes, Hana." He smiled. "Then I'm
Douglas."

"Yes. Douglas," she said. There followed a few
seconds of silence for the assimilation of the new
situation. Then Howard spoke.

"There isn't an outside staircase on the Tiesenhausen house by any chance, is there? Where one
could get to the upstairs terrace?"

"Of course there is. But you couldn't see it
unless you were in the middle of the backyard.
There is a large oak tree right in front of it, hiding
it."

The commander's eyes lit up.

"That's perfect. Perfect." He rubbed his hands.
"Why?"

"Because it means that we can enter the house
on both floors at the same time. The bedrooms are
on the first floor, aren't they?"

"No, they're upstairs. All of them."

Howard smiled.

"The first floor *is* upstairs in England. I must
have been there too long. I guess you don't have a
ground floor here."

"Oh, but we have a *parterre* and *mezzanin* to
further confuse things," laughed Hana, throwing
her head backward. Howard joined in the laughter, which was more the result of released tension

than anything else. Suddenly they both stopped
and stared at each other for a moment.

"I'm really sorry about this afternoon. I had no
right ..." Howard began but her finger placed over
his lips lightly silenced him. He pressed his hand
against it, moving his head to the side so that her
hand now rested against his cheek.

"Douglas," she whispered, "Douglas, Douglas."

He sat down beside her and she curled up in
his arms, feeling more secure than she had in
years.

"When will all this be over?" she whispered.
"I'm so afraid. I used to be a fairly good actress but
I can't feign courage forever."

"Soon," he said, "it will all be over soon." He
stroked her hair and she rose toward him until
their lips met. Then they were locked in an
embrace, oblivious of time and place, oblivious of
everything except to the sudden, exhilarating
release of their long pent-up passions.

Kamm had spent the night in his chair fully
clothed. His premonition was becoming stronger
without any real reason for it. Something seemed
to be happening in the Orlice Mountains and he felt
increasingly powerless in changing anything any
more. Downstairs in the cold slime of the basement
was Vitek, periodically hallucinating but completely off the subject of the telephone call. Kamm
was becoming convinced that Vitek knew nothing
more, that Kekl had been drunk, that there really
had been no parachutists. In the final analysis,
however, that all seemed unimportant. The danger
was somewhere else, independent of what was happening in the mountains. As if in a Greek play the
men who were part of the drama were all destined

for a tragic end. There was nothing they could do about it. All roads led to hell.

Kamm woke up with a start. The pain in his hip, which throughout the night had periodically woken him up, had increased. He got up and moved slowly across the cold room, hoping that the movement would ease the pain. It didn't do the job and in desperation he reached atop the cabinet and poured himself a glass of the potent Steinhaeger liquor. Only then did his pain as well as his anxiety subside a little.

He limped into the bathroom without his cane and washed his face, then began to shave. At that point Röhmer arrived.

"It's seven o'clock sir. Would you like some coffee?"

"Yes. Who's downstairs with Vitek?"

"Hammerberg, sir."

Kamm suddenly got an idea. He limped back into the living room with his face only half shaved.

"Take a couple of men and start searching for possible signs of the parachutists, Röhmer."

Röhmer clicked his heels in that annoying way of his. Kamm always had the feeling that when this corporal did it, it was more like a sarcastic joke.

"Yes, sir. With all respect sir, could you instruct us where we should start the search?"

Kamm thought for a moment.

"Start at Nekor and continue toward Pastviny," he said finally. "Look through the farmhouses near the main road."

"Yes, sir," Röhmer clicked his heels again. "I also wish to report, sir, that three more trucks arrived during the night. We put them up according to the list. I took one of them over personally."

Kamm nodded, thinking that Röhmer was too damn eager to please. That's more likely how he managed to get promoted to corporal, but he would not go any higher than that because the war was almost over. And chances were that Röhmer, the blue-eyed, blond, super Aryan will not be alive to collect any pensions. Not when all the hate of the Czechs in the region will be directed against the Gestapo. By then I'll be long gone, thought Kamm. At the same time, though, he had serious doubts about it. He would do everything humanly possible to be gone, that's all he could do.

Zahorelova came in as he finished shaving and started a fire in the kitchen on which she would cook breakfast. Kamm put on a clean shirt and without saying a word to her, he descended into the basement.

Vitek looked exactly the same as when had left him the night before: dirty, unshaven, ashen pale. But he was not yet broken; his eyes attested to that. Kamm motioned to Hammerberg to give Vitek some coffee. While the soldier held the cup in front of the innkeeper's swollen lips, Kamm spoke.

"Very well, a new day means a new way toward the truth. Now, we have to have truth, unless of course, you'd want your wife to be sitting right here beside you. You wouldn't want that, would you Vitek?"

The hatred in Vitek's eyes was immense. But Kamm liked hatred. It was a passion, a strong one, and as such it was a highly useful force. All sorts of things could be made to happen with its help.

"Let's concentrate on the people who were in your place Friday night. Name them."

Vitek's eyes jumped around the cellar in an intense effort to sidestep the danger. His mind was weary and the demands on it were excessive. But finally it responded.

"Kekl was there," he said barely audibly.

"I want only the live ones," barked Kamm. But he did not hit him. Vitek took his time thinking again.

"Pochdar and Matejka. I'm not sure, but I think they were there earlier that evening."

Good guess, thought Kamm. Both had applied for German citizenship as soon as the Wehrmacht marched into Czechoslovakia and both were refused it because of their criminal record. With their large families they lived in the poorhouse at Pastviny, primarily because of their frequent and costly visits to the pub. Nothing here worth hanging on to. Vitek was still ahead.

Kamm turned around and with an effort started up the stairs. He needed time. Time to think of something.

20

Sunday lunch was a pork roast with sauerkraut and dumplings, well-cooked and served by Hana herself. Ostensibly she had prepared the feast to celebrate the Allies' arrival at Orlice Mountains, but Howard couldn't help think it was also meant as a farewell meal. He had estimated fifty percent casualties.

They ate upstairs near the lookout window, holding their plates on their knees. Evans and Jaroscynski were briefed on their parts in the overall plan, while Hana served the meal and occasionally listened. Downstairs in the living room Hana and Howard were left alone with their chicory coffee. Hana took a bottle of home-made slivovice from the mantelpiece and poured a small glass for each of them. They settled in their seats around the coffee table.

"I would like you to know, Commander Douglas Howard, that I don't regret last night. Not at all," she said slowly.

Howard remained silent for a little while. Then he looked down at his glass and mumbled awkwardly, as if he were not used to such intimate situations.

"Neither do I. I meant everything I did and said, Hana."

They raised their glasses.

"I'm trying to work up enough courage to say it," she explained.

"Say what, Hana? What's the matter?"

"If you feel as strongly about me as I do about you, Douglas, why do you want me dead?"

"Dead? What're you talking about?"

"If I stay behind, if I'm not part of your plan, I'm dead. If I go with you I have a chance. Not much of a chance, granted, but some chance at least."

"Hana there's sure to be shooting."

"Do you really think that the Gestapo is so stupid? How long do you think it'll take them to put it all together, before they know that the headquarters was here, at my place?"

"Isn't there somewhere that Palka could hide you?"

Hana shook her head.

"This whole area will be hell after the Adam Hill thing is over. There will be no place left to hide in all of Orlice Mountains. You have the only plan of escape with some chance of success, Douglas, the *only* one. Keep moving. Into the Reich and through there into Poland. Because there is a possibility that the Germans will not be able to coordinate their search on the Reich's side right away. That might give you a day or two."

"You sound as if you've had experience with escapes."

"We managed to get some thirty officers safely through this region to fight with the Poles in 1939. I hope they will all be coming back with the Russians."

Neither said anything for a few moments.

"All right Hana," Howard finally broke his silence, "What should I do?"

"I can't go inside the fortress on Adam Hill
with you."

"No."

"But I can join up with you and the other two
afterward."

"A group of four is too big, Hana."

"I know. But while you and Stan Jaroscynski
are in the fortress, Evans will be guarding Frau
Tiesenhausen, is that right?"

"Yes."

"How will he get there — to the Reich — and
join up with you?"

"We'll meet at St. Stephen's Church in Glatz,
Wednesday night for vespers."

"Yes, but how will *he* get there?"

"He has a compass."

"He has never been in this region before so
he'll have to follow the main roads. The ones with
the signs."

Howard nodded.

"But I know the out-of-the-way paths, the
mountain trails, where the Germans can't get with
their vehicles and where there are no farmers who
could report you."

Howard thought it over for a moment.

"All right Hana. You win. Come here."

Howard took his Colt automatic out of its
holster.

"You'd better get used to this," he said, taking
the clip out of it.

At eight Palka arrived and unraveled a plan before
them which seemed technically faultless. After the
kidnapping of Tiesenhausen, accomplished with a
force of ten men, there would follow the penetra-
tion of Adam Hill with six of them. Three would
wear *Wehrmacht* uniforms acquired at Tiesen-

hausen's house, the others would pose as civilian advisers from Berlin on an inspection tour.

Halfway through the explanation Howard stopped him.

"I'm sorry, Jiri, but it can't be done that way."

"Why?" the Czech looked up in surprise.

"Because with that big an operation something is bound to go wrong. The idea of getting inside Adam Hill is highly improbable to start off with. Add the fact that there will be three men in civilian clothes and it becomes even less probable. And this cumbersome business of coordinating the actions of six men once inside, only places added stress on the whole operation. Do you know Tiesenhausen's rank in the Nazi party?"

"He is an Oberdienstleiter—the equivalent of a Standartenführer in the S.S. Your Brigadier General."

"Then it's more than likely that with that high a rank he would keep a uniform at home, isn't it?"

"Yes."

"That's all we need. Once we take the house we'll have three uniforms. Tiesenhausen doesn't need one, he's known at Adam Hill. It's hardly likely that anyone will ask for the identification of an Oberdienstleiter in the car with Tiesenhausen which is being driven by a Wehrmacht soldier, Jaroscynski here. You don't mind being demoted into the ranks, do you, Stan?"

The last part was designed to relax everyone, to take the edge of the next confrontation between Palka and Howard which might follow.

"Look, the main thing is getting inside the fortress to do the job," Howard continued. "Sure we all would like to survive, but it isn't essential. And there is something else: I would like to keep your group here intact, Jiri, even after the Adam Hill mission. The front is coming closer and you and your men will be needed."

No one said anything for a while. Finally Palka spoke up.

"I've brought the chloroform you've asked for," he said, handing Howard a small vial. It was clear he was in agreement. "What about Hana?" he asked.

"We'll do our best to get her through with us."

He nodded and rose.

"Then I don't think there is anything else," he said, but his voice was not convincing. Clearly there was much, much more to be said.

"We will be along your route tomorrow morning, but most of us you won't see."

"Thanks," said Howard.

Hana suddenly rose and walked over to the cupboard beside the fireplace. She took out a small box from it.

"Jiri, I would like you to have this. I got it for an essay I once wrote in tenth grade. I have always been very proud of it. Soon, I hope it will not be just a memory any more."

Palka opened the box. Inside was a bronze medal commemorating the tenth anniversary of the Czechoslovak Republic in 1928. Palka nodded without a word, clearly moved by the gesture. He closed the box again, put it in his pocket and was about to exit. At the last moment he stopped in his tracks. He turned around and embraced Hana, kissing her on the cheek. Then he walked over to Howard, Evans, and Jaroscynski, shaking each one's hand without a word.

"Good luck," he said finally, his voice nearly breaking. "We'll see each other after the war. Get a good night's sleep tonight. We'll keep a lookout."

Then he opened the door and disappeared into the icy stillness outside.

Douglas Howard felt it coming. That's why he went up to his room to be alone. First there was the familiar tingling in his fingers, followed by his left arm becoming numb. By that time he was upstairs in the dark room and under a heavy blanket, fighting off the shivers as best he could. His mind raced toward tomorrow. His fear was now mixed with thoughts full of excruciating pain about Hana, about the part she had been forced to play, about the havoc and reprisals which would descend on the peaceful countryside once Adam Hill had been attacked and the full force of Nazi fury turned against anyone who might have been involved.

It was really the first time that he had thought about the whole region's implication in Operation Lister, about the death, suffering, the tragedy of it all — like a big bubble full of dark blood that had burst over the snow-covered countryside. Like an opened Pandora's box that would be regretted but justified in London, but which would be something else entirely when it shattered the tranquility of this beautiful land.

Then came thoughts about Hana. He realized now that he loved her. In her, quiet courage, wisdom, and dignity came in a combination he had never encountered before, except, perhaps, on the pages of some exaggerated novel. Just like Palka and all the unknown and unseen Resistance members, she walked on through all this horror, even though all around them others were being felled by Nazi vengeance left and right. But they were always quietly replaced and the effort continued as if it were the most natural thing in the world. Howard tried to picture his own countrymen in a similar situation, but he couldn't. All the circumstances seemed too bizarre, too theatrical for Canada. He hoped it would always remain so.

What about Hana, what about both of them? Chances are that neither of them would be alive by noon tomorrow.

God, isn't there a way out? There must be.

He heard someone gently knock on the door and he realized that, exhausted by the fast-moving, criss-crossing thoughts in his head, he had fallen asleep. But he felt much better now. His mind was back to normal.

"Douglas," whispered Hana, entering the room, "are you awake?"

When Howard stirred and sat up in his bed she came closer. "I thought you'd like some tea. It's almost midnight and you wanted to take the supplies near to the Tiesenhausen place."

"Yes, we should do that," Howard answered, taking a sip on the hot tea. He was now fully awake.

"Hana, you can't go to the Tiesenhausen house with us tomorrow. You should leave right now, walk to the train station and hide somewhere in Prague. The war will be over in a few months."

She smiled and took his hand.

"I am an actress, a movie star, Douglas. I have a face that everyone in this country knows. I can't travel on a train without being immediately recognized. Even if I reached Prague, who do you think would take me in with the infuriated Gestapo after me? And what about Tom? How will he find his way from the Tiesenhausen house across the border by himself? Remember, you and Stanislaw are already in the Reich on Adam Hill. Tom will first have to make this way through several kilometers of Czech countryside to it. Without me he hasn't much of a chance, has he?"

Howard swung his legs from the bed, his head in his hands. Hana was right and he wished so much that she had not been.

The flames were dancing inside the small, mica-covered opening of the barrel stove in the corner. Otherwise the room was dark. But outside there was full moon which enveloped the countryside in its light and threw an intricate pattern of shadows on Howard's bed. They sat there in each other's arms for some time before he stirred, got up and put on his heavy sweater.

"It's time to get the supplies up to the Tiesenhausen house," he said.

With his hand on the door he heard her softly call him. He turned around, her figure now only one of the shadows across the room.

"Douglas, when you come back, could you do something for me?"

He nodded.

"When you come back will you spend the night with me? Tonight of all nights I'd so much hate to be alone."

He nodded again.

21

Just before daylight the four of them were lying on some pine branches placed on the snow in a small clump of trees about fifty meters from the Tiesenhausen villa. Howard was keeping watch, scanning the place with his binoculars in an attempt to determine if anything was moving. It was logical to expect that both of the bodyguards would be downstairs. Tiesenhausen was probably quite rank and class conscious. It wasn't likely he would assign one of the upstairs bedrooms to a common soldier. Besides, the guards were far more useful downstairs, where they could block anyone's way to the bedrooms.

Except for the light from a small desk lamp downstairs, the villa was dark. But there was a thin wisp of smoke coming out of the chimney. The bodyguard was probably keeping warm.

Before they had left Hana's house Howard had been plagued by frequent urges to turn and to start running. Now such ideas were gone. With the dark outline of the Tiesenhausen house looming in front of them, there was no longer a thought of turning back — only of how best to utilize the element of surprise they had so overwhelmingly on their side.

"All right," he whispered, "let's take the supplies across as quickly as possible, then assemble below the oak in the backyard."

First across the open terrain were Evans and Jaroscynski, dragging the box with the explosives behind them. In the deep snow it took them considerably longer than expected. Throughout it all Howard anxiously scanned the surroundings. Still no signs of life.

Next went Hana and Howard with a rucksack on his back in which he carried the chemicals. He paid attention to Hana who found it hard going in the drifts near the house. Finally they were all assembled below the willow tree, only ten feet or so from the outside staircase. On Howard's nod they moved to it. With Jaroscynski leading they started to climb the staircase.

Meanwhile, Howard reached the window. Standing slightly to the side of it, he looked in.

Next to a small table with a lighted lamp dozed a soldier with his tunic undone. He is young, damn young, thought the commander. From upstairs came two short hisses. Hana and the two men had reached the terrace. Howard looked at the soldier again, then answered with short hiss of his own, followed by the sound produced by the barrel of his gun shattering the downstairs window. The startled soldier jerked in his chair.

"*Hande hoch!*" the commander called in through what was now a fairly large hole in the window. He hoped to God the kid would obey and raise his hands. But the soldier's eyes strained to grasp the situation. Then, making out the outline of the figure with the gun in the window, the soldier reached for his own weapon.

The force of the five bullets which struck him almost simultaneously threw him and the armchair he was sitting in several feet back toward the wall. Howard reached in to unlock the door. Moments later he was inside, racing through the hall alongside the room with the dead soldier, frantically flicking on the light switches on the wall.

There was no one else downstairs. When Howard entered the living room the soldier was no longer breathing and a thin stream of blood oozed from beneath him. Only then did Howard become aware of noise upstairs.

The master bedroom was invaded by Jaroscynski. He threw the door open and the rays of his flashlight revealed a man and a woman rising in their beds, their stunned eyes wide open and focused on the terrifying figure.

"*Hande hoch,*" Jaroscynski screamed. Reluctantly they raised their hands. There was something comical about the pair sitting up in their beds with their hands above their heads but Jaroscynski was too busy to fully take it in. With his free hand he searched along the wall until he found the light switch, then turned it on.

Farther down the hall the door flew open in another room. Into it strode Tom Evans with Hana beside him holding the flashlight. In bed was a young man, both in texture and color as if made of straw. The invaders and the invaded stared at each other, assessing the situation and in the process trying to arrive at some way of dealing with it.

But only for a moment, because then Evans noticed on the chair beside the bed a neatly folded SS officer's uniform, with the cap resting on top. A bit farther away was a service revolver in a holster. The young man had followed the angle of Evans' gaze and instantly realized he was in grave danger.

"*Nicht schussen, ich bin der Sohn — Eric Tiesenhausen!*" he yelled in mortal fear.

It was exactly the right thing to say. Just as he cried out Howard had reached the upstairs in his frantic search for the second bodyguard. He heard the plea.

"Don't shoot, Tom." said Howard matter-of-factly. "He says he is Tiesenhausen's son." He worked his way inside the room and he grabbed young Tiesenhausen by his shoulder, telling him to get dressed. Then he reached for the revolver and slipped it into his own pocket.

Downstairs, the commander dragged the soldier's dead body into the cellar, then rearranged the disturbed furniture. The German participants in the drama started to come down, now dressed and accompanied by Hana and the two men. Howard placed them strategically in various chairs, explaining the plan as quickly as possible, in the end adding the part each member of the Tiesenhausen family would be expected to play in it.

The silence which followed was interrupted by Hana who announced she was going in the kitchen to make coffee. The expectant eyes of everyone in the room were now on the older Tiesenhausen.

Howard noted that the face of the gray-haired and moderately balding professor Tiesenhausen betrayed a touch of fanaticism. Especially around his eyes. He didn't expect much from him. Except for the younger Tiesenhausen introducing himself upstairs, no other member of the family had yet uttered a word. Now they would have to.

The scientist looked around at the three men around him with disdain. He finally spoke.

"So you think that you can break into Robert Tiesenhausen's house with impunity and frighten him so much that he will transform himself into a meek lamb, eh?" he began with a pompousness that, in the circumstances, seemed comical. "You are very much mistaken, Englishmen. That will not be the case."

"A few explanations, professor," said Howard, surprising the professor with his fluent German. "First of all, this is not your house but one which you occupy only temporarily. It is the house of Jakob Abeles. In a few months he will be able to claim it again. Second, none of us is English. You must have forgotten that Germany is now fighting the whole world. And losing, I think you will agree. But those are only minor errors. The big one you are making is underestimating us. We haven't shot your SS officer son because we are still negotiating. Not only for his life, but for your wife's, and your own as well. Everything is negotiable. If you refuse to accompany us to Adam Hill the entire Tiesenhausen family will die out right here on this cold February morning in 1944. There is no other way."

Throughout the explanation Tiesenhausen was staring at the floor in front of him, as if not listening. Now he looked up.

"Do you have any idea what will happen to me if I cooperate with you?" he asked suddenly. But it was a poor maneuver, one that betrayed weakness.

"I know that if you don't cooperate yours and your family's lives will be over in minutes. We will then put our alternate plan into operation which will not only destroy the germ cultures, but scores of lives on Adam Hill. Lives which otherwise might have been spared."

"I am a German, sir, please understand."

"The Germans have been very difficult to understand, professor. Almost always."

Howard motioned to Evans and Jaroscynski who cocked their guns. The deathly pale Eric Tiesenhausen suddenly got up to face his father angrily.

"Think it over carefully! What is it exactly that we are dying for?" he screamed into his face.

"So that we will not have to avoid mirrors for the rest of our lives," the old man shot back. He was recalcitrant now, angry for having shown a weak side, for momentarily giving the intruders the illusion of supremacy.

"My God, Robert, the war is lost. There is no hope any more for saving anything except our bare lives. It has all been a dream, a terrible delusion, a nightmare! And you want to end it with three more deaths. For what, Robert, *for what*?"

The scene was almost incredible. The dignified, tall Frau Magde Tiesenhausen was on her knees in front of the professor, wringing her clasped hands at him. Large tears rolled down her cheeks as she hysterically tugged at her husband's trousers. Finally she collapsed at his feet and remained lying there, totally spent by the effort.

"What do you want me to do?" the professor asked after a few moments, after he had helped his wife into a chair where she sobbed quietly, her face hidden in a handkerchief.

22

Five more trucks had arrived the night before. Something was about to happen on Adam Hill and everyone seemed to be increasingly nervous about it. It was up to Kamm to keep his wits about him.

Vitek was seated on a dirty mattress which had been placed for him on the floor against the slimy wall.

"All right," Kamm said in an unusually conciliatory manner. "Let me hear the whole story about last Friday night. From the beginning. I don't mind hearing it for the tenth time, I'm starting to like it."

The Gestapo man grabbed a chair, put it down in front of him with its backrest in the front so he could place his arms on it.

"Fine. Now I'm comfortable and you may begin."

"Well, it was a quiet night and ..." Vitek started reluctantly.

"Louder Vitek. I can hardly hear you. Shout it out!"

The innkeeper raised his head to show his swollen mouth and he pointed to it.

"It's difficult to speak. It hurts with every word."

"But you're an old soldier. You know how to conquer pain," Kamm couldn't resist a dip into sarcasm. "Start!" he screamed.

"We were cooking in the kitchen and it got hot. We kept the window open in spite of the cold outside."

"Get on with it!"

"That's why I heard Kekl coming. A few moments later I even saw him in some of the light coming from the kitchen."

Kamm was suddenly interested.

"Heard him? What do you mean? Was he singing or something?"

"Well, yes, that too. But I could hear his boots against the cobblestones. I think I also heard his bicycle. He wasn't riding it but walking alongside it. He has those solid tires on it, they're the only ones available now ..."

"Cobblestones! But the cobblestones are only on the bridge, the road to Nekor isn't paved. Besides it's the other way."

Vitek nodded.

Kamm tore out of his chair and grabbed the innkeeper by his shirt.

"Then he wasn't coming from home at all! He was coming ..." In front of his eyes flashed a copy of the report filled out by the Czech police on Kekl's death which had passed across his desk. *Of course!* He had been working on the road construction gang at Klasterec. His daughter lived in a house on the lake halfway between Klasterec and Pastviny. That's where he had been. He was not coming to the pub from Nekor but from Klasterec, from the opposite direction. That meant if he saw the parachutists they were in an entirely different place. No wonder Röhmer couldn't find any trace of them.

As fast as his hip permitted he climbed back upstairs, where he grabbed the telephone and shouted at the operator to connect him with Adam Hill in the Reich. But that was easier said than done. All communications with Adam Hill were to be routed via Prague, that was an order the operator quoted to him. When Kamm placed a call to Leimer there he was told that he was out of town. Then they connected him with some green official still on night duty at the Gestapo headquarters who knew nothing about Adam Hill, parachutists and sabotage. Finally Kamm decided the fastest way would be to go to Adam Hill himself. He left a message with the operator to alert the special anti-parachutist unit at Königgratz before the Praga, its tires screeching, shot out of the Zamberk square, the two motorcycles following close behind. He would stop at the Tiesenhausen villa on the way to warn them.

23

Tiesenhausen was a taller and thinner man than Howard. Fortunately though, most of the ill-fitting uniform was hidden by a heavy overcoat. Stan Jaroscynski put on the uniform of the dead bodyguard while Tom Evans quickly loaded the explosives and other supplies in the back of the Opel. The explosives were now stripped of their outer coverings and they rested in an ordinary medium-sized crate which should not arouse much suspicion. Professor Tiesenhausen would merely be bringing in some of his supplies. Next to the crate was a rucksack with the ampules containing the antibiotics and several thousand Reichsmarks. Finally, locked in the trunk, were bundles with Jaroscynski's and Howard's civilian clothes.

Frau Tiesenhausen was staring, eyes unfocused, into space. She paid no attention when her arms were tied behind her. Her son Eric, on the other hand, followed Evans' actions with smoldering, impotent hatred. His feet as well as hands were tied. Although Eric had dramatically opted for life twice already that morning, it couldn't be ruled out that, given the right circumstances, he would try to be a hero.

The preparations were completed. In the middle of the room stood the older Tiesenhausen, dressed in a dark brown suit with a long leather coat over it. Next to him stood Howard in the Nazi official's light brown uniform. He had made a slight substitution: instead of the ceremonial dagger supposed to be loosely suspended from the waist, he was carrying Eric Tiesenhausen's Luger, inserted in a shiny black holster.

Hana stepped closer to him, regretting that she had to say goodbye to Howard wearing the hated uniform. She had no illusions about it. This was their first and also final farewell. Howard's eyes rested on Hana only momentarily. He was making the utmost effort to concentrate on details of the plan.

"Well then everyone, all set?" the commander asked. One by one they nodded.

"Douglas!" Hana cried out when he was almost out of the room. She came running after him, carrying the ludicrously big revolver in her small hand. But halfway across she stopped as if she had suddenly remembered there were others involved. She did not want them to see any sentimental weakness.

"Good luck! Damn good luck, commander!" she said softly, looking at the floor. A slight smile flew across his lips. Then he turned around, disappearing without a word.

After a few tries the Opel's engine finally caught. Jaroscynski carefully eased the car into low gear and they started winding up the path toward the main road. Soon they were nearing a cluster of houses which formed the core of the village. These appeared deserted, but Howard was certain that in one or two of them he caught a glimpse of a grim face peering at the hated car from behind a snow-white lace curtain.

Then they were past the village, turning left at

the fork of the road and climbing away from the lake toward the Reich. All was exactly the way they had memorized it in England. The road still had a thin covering of snow but the chains on the Opel's tires provided the needed traction. The car was slowly climbing the hill when they passed a wagon pulled by a lethargic horse and loaded with milk cans. On the box, huddled in a heavy coat with a visor cap with its earflaps down, sat what was unmistakably Palka. He scarcely gave them a glance as they drove by.

At the top of the hill they passed a man pushing a bicycle laden with shopping bags. It must be another of Palka's men, thought Howard, but it would be the last one; they were entering a curve and when the road straightened out again they would see the Reich border control point.

Two men came out of the small hut but no explanations were necessary. Obviously the guards knew the professor well and they were not about to ask the identity of his friend in the uniform of a high official of the National Socialist German Workers' Party.

Five minutes later they were approaching the first bunker, the gate to Adam Hill. Howard felt his entire body become tense.

"I don't know who I should say you are." The professor suddenly interrupted Howard's thoughts. It was true. They had forgotten to brief Tiesenhausen on that part of the plan.

"I'm Oberdienstleiter Johann von Horwath of the NSDAP, here from Berlin on an inspection tour," Howard quickly improvised.

The officer at the bunker was a young lieutenant of slight build who came out with another soldier as the car came to a full stop in front of the red and white striped barrier.

"Good morning, professor," he called as the professor rolled down the window. Howard noticed that the lieutenant gave no Heil Hitler salute. Perhaps it was too late in the war for it.

"May I ask who is your guest?" the lieutenant asked with as much servility as he could possibly muster.

"This is Oberdienstleiter Johann von Horwath of the NSDAP, here from Berlin on an inspection tour," Tiesenhausen repeated Howard's instructions verbatim.

The lieutenant seemed slightly embarrassed. "I'm sorry sir but we have not been alerted that ..."

"The Führer doesn't alert lieutenants when he sends his personal emissaries on inspections of highly secret installations!" Howard barked angrily at him.

"I didn't mean it that way, sir," the hapless young man tried to explain, "it's just that had we been alerted we could have had an escort waiting for you and ..."

"The professor, I'm sure, knows his way around Adam Hill quite well. Now kindly call the area commander, lieutenant and tell him we will be in to visit him in a few minutes. Go on driver," Howard haughtily instructed Jaroscynski.

The soldier quickly started raising the barrier, while the lieutenant saluted rigidly as the car passed him by and for a few moments more until it disappeared up the hill and around a curve.

The Opel continued up the winding road in low gear. Periodically they passed other small bunkers hiding the approach, sometimes with one or two soldiers standing beside them. The commander knew why. The cold damp inside of a concrete bunker installation tended to become unbearable after a while.

The scene when they made their last turn looked as if someone had shaved a bald spot atop the hill, thought Howard. Not too far from each other were two gaping holes of maybe thirty feet in diameter where the Czech guns used to be. But they had been melted down a long time ago for the Nazi war effort. This part of the fortification was not in use anyway. What was used was a large round pillbox which served as the entrance to the underground part. There were several vehicles parked near the entrance and people mingled around them. Some were civilians in white laboratory coats but most were Germans in uniform. To the right, almost where the bald spot ended in the woods, were stacks of the containers, twenty feet long and shaped something like torpedoes but much wider. Howard estimated there must have been over 300 of them.

"Where is the military headquarters?" Howard asked Tiesenhausen, but he didn't have to wait for an answer. A dapper major dressed in an impeccable uniform stood before a wooden barracks to their right, smiling and beckoning to them. Obviously the military didn't want to be caught underground, thought Howard. Jaroscynski looked at the commander questioningly.

"Go on, let's pay our respects to the commandant. It's only good manners."

This time they got out of the car. The major introduced himself by some long name as the adjutant of Colonel Ritter von Streiwitz. It was unfortunate, he regretted, that they had not been informed of Herr Oberdienstleiter's impending visit because Colonel von Streiwitz would certainly have been at his post. At the moment he was away, attending to some urgent business, but the major had already sent a motorcyclist after him.

This time the commander was more conciliatory.

"Surely you understand, major, that an inspection tour loses much of its value if it is announced beforehand?"

The major nodded uneasily.

"Would you like to come to the headquarters for a cup of coffee — or perhaps something stronger?" he asked with a wink of his right eye which the commander found easily as the single most unpleasant thing about his singularly unpleasant personality.

"No, thank you," the commander answered, "I must leave for Berlin this afternoon. The Führer is leaving for his Bavarian headquarters tomorrow and he must have my report before he departs."

"I see," the major said, obviously awed by the heady conversation. "Are you interested in security, Herr Dienstleiter, are you with the Sicherheitsdienst?"

Jaroscynski looked up in alarm. He understood German only sporadically, but it was clear to him that the major was asking about Howard's organization. How well briefed was Douglas Howard in Nazi administration?

But he solved the problem with considerable aplomb.

"I'm on the Führer's personal staff, major. My special assignment is secret weapons."

It seemed to have the desired effect. Jaroscynski thought that he saw the up-to-now confident major cringe slightly. He meekly offered to accompany them on a tour but was quickly rebuffed both by the professor and the commander.

They got back into the car and Tiesenhausen

directed them to the entrance of the largest
bunker. Jaroscynski took hold of the crate with the
explosives. Rivulets of perspiration began trick-
ling down his forehead as he tried to maneuver it
inside. Howard noticed Jaroscynski's effort and for
a moment thought of helping him. But he couldn't
have done it without attracting attention. Not even
in democratic Canada do Brigadier Generals help
common soldiers with manual labor.

Long rows of bare bulbs provided light inside
the wide corridor. And there were people,
hundreds of people milling about, emerging and
disappearing into openings in the sides of the corridor. Tiesenhausen directed them toward one such
opening. They entered a huge room about fifty by
twenty feet, filled with laboratory equipment,
including test tubes, petri dishes and large glass
jars with a yellow, jelly-like substance covering
their bottoms. Howard guessed they contained the
concentrated germ cultures, which would then be
diluted and transferred into the torpedo-like containers outside. About ten people moved about with
notebooks, testing the material in various ways and
noting down results. One or two of the white-coated
workers came to the professor with questions or
reports. He brushed them aside, pointing to his
high-ranking visitor.

Howard carried the vials of chemicals in the
briefcase. He directed the professor toward the
first row of the jars. Tiesenhausen suddenly
stopped in his tracks. He realized that this was
absolutely the last moment to resist. There was a
good chance that if he started to run among all the
apparatus, in the resulting melee he would save his
life if no culture was spilled. But what about his
wife and Eric? He didn't have the right. According
to the agreement he had to be seen reentering the

Czech Protectorate with the Canadian and the Pole. They had to give a certain sign to the underground member before his family would be released. Failure to give the sign would mean death for his family.

Jaroscynski had placed the crate with the explosives into a corner of the laboratory. He gingerly pried open one end of it. Then he reached inside, feeling for the timer. Because he was concentrating on his job so intently he failed to notice two soldiers who stopped by him.

"*Was machst du denn da?*" One of them demanded to know what Jaroscynski was doing. Stan looked up, startled. His eyes rested on the SS insignia on their collars. Stunned, he stared at them with his mouth opened.

"What is it you wanted?" he heard Tiesenhausen's voice from far away. "This man is my driver. He has brought in some supplies for me."

The pair hesitated a moment. Then they looked at Howard's uniform, saluted and headed toward the door. The professor had made his decision. It was irrevocable.

"What's in the next room?" the commander asked.

"Same as this. These are the two laboratories where the germ cultures are stored."

"Leave it here," said the commander to Jaroscynski. "Let's go next door."

Jaroscynski reached inside the crate and turned on the timer. They had half an hour.

24

Tom Evans stopped pacing long enough to look out of the window. He was stunned by what he saw.

"*Jesus*! There's a car coming. The one that came to your place."

Hana looked in the direction of Evans' gaze. "Kamm. The Gestapo."

For a moment the room was silent.

"Leave. Please go. Through the back while there's still time," Frau Tiesenhausen pleaded.

Tom hesitated. His mind was feverishly at work, trying to come up with a solution.

"No," he said finally, picking up from the table the dagger that had been a part of Tiesenhausen's Nazi uniform. With two steps he was at the side of Frau Tiesenhausen, cutting the rope around her wrists, then doing the same for her son's wrists and feet.

"Does the Gestapo often come to visit?" asked Evans. Hanna translated the question for Frau Tiesenhausen.

"Sometimes," was the answer.

"That's what I think it is, a visit. They wouldn't charge the place so openly if they knew we were here. I'm going out on the terrace."

"There is no hope, sergeant. Why don't you give yourself up? You'll find us Germans magna-

nimous in such circumstances," said Eric Tiesenhausen. Hana translated.

Tom stared at him for a moment. Just before
leaving he turned to Hana.

"You know, I wonder if that isn't their main
problem. That they still today regard us as such
blithering idiots."

Kamm had originally planned to stop at the Tiesenhausen villa for only a moment, but when he
discovered Hana there, he decided to stay for a cup
of tea. Theoretically, at least, she was not supposed
to be there at all. The Tiesenhausens' presence at
Pastviny was to be kept secret. There had been a
directive from Berlin, signed by Himmler himself,
which stated there was to be no fraternization
between anyone connected with Adam Hill and the
Czechs in the area.

But, of course, Hana Dykova was not just
another Czech. She was a beautiful artist, above
nationality, the nearest thing to perfection that
Kamm had ever encountered, a true lady who put
most German women to shame. No wonder the
aristocratic Frau Tiesenhausen befriended her.

Hana was describing the great cultural influx
that the arrival of the Germans in 1939 had meant
for the Czechs.

"I can best speak about the influence of the
National Socialist philosophy on Czech films. Until
1939 we used to make very inferior things, 'lemonades' we usually called these films. But things
have certainly changed since we have been inte-
grated into the Reich. The 'lemonades' were amus-
ing, I suppose, but it was empty-headed
amusement, without any thought behind it at all.
Quite like the Jewish-Negroid banalities of Holly-

wood." She was quoting from some Germanized film magazine almost verbatim.

It is getting cold, thought Hana. The part of the window earlier broken by Howard was hidden by a curtain, but it let in a steady stream of freezing air. Outside huddled Tom Evans with his grease gun.

Kamm glanced at his watch. It was past eleven thirty. Frau Tiesenhausen offered him more tea and he rose to cross the room for it. That's when his eyes caught sight of the holes in the armchair beside the lamp. And near them, what from across the room seemed like some highly modernistic pattern, was now clearly visible as a spot of scarcely dried blood.

The moment of his realization produced a lull in the conversation which caught Tom's attention. When he looked into the room he was staring straight into Kamm's widened, hateful eyes. But while Kamm only started to reach inside his coat for a gun, Tom's was ready. He directed his first burst, mixed with the sound of shattered glass, toward the left side of the room. Away from Hana and Frau Tiesenhausen seated on the couch.

Kamm and young Tiesenhausen collapsed almost simultaneously. Tom was about to enter the room from the patio when he saw through the window that Kamm's two companions had reached the house on the opposite side. One of them panicked. Seeing Tom, he fired a burst in his direction, but the shots were deflected by the glass, one of them hitting Hana in the shoulder. She fell on the carpet without a sound, one of her feet twisting unnaturally in the fall.

The two soldiers then entered the house, cautiously approaching the bodies scattered throughout the living room. There were puddles of blood seeping from underneath the bodies of the young Tiesenhausen, Kamm, and Hana Dykova but Frau Tiesenhausen, slumped to one side on the couch and apparently no longer breathing, did not seem to have been felled by a bullet. Must have been her heart, concluded Röhmer. Leaving his companion behind, he walked out on the patio.

Below him, desperately trying to trudge his way through the deep snow toward the lake, was Tom Evans. Periodically he kept turning around to scan the Tiesenhausen house, but when he spotted the German above him, he stopped. There was nothing, absolutely nothing that could be done any more. Röhmer rested his gun on the railing to take better aim.

Tom's own weapon was empty. He had used up the entire clip and as yet had not found time to insert a new one.

25

Methodically advancing from jar to jar, Professor
Tiesenhausen played his role unexpectedly well.
Pretending to be engaged in a lively conversation
with Howard, he occasionally even used hand gestures to make the whole thing more believable. As
a result, Howard was unobserved and able to drop
some powder into almost every jar they passed.
The commander also noticed that white-coated
technicians occasionally passed by who did not
seem to be particularly interested in them. Then
the dapper major with the long name, von Streiwitz's adjutant, appeared at the entrance to the
laboratory, pausing for a moment to look around.
His eyes lit up when he spotted the trio.

"Get outside and start the car," Howard
instructed Jaroscynski under his breath. "If you
hear gunfire then get out of here fast!" There was
no time to argue. Jaroscynski carried out the order.

Howard estimated that over a half of the jars
now contained the antibiotics. This, combined with
the destruction produced by the bomb next door in
a tightly enclosed space, and along with the bombs
which would soon fall on the containers outside,
meant their mission had been accomplished. What
remained now as their objective was survival. And
that was definitely uncertain at the moment,

thought Howard, with the major only some ten feet away. Howard looked at his watch. It was 11:40 A.M. Almost twenty-five minutes had elapsed since Jaroscynski had set the timer.

"Aaah, gentlemen," the major smiled, "Colonel Ritter von Streiwitz has just returned. He would like you to join him for some refreshments."

Obviously the major was terribly proud of the aristocratic background of his commandant and also quite obviously they could not take the chance in sipping schnapps with him, trying to answer his prying questions which were bound to reveal the commander was an impostor. Besides — the time!

While they were walking underneath the endless row of lightbulbs in the corridor and breathing in the foul air, the commander was trying to decide what to do. They passed a stand of some kind around which milled white-clad civilians, drinking liquid from military utensils and eating slices of brown bread. Professor Tiesenhausen, who up until then had been playing his role so well, was beginning to show signs of strain. The major's arrival had made the whole charade infinitely more difficult. Torn between his loyalty to the cause and the survival of his family, Tiesenhausen seemed to be desperately searching for some way of reconciling the two.

Approaching the wide entrance they could now see daylight. While the major insisted on explaining some highly technical data, Tiesenhausen's eyes jumped wildly from one face to another, attempting to anticipate events.

Outside, Jaroscynski stood next to the car, holding its back door open. The major noticed him.

"No need to take the car, Herr Dienstleiter. It's only a few steps," he explained.

At that desperate moment the commander

heard in the distance the faint rumblings which heralded the arrival of his guardian angels. It was unmistakably the engines of the lead B-17s and they must have been very low. No one else seemed to have heard them yet. The morning had turned out to be one of those crisp, sunny winter ones, perfect for this type of a bombing operation. As yet no alarm had sounded. In spite of the fact the planes must have been spotted as soon as they crossed into Germany, a bombing raid on Adam Hill was not anticipated. After all, the Allies couldn't have any idea what was inside the fortress. Howard decided to stall for time.

"Excuse me, major," he said. "I'd like to get a small present for the commandant. It's in the car."

But when Howard was about halfway to the car the major heard the planes too. As he anxiously scanned the sky for a moment or two the commander saw his chance. Before the major's eyes returned to earth Howard's Luger was out.

Several gigantic shadows of the bombers flying at tree-top level crossed the bald spot atop the hill with a defeaning roar. It was their first, familiarization pass and they were quickly followed by other bombers, accompanied by fighters. It was during the second wave, when the ear-splitting explosions filled the air along with the flying debris, that Howard pulled the trigger twice, watching the major collapse first to his knees, then on the ground. Few people in the immediate vicinity heard the shot. Howard assumed that those who did must have reacted in some way but he did not take the time to look around and see how. None of the military seemed to have been aroused by the shot. There already was the beginning of a wild panic anyway, as soon as more people saw the white stars on the bombers' wings and realized they themselves were the target. Some scampered into the wide jaw of an opening to the underground bunker, others sought refuge in the surrounding woods. Howard and Tiesenhausen reached the car. Jaroscynski expertly put in gear and within moments they were away from the bare area at the top of the hill along the narrow road, hidden in most places by tall pines.

"Where are we going?" shouted Jaroscynski over his shoulder above the roar as they passed a startled group of soldiers next to their approach bunker. One of them made a half-hearted attempt to stop them but desisted as soon as he recognized Howard's uniform.

"We can't get by the first bunker. They will have been alerted now."

Actually the decision had been made for them. First to see the plane in his rear-view mirror was Jaroscynski. He stomped on the brake. Using the emergency brake as well, he brought the Opel to an abrupt halt.

"Get out!" he yelled, opening his door. "Get out fast!" They had already heard the roar of the low-flying plane and the counterpoint of its cannon. Howard opened the door on his side and rolled up in a ball. Protecting his head, he remained lying in the snow alongside the road until the plane had roared over them.

"Stan, are you all right?" he yelled. Instead of a reply he was rewarded with the view of an almost totally white figure, ferociously spitting snow from its mouth. In spite of their predicament it was difficult to keep from laughing. But only for a moment.

"Let's get out of here," the commander yelled, reaching the car with two long steps and opening its trunk. He threw a bundle with civilian clothes and supplies at Jaroscynski, then pulled out another for himself. As he was taking out the rest, Stan spoke.

"Where's the professor?" he asked. Only when Howard stepped over to the other side of the car did he see the body. Tiesenhausen was lying there, his face turned sideways, the snow around him crimson red. The gunner must have set his sights for the middle of the road and Tiesenhausen had paid with his life for sitting on the right side of the car. Stan had pulled over to the left so he would be as near the forest as possible, but the professor as result had to run across the road which the American plane was spraying with its bullets.

Howard sensed danger in the distant drone of the airplane which had completed its circle. It had stopped climbing and was getting ready for another pass. Grabbing the bundle with their supplies, Howard threw himself into the woods just as its guns started blazing, kicking up particles of snow and dirt from the road. He quickly followed Jaroscynski deeper into the woods, away from the car. Almost a quarter of an hour later they stopped to change their clothes and to bury their uniforms in the snow.

Then they continued northward, toward their rendezvous at the church in Glatz.

26

She was being painfully lifted off the floor by two
soldiers. Someone had already bandaged her
wound while she was still unconscious, but now she
almost screamed with pain as she was being carried to the truck with canvas awning waiting outside of the Tiesenhausen house, surrounded by
military uniforms, motorcycles and khaki-painted
vehicles of all kinds. The truck started on its way,
but soon it was intercepted by someone who yelled
orders at the driver and the escorts. The canvas
flap was thrown aside and in climbed a thoroughly
terrified doctor from Zamberk, whom Hana knew.
Immediately after greeting her he was roughly
told to keep quiet by someone outside, to get on
with the examination. His hand shook so much that
he found it difficult to give her an injection.

And all the time Hana was hoping to hear that
all had gone well on Adam Hill, that Douglas and
Jaroscynski had somehow, miraculously, found a
way to escape. It was impossible to deduce anything from what the men around her were saying.
They communicated mostly in short grunts whose
muffled sounds she was unable to decipher.

In Zamberk she was placed aboard a train.
Several times she tried to ask what was happening,

what was being done with her, and each time was sharply rebuffed.

The curious thing was that she was fully awake. The injection did not make the pain in her shoulder disappear; it only somehow depersonalized it. In a strange way she was still aware of it being there, but it was as if it were happening to someone else. It was also as if someone she was watching had been put into the strange railway car with two compartments joined together to make room for a stretcher, with a silent German soldier sitting on a wooden bench beside her, another one periodically looking in from the corridor outside.

The compartment became darker, eerily lit by a single weak blue bulb in a far corner. She counted at least three stops before the train pulled into what seemed like a larger station. A blond-haired civilian who must have been a Gestapo man entered the compartment. He sent the guards away and gazed at her wordlessly for a few moments while Hana, hoping he would go away soon, kept her eyes tightly closed.

But shortly after he left he came back, this time with another doctor. He silently examined her, then gave her another injection. She searched his face for some sort of an expression because somehow she was sure he was Czech. But the Gestapo man remained in the doorway, watching the doctor's every move. In spite of it, just before the doctor left, she was certain that she detected a slight softening in his face, even an almost imperceptible friendly nod of his head. As if to give her courage, to say that all would be all right soon.

That was exactly what she needed as the car started to move again. With darkness her apprehension increased by leaps and bounds. A harsh interrogation by the notorious Prague Gestapo in the Petschek Palace probably awaited her. Was she strong enough to withstand it?

She had her doubts.

Valery Semlyonov stood a few paces away from the large cauldron with hot soup, sipping on his portion and savoring every morsel of the black bread he was chewing along with it. He had been at Adam Hill for several weeks now, but he still couldn't get used to the unspeakable luxury of these snacks. A few weeks ago at the Birkenau camp — part of that vast complex called Auschwitz — he had been marked for quick extinction along with a group of other Russian officer-prisoners. But, dirty, starving, and exhausted, he had been called out of the ranks one morning and given a short test in what seemed to be elementary biology. The same night he was shipped to Adam Hill. Along with his incessant mortal fear he had also left behind all of his friends, most of whom were probably dead by now.

And here he now stood in warm clothes, sipping on a large bowl of pea soup with pieces of sausage floating in it, allowed to go back for seconds, thirds, or whatever other helping he desired. At Adam Hill his job was recording temperatures. All day he walked through the insides of the fortress, lifting the covers of the labeled jars and recording in his book the numbers on the thermometers inside them. It was an unobtrusive job, perfectly suited to his main goal, which was survival.

Of course he knew that the germ cultures would be used by the Germans. Even a child could have figured that out, what with the tight military security around the place and the fact they were forbidden to talk either about their work or where they came from. Except for a few supervisors, the white-coated laboratory technicians were all East Europeans. There were Czechs, Slovaks, Russians, Poles, Yugoslavs, and Romanians among them, some so emaciated it was clear that they had, like Valery, arrived at Adam Hill straight from concentration camps. They soon realized just why they should not discuss either their work or their backgrounds. The technicians' ranks were full of informers. A day after his arrival at Adam Hill Valery had seen two East Europeans taken into the nearby woods and summarily shot for discussing their concentration camp experiences.

Then and there Valery Semlyonov vowed that it would not happen to him. The best way to keep his vow was to stay away from everyone else. To be a lone wolf, recording temperatures, sleeping and eating. Nothing else mattered. Everything else meant death.

Valery Semlyonov was convinced now that for some reason he had been destined to survive. But he was also convinced that he had to do his utmost to help with the task. He had been given a start by being released from Auschwitz. The rest was up to him. His good fortune had befallen him supposedly because he had studied biology at the University of Moscow before the war, but the real reason was far more mystical than that. As a life-long Marxist, Valery did not believe in God. What he did believe in, more and more now that the war was drawing to a close, was fate. He was being spared because of something he did not understand but which he found awesome.

He heard the first explosions as deep, muffled sounds from the outside, but resisted his first impulse to run and see what was happening. Whatever they meant, it was much safer in here. Then the force of an explosion threw him back against the concrete wall. He vaguely felt pain in his left shoulder against which he had fallen, but he was far more concerned with the pandemonium that had broken loose around him. A mass of people entered the corridor from outside where the explosions grew louder, terror in their eyes. Another wave of humanity was approaching the snack bar from the opposite direction, from the inside of the fortress, along with a cloud of dust which made it difficult to breathe and see. Some were hurt, bleeding profusely from their wounds, pushing toward the open air and the safety of the dark woods. They didn't seem to be aware of the sounds of explosions coming from outside.

In a split second Valery made his decision. It was likely that there had been sabotage and there would probably be more bombs exploding inside the fortress. That spelled doom. A far better chance was outside. An air raid was lethal only if one suffered a direct hit or if one were confined to a small space. The vast, wooded Adam Hill was the answer.

He was lucky to have made his decision fast. The full impact had not yet reached him from the inside explosions, so far only individuals kept emerging from the dusty fog. Also, the number of incoming people was great but not yet a stampede. Most people caught outside must have been too stunned to look for shelter in the fortress right away.

Valery reached the entrance and leaned against the concrete wall of the bunker to catch his breath. Among the people who seemed to be running aimlessly across the open area in front of the bunker his attention was caught by two figures who seemed to ignore the tumult. A Wehrmacht major with his back to him had his hands at his mouth and yelling something at a man in a brown Nazi uniform who only moments before had passed by the snackbar where Valery was having his soup.

Another flight of bombers cast their shadows across them and the major looked up into the sky. Valery was about to follow suit but at the last moment his attention was drawn away from the bombers by an awkward gesture on the part of the Nazi party man whose holster was now opened and who held a gun in his hand. Valery's breath was taken away momentarily by the fact that the man's stance was so unusual and that he, standing directly behind the major, was in grave danger. In rapid succession three times a flash licked the end of the Nazi's gun barrel and the major fell, holding his chest. The Nazi then jumped into his car and disappeared toward the forested area.

Stunned, Valery looked around him. Where before the containers had been piled at the edge of the woods was now a pile of twisted, smoldering metal. The open space atop the hill was full of smoking craters. The bombers roamed above it all at will, unhampered by any air defenses.

He realized he should not run toward the containers. They were the primary target. In the other direction he would be some fifty meters in the open before he could reach the safety of the woods. Through the corner of his eye he caught sight of a group of planes lining up on a target to his right. In a few moments they would be above it, spewing large calibre bullets all over the area. The decision had to be made immediately. He looked toward the woods for the last time, then he crouched to present as small a target as possible. Then he started running.

Seconds later, watching the growing holocaust

from his position on the edge of the woods, he realized that whatever the Nazis were manufacturing
and storing there was now destroyed. That there
would no longer be any need for East European
laboratory technicians at Adam Hill. In addition to
all that there was now the murder of the major
Valery had witnessed a moment ago. It had certainly not been meant for the eyes of Russian prisoners of war. What awaited him was an
immediate execution at worst, a return trip to Birkenau at best.

He was alone. A moment ago, soldiers and
civilians had been running about to save they
didn't know what; that was a drama taking place a
fair distance from him now. Again he made up his
mind instantly. Turning, he started deeper into the
woods, away from the bunkers. His last quick decision inside the corridor of the fortress had been
right. He hoped that this one would be as well.

Shortly after sunset he stopped on the doorstep
of a small farmhouse. He did not have the strength
to go any farther. He had to trust someone now. He
knocked at the door. An elderly man opened it, his
wrinkled wife, wrapped in a black shawl, peering
over his shoulder.

"Help ... prisoner of war ... Russian," he said
in a universal Slavic language he hoped would
sound more like Czech than Russian.

The old farmer stared at him for a moment,
grabbing him just as Valery was about to collapse
from exhaustion. He quickly closed the door
behind them, at the same time saying something to
the woman, who disappeared into an adjoining
barn. There she grabbed a pitchfork and energet-
ically began removing piles of hay to the side until
she uncovered a sort of wooden cage, measuring no
more than two by four meters. The woman helped

Valery inside, on a bed made up of two folded blankets.

But not for long, dear God. Make the war end soon, she thought.

27

Willy Leimer, Chief of the Anti-Parachute Division of Prague's Gestapo Second Department, stood on the platform of the station which the Czechs still unofficially insisted on calling by its prewar name, the President Wilson Station. His arms folded across his chest, the Gestapo man stood arrogantly on platform one, periodically taking small steps on the spot to warm his feet.

To his left stood a Czech doctor and two ambulance attendants, one of them holding a folded canvas stretcher. Farther away stood four soldiers with submachine guns hanging across their chests. The few travelers who inadvertently appeared on the platform quickly recognized the situation and gave the group a wide berth. Leimer's long leather coat, his boots, and hat with its turned down brim practically constituted a Gestapo uniform by now.

The doctor and the ambulance attendants were visibly frightened; the soldiers were bored. But Willy Leimer stared eagerly into the darkness beyond the station, awaiting the express train bearing the legendary Hana Dykova. She had lost a lot of blood, a doctor in Zamberk reported, but she would live. All she needed was rest and for that purpose Leimer had already cleared half of a floor at Prague's Bulovka hospital — the same floor on which Reinhard Heydrich, the Reichsprotektor of Bohemia-Moravia, died after he was assassinated by Czech parachutists from London a year and a half ago.

And Hana Dykova would eventually die as well now that it was clear that she had been working with the Czech Resistance all along. In a week or so she would have regained enough strength to start unraveling the story of all the parachutists in the country — the ones that had already been dropped and the ones that were yet to come. The amount of information that the beautiful red head of hers must hold! She had quite likely been in on the planning of most Resistance operations that took place in the Protectorate in the past five years. True, the two parachutists who had infiltrated Adam Hill were still at large — mostly due to the stupidity of the corrupt Kamm — but they really had nowhere to go. They would be caught because eventually Hana Dykova would be made to tell exactly where they were.

That's why Leimer didn't bother to join the special battalion from Königgratz, which right now was combing the countryside around Pastviny. Hana Dykova was much more important than poking about farm houses and frightening peasants. She was part of that Czech democratic intelligentsia which couldn't be bought off with an extra ration of tobacco or a half a pound of butter like the workers.

The Communists had obliged the Gestapo by organizing their Resistance cells exactly along the lines they had organized their party before the war. As a result, they were picked up one by one. Occasionally some of them even agreed to act as decoys for other Resistance members. But the more educated Czechs usually used all their craftiness to confuse, delay and even temporarily elude the Germans. And they were proud patriots, ready to die if necessary. Teachers, lawyers, businessmen and journalists were among them as well as artists. Now, though, it was all over for Hana Dykova, the proud, glamorous Czech who had once hobnobbed with the mighty in Berlin and thereby managed to set up a very nice alibi for herself. Hana Dykova was now his — Willy Leimer's.

He reached into his pocket for a cigarette. It was a Player's, taken from a downed British pilot. The tobacco was of much lighter color than that of German cigarettes and it was heavily perfumed. When rapidly and deeply inhaled it produced a highly pleasant feeling of giddiness that was well worth the ungodly amount one had to pay for them.

He looked at his watch. The train was now almost half an hour overdue, but that was to be expected — troops and munitions transports for the front had priority and the slightest chance of an air raid slowed down rail traffic to a crawl. It was becoming unpleasantly cold now. The doctor and the ambulance attendants kept up their steady movement from one foot to the other, periodically clapping their hands to keep their blood circulating faster.

As Leimer started to put out a cigarette stub with the tip of his boot, he noticed someone running along the platform toward him. He strained through the semidarkness to see who it was. He recognized Pfitsch, one of the men in Division II — a coward, drunkard, and a sadist, but most of all an opinionated fool. To run messages, that's really what he was best suited for.

Pfitsch, huddled up to his ears in a heavy overcoat, reached Leimer. Without a word he handed him a folded piece of paper. From its color and shape Leimer already knew it was a telegram. He took off one of his gloves and unfolded it.

SEND DYKOVA TO GRUPPENFÜHRER LUDOLF VON ALVENSLEBEN IN DRESDEN TONIGHT
SS OBERGRUPPENFÜHRER KALTENBRUNNER

Puzzled, Leimer looked at Pfitsch, convinced that he detected a slight smirk on his face.

"It came from Berlin half an hour ago," Pfitsch said. "It's a good thing that headquarters is just across the park from here. I might have missed you."

"Does Gehrcke know?" Dr. Gehrcke was chief of Prague's Gestapo.

"Of course. He also orders you to go to Adam Hill and take charge of the investigation there. Tonight."

Leimer stamped his foot angrily. Then he turned on the heel of his boot and started toward the exit. Just before he disappeared from Pfitsch's sight he called over his shoulder: "Make sure she gets to Dresden, will you Erich?"

Heinrich Himmler, Reichsführer of the SS and Chief of the Gestapo, stood grim-faced outside the main fortress at Adam Hill. The bomb which had exploded in the first laboratory had littered the area with thousands of pieces of glass, infesting it with deadly type BB bacteria. Since then the bunker had been sealed off and before the Reichsführer had been allowed to enter the complex, extensive tests had to be made to make sure the area was safe. It had been discovered that the remaining cultures in the second laboratory had also been tampered with and that most of what the jars contained was now worthless. The Allies now also knew the location of the production center. Added to the damage inside and outside was the fact that the genius behind the project, Professor Tiesenhausen, was now dead. The effectiveness of the germ program for the near future was finished. Before the program could be resumed it would have to be moved somewhere else and by then it would probably be too late.

Himmler heard the droning voice of the junior officer from Adam Hill headquarters who was explaining the extent of the damage, but he was not paying attention. Details were no longer interesting. Soon after his arrival Heinrich Himmler had assessed the situation and found the rest of the lectures boring. What, however, he had not found at all boring were plans for the punishment of the guilty ones. They had occupied his mind almost constantly ever since his arrival at Adam Hill about two hours earlier. Even before, while still in Berlin, he had ordered the immediate arrest of the major (he had long forgotten his name) who had allowed the impostors into the area. When it was established he was responsible, Himmler personally ordered him shot. Later, however, he changed the verdict to hanging, with the provision that a tree from which the major could see the damaged fortress as he was dying would be used. Himmler dismissed as unimportant a report that the man had been wounded and could not walk.

"If necessary a stretcher should be used to bring the officer to his place of execution," the Reichsführer's order clearly dictated.

By the time Himmler arrived at Adam Hill, its commandant, Colonel Ritter von Streiwitz, had already been taken to Berlin's Plötzensee Prison. The commandant was, of course, a much bigger

fish than the incompetent major and Himmler definitely wanted to have a few words with him. But
not at Adam Hill, where the aristocratic colonel
would still be at a slight advantage before a former
schoolteacher. At Plötzensee on the other hand,
appropriately starved and in a dirty remnant of a
uniform (with all the insignia torn off, of course)
and with a several-days-old beard, the proper rela-
tionship between Ritter von Streiwitz and the
Reichsführer of the SS would instantly be established. Von Streiwitz would hang, but only after a
spectacular trial. That, naturally, would require
permission from the Führer himself, but Heinrich
Himmler was confident that, if properly presented
with the pertinent facts, the Führer would readily
give such permission.

Taking off his pince nez, he rubbed the bridge
of his nose in an effort to increase the blood circulation. He was beginning to feel uncomfortably cold.

"Captain," he suddenly interrupted the Wehrmacht officer giving the lecture. "Where are the
foreign civilians who worked here?"

"This way, Herr Reichsführer." The servile
officer directed Himmler's party to the temporary
barracks in front of which stood, as they had been
standing for several hours now, a group of some
200 men and women. They no longer wore their
white coats but odd bits of clothing they had col-
lected from the warehouses of the various concentration camps where they had been recruited,
ill-fitting garments of various types, often ludicrously altered to provide as much warmth as possible. Their expressions betrayed fear. Most of
them recognized the Reichsführer and after weeks
of relative comfort and warmth they rightly suspected that his presence here signaled a radical
change for the worse.

He said nothing. Standing in front of the
crowd, and studying their faces he found them
stupid — revoltingly Slavic. It had been unfortunate that the development of the germ weapon had
depended on their help. At least one good thing
came out of the destruction at Adam Hill though:
the services of this inferior rabble would no longer
be required.

Himmler suddenly felt even colder. He
turned on his heel and motioned to Leimer, the
anti-sabotage specialist from the Prague Gestapo.
On the way to the headquarters hut, most of
which had miraculously remained intact in spite
of the air raid, the Reichsführer spoke to Leimer:
"Have you discovered any connection between the
East Europeans and the parachutists yet?" he
asked.

"Not yet, Herr Reichsführer. If I may be permitted to say, sir, with 200 of them, there isn't
much hope."

"No, there isn't, is there," Himmler momentarily stepped out of character and commiserated
with Leimer. "But try."

"Of course, Herr Reichsführer. Five died in
the explosion and four of them are missing. If they
weren't killed in the air raid it is likely that they
were the ones who provided the connection
between the parachutists and Adam Hill."

"How is your search of the area progressing?"

"Very well, Herr Reichsführer. We are pro-
ceeding with great care. In a day or two we should
have both the parachutists and the escaped East
Europeans apprehended. As I always say, sir, the
success of a search rests primarily in its preparation, not in its execution."

Himmler nodded.

They had reached the headquarters hut. Just

before they entered, the captain caught up with them, saluted and asked,

"Begging your pardon, Herr Reichsführer, but what should be done with the Slavs?"

The Reichsführer looked at Leimer who shrugged his shoulders. "We have some trucks in the area which were to be used for the transportation of the containers, Herr Reichsführer," Leimer suggested.

Himmler allowed one of his rare smiles to cross his face.

"Then there you have your answer, captain. These people are no longer of any use to anybody. Final solution. I suppose Auschwitz is the most convenient place to take them from here, isn't it?"

The problem solved, the Reichsführer turned around to walk up the three steps into the hut where he was certain to find warmth, some hot tea and cakes.

Part Two:
The Hostages

28

About three hours out of Prague the train stopped
somewhere at another darkened station and she
was brought a bowl of beef soup with two pieces of
bread. The soldier on the bench next to her
propped her up, then fed her as if she were a baby.
He seemed to be studying her intently with each
spoonful that he raised to her lips. Was it because
he thought she had been a traitor to the Reich or
because she was a movie star, she wondered. With
her stomach now pleasantly warm and full, she fell
asleep.

But it was not an easy sleep. She kept waking
with a start, her thoughts disturbed, even panicky.
The soldier beside her, the blue light, the monoto-
nous rattle of the train — it all combined in an
ominous, terrifying, anxiety that at times seemed
almost unbearable.

Then, shortly after the sun rose, the train
slowed down, entering some sizable station.
Moments later two men in white entered the compartment and she was placed on a stretcher again.
And as they carried her out onto the platform, she
caught sight of a sign above her: DRESDEN. The
city of porcelain, of gentle music. What was she
doing here? Through the great hall of the station
where people stared at her with unabashed curios-

ity, she was carried out into a waiting ambulance, followed by her four escorts. The ambulance then wound its way through the city and into the suburbs, past high-walled villas with towering chestnut trees and wide, wrought-iron gates. They stopped in front of one of them, the gate opened, and she was carried up a wide staircase to the first floor, and into a luxurious room with a carved mahogany frieze near the ceiling.

Another doctor examined her, this time a German, asking questions about her health in a clipped, disinterested tone. Then a nurse came in; she washed Hana, rebandaged her wound and dressed her in a nightgown, finally sitting her up against the wall, but totally ignoring all her questions.

Nothing happened for about ten minutes after she left. Then a noise downstairs heralded another arrival, followed by the sound of footsteps muffled by the heavy rugs. Finally there was a soft knock on the door and Hana deduced she was to answer. When she bid the visitor to enter the door slowly opened and revealed a man in a meticulously pressed suit, his overcoat carelessly thrown over his shoulders. He was unusually short and thin, his dark hair was heavily brilliantined and as he advanced toward Hana's bed she noticed his limp.

He was Adolf Hitler's Minister of Propaganda and Enlightenment, Dr. Josef Goebbels.

What he said made Hana wonder at first if it all was some sort of a joke or perhaps a trick — if the luxury and comfort by which she was surrounded was meant to throw her off her guard, to confuse her. Because what he outlined was an incredibly ambitious scheme, designed to show the world that the people of the lands conquered by Germany were solidly behind the Führer, that they were ready to die for him in droves if necessary. He talked of the production of several major films, of radio and personal appearances, theatrical presentations and the launching of new magazines with the help of prominent personalities from the world of art. From what Josef Goebbels seemed to suggest, Hana herself would be in charge of the film's undertaking. There was no mention of her health. It was almost as if the minister didn't want to be bothered by trifles.

The scheme was preposterous considering Germany's situation. The required personnel and material were unobtainable. Above all, it would require a degree of enthusiasm, even optimism, which the Reich had not possessed for several years. Certainly not with the Russians on the offensive, Africa lost, and the Allies steadily advancing up the boot of Italy. Not to mention the most obvious flaw: it would be impossible in 1944 to find the necessary number of collaborators among the conquered people.

But the Reichsminister droned on in his formal, almost officious way, anxious to be respected, lauded, and esteemed. Hana gradually began to realize that he was deadly serious, that she only had to agree, to praise him, to seem optimistic, and she would be taken under the protection of this extremely powerful man. It was also clear that he did not want to be bothered by her supposed role as a member of the Czech Resistance. He simply dismissed it as only extremely powerful men are able to.

"I suppose you know that in the Protectorate there have been some who seriously suspected you may have been with the parachutists, but that was only to be expected. After a monstrous bit of sabotage like that, everyone is looking for scapegoats.

And things are in a dreadful state there since the death of Heydrich. Daluege is a gross incompetent and he is constantly fighting with his State Secretary Frank. I knew they would try to use you for their own purposes, so I asked Kaltenbrunner to have you brought to Dresden. Here you are under the personal protection of Nationalist Socialist Gauleiter, Lieutenant General von Alvensleben, a very good friend of mine."

He rose and patted her hand with a smile.

"Of course, the first thing is to get you well again, but while you are resting think about all things I told you. It could mean the turnabout in the war."

Then he was gone, the incredible, fantastic Minister for Propaganda and Enlightenment, who seemed to be so thoroughly dissatisfied with the world in which he lived that he had created another.

Now he was asking her to join him in it.

Hana slumped down in her bed, exhausted by the turn of events. She had to think carefully about all the ramifications of it but she was unable to do that now. She closed her eyes.

29

First there was the excruciating, practically non-stop thirty-six hour trek to Glatz. It led over trails where Howard and Jaroscynski at times fell waist-deep into snowdrifts, where needle-like snowflakes made them change places every few minutes since the lead man's eyes were not able to take the punishment any longer than that. When they finally arrived at their destination their food was almost gone. They remained seated on the hard pew of the dim church long after the hour for the meeting had passed. Slowly the realization came to the dead-tired Howard that Evans and Hana would not be coming, that they were dead or worse, in the hands of the Gestapo. And their impotence to do anything about it as they sat inside the cold church, brought the commander almost to tears. Sadness was replaced with a frustrating, deep anger, which made him long to turn back to Pastviny and certain death in spite of everything rational inside him telling him to go on. But there was Stanislaw Jaroscynski, who in his understanding yet firm way convinced him that they must get away, that their own escape had been nothing short of miraculous, that either staying in Glatz or returning to Pastviny would not help anyone at all.

As if through a haze Howard remembered

being dragged by Jaroscynski to a railway yard where they boarded a freight train bound for Breslau and from there another, heading east.

Finally they were out of the Reich and in German-occupied Poland, only kilometers away from Jaroscynski's home town of Czestochowa. Though still far from the front, military convoys became more frequent. Howard and Jaroscynski traveled at night, across fields, forest, and countryside which Stan knew so well that sometimes he chose in which barn or haystack they would spend the night, hours before they actually reached it. Like a dull ache in his heart the sorrow of the loss of Hana stayed with Howard. It grew more pronounced along with the lessening of the tension as they got farther and farther away from Adam Hill. The mission had been successfully completed. What remained now was bare survival — something Howard was not too sure he really wanted without Hana.

From far away Jaroscynski's home seemed unchanged. But a closer look revealed a house with its back badly damaged by shrapnel. Windows were covered with pieces of wood, which produced an eerie half shadow inside. The old oak tree in front had been cut down. It had been burned during the German advance. The once neat garden was thick with debris.

Stan's parents were haggard. Almost dour. Their furtive glances sideways now and then betrayed their nervousness. They must have been through a lot.

They welcomed them with surprise and genuine happiness. Within moments though, it was obvious that there otherwise was little joy over Stanislaw's return. The house was filled with relatives and friends — refugees from the East who waited anxiously for the front to near because they were without adequate documents. Even if caught by the Germans, however, they could still hope to survive in a camp somewhere. But to be found with the parachutists meant certain death. Besides, there was little food and two extra mouths to feed were not exactly welcome.

Under the circumstances Howard and Stan were on their way again almost within hours. The countryside where, in return for all their Reichsmarks, a friend had agreed to hide them on his farm, seemed a safer bet. But soon the first signs of malnutrition appeared. Howard now tired quite easily and he suffered from frequent spells of dizziness. To make things even worse, he did not feel hungry. The loss of Hana had been such an immense shock that he spoke little. He had withdrawn into himself, frequently catching himself wondering if the enormous effort needed for his escape and now his survival was really worth it all.

And it was again Stan who took charge, who managed to get them safely to their new refuge and to help with the chores on the farm so they could have a legitimate claim on the steadily dwindling food supplies. Eventually Howard spent most of his time lying down. He rested on a wooden platform crudely constructed in the cellar, tiring even after a few steps.

One night Stan came down into the cellar to tell Howard that the owner of the farm was leaving. It was October and the artillery din from the east was deafening. Long lines of Germans — almost crawling with fatigue — who passed by the farm indicated that the front had collapsed. For some reason the owner of the farm felt he and his family would be safer some ten miles to the west

with a group of his friends. Stan Jaroscynski and
the commander were left alone.

But the Red Army was in no great hurry. First
days then weeks went by passed during which the
artillery still thundered but no soldiers came by.
The farm must have been located between two
thrusts. While the Russians were straightening
their lines to the south and north of them, in the
middle there was a lull. The small pile of potatoes
they had been left was now gone. And had there
been food somewhere in the vicinity it would have
made no difference: even Stan was unable to climb
the stairs out of their prison any more. A well with
a pump was nearby. They had water, but little else.

Now Jaroscynski and the commander spent
their days huddled in rags on the wooden platform,
sometimes remaining silent for hours, convinced
that the end had come. Then Howard began hallucinating. Repeatedly he saw Hana running away
into a thick mist or being dragged away by faceless
figures. He was powerless to help, powerless even
to raise his hand against the outrage.

There was only a small, dirt-splattered window in the cellar and they lived in perpetual dusk.
After a while they were no longer able to distinguish between day and night, morning or evening
or summer and winter. Time had become a long
dark ribbon along which they were sliding to the
end, steadily downward without interruption,
without a change in sound, temperature, and feeling. They slept more and more until they were
unable to separate sleep from wakefulness, dream
from reality. It was all the same, a semidark road
into oblivion, without pain, without concern, without a desire to alter anything any more.

Howard thought he remembered the dirty,
round face of the soldier quite clearly, but chances

were that most of his memory was really imagination. Because in the darkness of the cellar he could not possibly have noticed (as he thought he did) the soldier holding one of those submachine guns with holes all over the barrel.

He wore what seemed to be a very loose pyjama top. But the most obvious thing about him — at least in the commander's memory — was the shiny red star on his cap. The Russian looked cautiously around the cellar then asked something for which Jaroscynski provided an answer and caused the soldier to break into a wide grin.

Later there was the makeshift stretcher on which someone took Howard somewhere. A train ride followed (already without Stan) and then an airplane, which Howard suspected was taking him home, broke through the clouds in his mind. Suddenly everyone spoke English but all that Howard registered was that the invasion had been successful somewhere in Normandy. Then he was sleeping again in a bed with white sheets which were kept scrupulously clean. Someone in the hospital finally answered his questions, told him it was spring in 1945. Shortly afterward his mind sporadically started accepting things again. There were even attempts to arrange them properly according to time, importance, and his own relation to them.

Howard was fairly certain it was not a dream as one day he recognized the short, sharp-nosed Montgomery with an impressive retinue at the side of his bed, pinning some sort of a decoration on his pyjamas and smiling for the photographers. He even vaguely remembered shaking the field marshal's hand, but immediately after his departure he fell asleep again and stayed like that for the next sixteen hours.

Eventually he woke up to a very pleasant voice, saying:

"I took if off again Commander, if you don't mind. It wouldn't do to have you spear yourself to death with the Victoria Cross, would it? By the way, there are a whole lot of other commendations and medals awaiting you in the office safe. From what I hear you were so blasé about the whole thing, you even refused to wake up for the presentations. So all the visiting international brass just left them behind and quietly tiptoed out again."

The voice was vaguely familiar and she knew it because she immediately introduced herself as Sybil Hawthorne, his cousin Roger Stillwell's friend. She told how they had come to visit him together and how, when Stillwell's squadron was transferred to the Pacific, she asked to be assigned to the case.

"Sybil, you should know that in the States Roger has a ..." Howard started to explain with considerable difficulty.

"Wife? Come on, commander, I wasn't born yesterday. I know. He needed someone here to be waiting and so I played the role. We were just friends, but damn good ones."

Howard smiled.

"But listen, while we're on the subject, I couldn't find any mention of your wife anywhere. And because should the situation arise, I'm not ready to play act any more, I would sort of like to be clear on that score. Is there a Mrs. Howard — besides your mother, I mean?"

He smiled and slowly shook his head.

"That's good. That's actually damn good. Because I hate writing those awful, mushy letters for patients."

From then on the name Sybil became synonymous with his recovery. Her crisp uniforms and irreverent humor, her practical approach to life and trim figure, all became a beacon toward which Howard gladly headed. With Sybil his hospital day at Sevenoaks began. It was she who took his temperature, who brought him breakfast, propping up his weak neck, and who eventually helped him out of bed, providing support as he took his first, uncertain steps after the long months on his back. It was Sybil who offered encouragement, who quietly stood nearby because she might be needed, or who was noisily telling ribald jokes in the New Zealand accent she had learned to imitate in a North African hospital. As time went by Sybil became no longer just a symbol of his recovery but of life itself.

"It's time we were a bit more frank with each other, commander," she said one night in August as they sat together in the darkened recreation room following a particularly boisterous celebration (at least the tenth since V-J Day) of the end of the war in the Pacific. "I didn't just happen along."

"Meaning?" His curiosity was aroused.

"Meaning that in spite of all the learned doctors around you, you weren't getting any better. You weren't putting on any weight, you weren't interested in permanently coming back to reality, or even making the trip to the loo on your own. Obviously you weren't interested in living. I was meant to take the place of some wonder drug."

They remained quiet for a moment while Howard mustered enough courage to ask the next question.

"And are you leaving now that the mission has been accomplished?"

"I was supposed to have left a month ago," she

answered softly. Even through the darkness Howard could see that she was smiling. He reached toward her, found her hand and held it for a very long time.

30

Hana reached for the small piece of chipped concrete underneath her bed and then, listening for any noise in the corridor which would indicate an approaching guard, she carefully scratched another line into the wall near her bunk. Again she counted the crossed sets of lines — there were thirty-two. Thirty-two times five. That didn't mean that she had been in Schwachstein 160 days. Only that it had been 160 days since she had started counting.

She thought that at first she considered the prison to be temporary, but she really couldn't remember too clearly just what it was she thought at first. She might have thought that she would be taken to Prague or merely into the courtyard to be shot by her Russian captors. But neither happened. Instead, she was left and for all practical purposes forgotten in her isolation cell.

It really wasn't that much out of keeping with all the bizarre turns in her life since she had left Pastviny. Instead of the expected interrogations and torture by the Gestapo she had been placed in the midst of luxury inside a Dresden villa. The only requirement was that she would periodically listen to Josef Goebbels' fantastic dreams, meticulously unraveled before her either in the plush salon or the fragrant garden, an eerie series of confessions delivered with an intensity which clearly indicated the stress to which he was being increasingly subjected.

The Gestapo did come to the villa once or twice, asking for information about the parachutists. But these were polite visits by men with impeccable manners addressing an ally. She gathered from their questions that Howard and Jaroscynski may still have been alive, but it seemed too fantastic an idea to even consider.

Josef Goebbels never made any advances to her, although he was quite aware that she was in no position to resist them. He simply showed need for a place where he could talk and act as he once used to. The hopes for the erection of a great German cultural empire now lay in smoking ruins everywhere but inside the walls of Hana Dykova's Dresden villa.

And even that refuge was destroyed in February 1945. Thanks to a frightened cook Hana had been in the basement shelter when the incendiary bomb struck. They were pulled out of the burning ruins by passersby. By nailing planks together and using doors that had been torn off their hinges a part of the kitchen had been made habitable. Hana set up housekeeping in the freezing cavity, alone, totally ignored by the local Nazi Gauleiter who now had other things to worry about. And as the front neared Berlin, Goebbels, who had just been appointed Reichs Commissioner for Total Mobilization, found it impossible to get away.

Not that he would have likely wanted to anyway, Hana thought. The remains of the villa on Marksgasse was no longer an ethereal haven but merely an unpleasant reminder of the harsh present-day reality. By trading for bread some of the cans of food with which the basement had been stocked, and on occasion even for eggs and milk, Hana managed to stay alive. But what sustained her most of all was hope — hope for the end of the war, of returning to Czechoslovakia and — above all — of seeing Douglas Howard again.

When the end to the war came, it was all quite different. The two Red Army officers she spoke with at the Grosser Garten park on May 9, a day after the city fell into Russian hands, seemed quite sympathetic to her plea. They told her that she would be taken to Prague the moment it was clear that the Czech city had been liberated and that the necessary transport was available.

The same night, though, one of them came for a visit. He started off quite innocently, arriving with a box of American-made chocolate bars. But he also brought with him a bottle of vodka which he quickly opened and insisted that Hana join him in a toast to Allied victory. She had not tasted alcohol for over a year and the first sip already sent her head into a spin. The officer insisted on more toasts, refilling their glasses almost continuously. She felt her grasp on reality slowly receding and alarmed she tried to make her way out for some fresh air. But it was obvious as he stood by the door that he had other plans.

And she struggled to resign herself to what was about to happen, knowing that she could not possibly get by him, that perhaps if she tried to convince him she was submitting willingly, it would at least be less violent — more human.

But she saw that he had been killing and maiming much too long; that he had long ago learned all that counted was brute force, that with it one could take villages, towns, even once-proud world powers. Her terrified screams may have been heard by others living on the street, but no one would come and help, she realized, because law and order was in the hands of the man before her with a wide belt over his tunic which buttoned at the shoulder, the man with stiff cardboard epaulets, the man tearing at her clothing, whose face, with several days' growth of whiskers, smelled of alcohol and had probably not felt a gentle touch for years.

Her terrified screams of utter helplessness he mistook for angry resistance, hitting her again and again across her face with the back of his hand until he clenched it into a fist and struck her in the mouth full force, quieting her by filling her mouth with a mixture of bloody mucus and parts of broken teeth, throwing her on her makeshift bed and holding her there with one hand while opening his trousers with the other. And then came the painful jabs mixed with short, audible, and hot breaths against her face, his hands fondling different parts of her body, roughly, hungrily seeking unilateral pleasure as payment for all the long years of misery, fear, and discomfort, jabbing, jabbing as if with a deadly weapon instead of the pleasurable organ with which he had been endowed.

In the end he lay heavily upon her, spent, resting, perhaps even slightly embarrassed. Then, without a word he rose, straightened out his tunic, and still without looking back he pushed aside the makeshift door, a moment later disappearing into the dark hopelessness of the night.

Except for pulling a blanket over her, Hana didn't move for hours. She remained there in the dreariness of her lair, a puddle of blood and saliva mixed with the remains of her teeth beside the bed, staring with unfocused eyes at the crossboards above her that propped up her sagging ceiling.

In the morning she rose, put on a cotton dress she had sewn together from dyed sheets, then made herself a cup of herb tea. She heard a screech of tires, followed by the sound of several pairs of boots on the walk outside. Then the door opened abruptly and two Red Army privates ordered her to come with them. She didn't resist, mechanically putting on her coat and following them out through the garden and into the street. Exhorting her to move quickly, they roughly helped her inside their jeep; it then pulled away from the curb. She didn't look back. It didn't matter any more, nothing mattered. She actually preferred her stupor; anything else would have required an exertion of strength she simply didn't have any more.

No one spoke to her during the hours they drove, first through the rubble of what had once been Dresden, then on one of Hitler's *autobahns* which, however, they periodically had to leave because most of the bridges had been destroyed. Shortly after noon the ugly outline of a castle emerged before them; they entered the courtyard through a massive gate that someone had opened from the inside and immediately closed again behind them. She was led up the stairs to what she vaguely expected to be some sort of an administrative office, but she was wrong. The soldier who had brought her up unlocked the door to her cell, then without a word pushed her inside. Not with malice though: with indifference.

During the first few days she didn't eat. It was as if the uncertainty and misery of the past few months had taken their toll, as if she was powerless to break out of her shell that had so effectively kept out all feelings.

But then, slowly, the flow of life began to

return to her. She took a bite or two on the dark piece of Russian bread she received each morning, she got up from her bunk and glanced at the empty courtyard below; finally she scratched the first line on the wall beside her bed. The name Schloss Schwachstein she noticed engraved on the metal dish in which she received her soup each night. The swastika sign below it indicated it had been some sort of a military facility before the Russians came. But more she didn't know. Food was distributed by civilians who, she assumed, were Germans. But in the corridor always stood a Russian soldier with a submachine gun strapped across his chest, making sure that no words were exchanged with the prisoners.

With the uninterrupted routine of the forgotten prison she had time to think, to revisit all the scenes left by the past year, trying to wean some sense from them, to find an explanation for it all.

But there was no indication of a certain or even probable last act. The only firm and secure factor that kept emerging was Douglas Howard, the confident, stocky, and not-at-all handsome Canadian Navy commander who had come to her as a harbinger of peace. She probably loved him. The man had become to her a symbol of the end to suffering.

31

Howard had called the military authorities in London three or four times to find out about the aftermath of Operation Lister, but no one could give him any information. Before being disbanded, the Supreme Allied Headquarters had moved twice, each time leaving a monumental confusion in its wake. The British Chief of Staff's office was not much help either. Telephones there didn't work properly, responsible officers had already been posted to occupied Germany and total ignorance of Operation Lister seemed to reign supreme throughout the place.

Once a lieutenant with a Greek name assured him that the operation had indeed been successful, that the 2,000 paratroopers had done their job, as could after all, be seen by the fact that the invasion of North Africa had gone on without a hitch. Another time a young captain with a clipped Oxford accent stated in a somewhat imperious manner that he had it on the best authority the entire operation had been aborted only hours before it was to have started because one of the commandos who was to have taken part in it was uncovered as a German spy.

The commander's letters to the new U.S. Headquarters in Frankfurt remained unanswered. Even stranger was the fact that not a word about Lister appeared anywhere. English newspapers and magazines almost daily ran some daring story which "until now had been unknown to the public for reasons of security," but Operation Lister was never one of them. When an American picture magazine ran a three-part story on D-Day with the first part concerning preparations, there wasn't a word in it about Lister. Howard was confused.

But before he had a chance to send out a new barrage of quizzical letters, the door flew open and in walked Harry Mindon, now a lieutenant colonel, resplendent in his uniform, which included a swagger stick.

After Sybil was introduced there followed a few minutes of pleasant chatting in the hospital garden under the trees with their fall foliage. Then she excused herself and disappeared inside.

Mindon looked in her direction as she left, then gave Howard a meaningful look.

"Well," said Mindon, cleaning the leaves from a garden chair and sitting down. "We'd better get down to business."

Howard took a seat opposite him.

"First of all I should explain that I am not here in England on leave. That doesn't come until next year. I've been sent here especially to talk with you. You see two weeks ago I was transferred to Berlin. Someone found out I was in on the start of Lister and the Americans considered me as something sent from heaven. They now know you're back in working order and at the end of this week they were to have a draw: whoever got the short end of the stick would have to fly here and explain to you what happened. And in the middle of it all I walked in — a personal friend of the great

Howard."

"Is the news *that* bad?" asked Howard anxiously.

"No," said Mindon, lighting a cigarette. "At least I think you already know the worst of it. What is perplexing is that there are some incredibly large holes in our knowledge.

"What happened to Hana Dykova — the Czech actress?"

"I'm afraid there isn't much doubt that she is dead. She died in the Tiesenhausen villa, along with Tom Evans, Frau Tiesenhausen, and the Gestapo man Kamm."

"How do you know?"

"It has been corroborated from Czechoslovakia. I'll show you the letter in a minute. In March of last year — two months before the end of the war — there also appeared an article in *Der Neue Tag*, the German language newspaper published in Prague. Of course, it all has to be taken with a grain of salt from a source like that, but some of the things in the article we know to be true from elsewhere."

"What did it say about Hana?"

Mindon rummaged through his briefcase.

"Sorry Douglas, that's one thing I didn't bring with me. But I do know that in it Hana was described as something of a martyr. It said she worked faithfully with the Germans only to be brutally murdered by a group of American gangsters who were dropped from the sky for that purpose ... I assume she was *not* a collaborator, is that right?"

Howard shook his head.

"She helped us a lot, Harry, precisely because she *was* willing to play the part of a hated collaborator. Few people in the region even spoke to her. Well, at least now her memory will be vindicated."

Mindon looked at the ground.

"That hasn't exactly been the case. You see, the Czechs haven't been what you might call exuberant in posthumously clearing her name. In fact they haven't been saying anything about Hana Dykova, about Adam Hill or Operation Lister. Nor have the Nazis. According to them, Hana and the Tiesenhausens had been killed by American gangsters. Because in saying that the local citizenry had been involved they would have hinted at the existence of organized resistance — something that the Nazis wanted to avoid at any price."

"But why are the Allies making such mystery out of the whole thing?"

Mindon took a letter out of his briefcase.

"Here, read this. It may explain a few things. It also may have exactly the opposite effect, I don't know. It arrived at the American headquarters in Berlin last week. I'm afraid they took the liberty of opening it."

Howard nodded. The letter had an unusual format. It was typed and folded into four equal parts in the European style. His eyes slid down to the bottom of the page, where the signature stood out quite clearly: Bozena Palkova.

Howard raised his eyes questioningly at Mindon.

"Palka's wife. Take your time. I'll take a walk, then we'll talk again."

As Mindon strolled off, Howard returned to the closely-spaced letter, written in German.

Dear Commander Howard:

We have never met, but my husband Jiri often spoke about you. He considers you one of the bravest men alive. It is my fervent hope that you are still alive, although I am not at all sure.

This letter is being taken out of the country by a friend who often goes to Berlin. He will mail it there and with the help of God it will reach you.

Jiri, my husband, is gone. I haven't seen him since May. No one knows where he is, but it is likely he has been taken away by the Russians. Why? No one knows here. Or, if they do know, they are not telling.

This we certainly didn't expect from our liberators. I have been twice to Prague with his underground friends. We have been to the Ministry of Defense and also to the Ministry of the Interior which is in charge of state security. But all that happened was that we have been passed from one official to another. Long protocols have been put together with us and then filed away. I am sure they have been forgotten and nobody has looked at them since.

At the Interior Ministry they also suggested quite seriously that my husband may have joined the Bandera fighters for an independent Ukraine who are roaming Czechoslovakia these days. But they didn't say why Jiri would want to do this. What interest would he have in the Ukraine?

Commander Howard, there is no one else I can turn to. Hana Dykova is gone. The priest at the church in Klasterec saw her body on a slab there, along with the Gestapo man Kamm and your friend Thomas Evans. (Was that his name, did I spell it correctly?) They are all gone, there is no one to turn to except you. I pray to God that you are still alive, that you can be found, that you will help find my Jiri. After all he has done during the war for this country and for the Allies he deserves better. Much better.

Mindon strolled up the hill again when he saw that Howard had finished reading and that he was sitting there as if stunned, holding the piece of paper lifelessly in his hand. He sat down and waited until the commander asked the obvious question:

"Why, Harry? Why all this secrecy and intrigue?"

"Hmmm ... Well, they aren't quite clear about it all in Berlin yet. But they do have a theory or two."

"Do they think Palka is still alive?"

"Surprisingly enough, they do. You see they checked in Poland although, you can well imagine, it's even more difficult there to get any reliable information. But it seems Jaroscynski has also disappeared. Except that in his case we know that he is alive. In Krakow somewhere. His friends have seen him. He is under arrest, but it seems his incarceration must be fairly tame. He is even taken out for walks occasionally."

"Should I write to tell that to Palka's wife?"

Mindon shook his head.

"*You* shouldn't write to anybody. We will let her know."

"Is this why no one says anything publicly about Operation Lister?"

Mindon nodded.

"While he was still Commander in Chief, Eisenhower ordered complete secrecy. Nobody has lifted the order since then. Let me put it all together for you chronologically, maybe that will help. After you messed up the germ cultures no one wanted to talk about Adam Hill very much, not the Germans, who had suffered a major defeat, and not the western Allies because — but you know why. Eisenhower didn't want anyone to know that the threat of germ warfare ever existed, not until the war was over, because his troops might have come to the conclusion that if the Germans were going to use germs to keep the Allies away from Normandy they might also try to use them in order to keep the Allies from crossing the Rhine. Or other places. And on top of all that something else happened. The Russians or the Czechs or Poles or somebody must have found things about Operation Lister that they did not want to leak out. And we complied with their request. After all, we are all Allies — still."

"What are the theories?"

Mindon scratched his head.

"One is that the Russians are developing germ warfare techniques of their own. That they are studying what happened at Adam Hill. Bringing attention to what happened there in 1944 might also bring attention to what the Russkis are doing now. The whole area is sealed off now and designated as a military objective by the Russians."

"What's another?"

"Operation Lister was a mission planned and executed by the Western Allies. Stalin is highly suspicious of any Western doings on territory he considers within the Soviet sphere of influence. Hence the arrests and interrogations of all the participants that are under his control. Next week the Red Army is scheduled to leave Czechoslovakia. We will then see if Palka is returned to his home. They probably won't send him back, though. You see, both of the ministries his wife writes about are in the hands of Czech Communists.

The wealth of information provided by Mindon made Howard's head spin. The postwar East European situation was so complicated and fluid that it seemed impossible to build any rational theory based on it.

"Is there any theory, Harry?"

"Well," Mindon paused with certain amount of reluctance, "we were sort of hoping that you could provide us with some clues. Can you?"

"I don't know exactly what it is you are looking for."

Mindon chuckled.

"Neither do we. But you are the only survivor in the West who has been to Adam Hill."

"It seems like a million years ago," said Howard tiredly. Mindon suddenly became much more serious.

"I know. I don't think any of us could possibly imagine what you've been through. But you are our only hope. And that is precisely why I am here."

Howard looked up, surprised. He didn't expect now, almost at the end of Mindon's visit, to be let in on something like this.

Mindon rose from his chair and came closer to Howard.

"The Americans and the British have so far played along with the Russians because with you half unconscious we had practically no facts at our disposal. But somewhere in that highly capable Canadian brain of yours is hidden the cause for Russian fears in connection with Adam Hill. Chances are none of us in the West would normally regard it as anything that would keep anybody awake at night. But that, of course, is beside the point. If we have a report on the mission — a thorough, detailed report from you, one that would account for every minute from the moment your parachute hit the ground to the moment that your plane landed in England again — we will know what is scaring the Russkis; I will guarantee you that. By the way, we have a bit of a trump in our hand: the Russians don't know that you're still alive. They know that you were near death when we flew you to England, that you were in a coma. Of course, they have been sending out feelers about you ever since, but we have not been reacting. The same way they have not been reacting when we asked about Palka and Jaroscynski. It's all still a little bit of a game — admittedly with somewhat ominous overtones."

Howard nodded and rose. It was getting cold.

"How long will you need to write the report?" Mindon asked.

"Three months."

"Fine," agreed Mindon, getting up too. "Here's my card. When you are finished please get in touch *only with me*. Meanwhile, if there is any news about Jaroscynski, Palka or anything else, we'll get in touch with you."

Douglas Howard suddenly felt deathly tired. After he said goodbye to Mindon he found it quite a chore to make his way back up to his room.

32

The routine at Schwachstein prison now included a visit to the barber every two weeks where each male or female prisoner's hair was clipped down to the prescribed centimeter length. The Russians were afraid of lice. The first time Hana had been brought to the barber she considered it a kind of holiday. She hoped to find out something about the place from the pleasant-faced man in a dirty white smock who cut her hair, but the guard who brought her seated himself in the room as well. It was obvious that here too all communicating was forbidden.

Still, the barber seemed friendly. He smiled and now and then she caught him staring at her. Not that there is that much here to look at any more, she thought sadly. The first time she had seen herself in the cracked mirror beside the barber's chair she was faced with a pallid, middle-aged woman with uneven tufts of hair sticking from her scalp, whose cheeks were sharply concave and whose eyes seemed to have receded deep into their sockets. She had never been plump, but now she was skeletal, her gray calico dress hanging formlessly from her shoulders.

There were three more visits before the opportunity came. But when the barber first whispered into her ear she was totally unprepared for it. Startled, she twitched and looked at the guard seated against the wall. And then she knew why the barber had spoken. With his head on his chest the Russian was fast asleep.

"How do you like the House of Ghosts?" the man asked, in the next moment explaining that Schwachstein was just a few kilometers west of Cottbus, that the local townspeople had christened the mysterious castle with its twenty or so carefully guarded prisoners as the House of Ghosts.

"Who are the others here?"

The man smiled.

"All kinds. There are Lithuanians, Germans, and Bulgarians. All kinds."

"But why? Why are we here?"

"Because the Russians haven't yet quite made up their minds if we are more valuable dead or alive. I would say that at the moment we are really neither, are we?"

"Who are you?"

"The name is Franzl. Until recently I was just an insignificant Wehrmacht corporal. Except that my unit was there when the graves at Katyn were discovered and the Russians are pretty touchy about any witnesses to that."

Hana studied him for a moment.

"Why haven't they simply killed you?"

"If I knew that maybe I could also help myself by playing the right cards."

"Would it be possible to get the word out that we are here?"

"I suppose so. But why?"

"So that we could be helped."

"By whom? Our best chance is in keeping as quiet as possible. Not by attracting attention."

Hana thought for a moment.

"Not mine. I am a film actress. My name is Hana Dykova."

The man slapped himself on his forehead. Then, worried, he looked at the guard. But the Russian continued sleeping peacefully.

"So that's where I know you from! Of course. But you have changed."

"Yes, I have," Hana agreed. "Could you let someone in town know about me? I will make sure they are paid well if the word gets to Prague."

"It could be done, I suppose. But you *do* realize that the whole thing is very risky, don't you? For you I mean. If the Czechs ask the Russians to send you back the Russians may panic and cover up the evidence. You know how."

"Yes, I know. But I have to take that risk. I would be very grateful if you passed the word."

Less than two weeks after Mindon's visit to Sevenoaks, Howard and Sybil were on their way westward to Cornwall. There Sybil had rented a small thatched-roof cottage on a weatherbeaten cliff. Two weeks before Christmas, 1945, on a Thursday afternoon full of wind and drizzle, they made their way to a centuries-old stone chapel to be married by a deaf, white-haired vicar dressed in knickers. A couple of fishermen Howard had found in a nearby pub gladly stood as witnesses for a guinea each.

It was as if someone had, after a mad ride lasting several years, finally thrown his life onto a siding. Mornings were now marked by the foot-shuffling milkman who arrived at seven, his cart pulled by a highly disinterested, emaciated horse. The fog usually lifted shortly afterward, exposing a gray, almost mystic sea below them in a gloomy, wintry mood. Sybil cooked breakfast, providing also a much needed warmth from the wood stove. And the stove remained in use throughout the day, after Sybil had cleared the kitchen table of dishes and Howard began scattering his papers across it to begin his work.

His writing went more slowly than he had expected. There were days when the sun would timidly emerge from behind a fluffy cloud and the two of them would then bundle up against the breeze and set out along the rocky seashore, on mostly wordless treks with the unceasing surf in the background.

Sometimes Howard would not write for days. This was when they escaped even farther into the countryside in Sybil's rickety, damp Morris, when they surveyed picturesque villages, ate their steak and kidney pie in tiny pubs under heavy beams and a faded picture of King George. They talked with people for whom the war seemed to have ended hundreds of years ago, whose thoughts were now exclusively on this year's mackerel catch. They sat in the local school house through a charmingly inept production of Hamlet in which the hero was not only indecisive but forgetful as well.

In town they visited the cinema (carefully avoiding war films), a dance hall, or an antique shop. Cornwall had been Sybil's idea and a damn good one, Howard repeated as often as the occasion called for it. It had freed them from the military discipline of the hospital, taken them away from uniforms and daily reports, from the thoroughly uncomfortable feeling that their lives were being regulated.

But the report grew. And as the whole story of Lister began to unfold in front of the astounded Sybil, who was typing the final copy, she began to view her husband with increased awe.

"You know, Douglas, it isn't because you have done a heroic thing. I knew damn well you must have been a fairly brave man from the moment Monty came to pin the Victoria Cross on your pajamas. And it isn't because I married a man whose life is like a film scenario in the size of the adventure he has lived through. Both of those things are basically human; there's nothing ethereal about them. But what is most awe-inspiring about you is that you are, after all this, still sitting here in 1946 in a seaside cottage in Cornwall. I mean, you're still alive, in spite of all you went through. You were fired at in that Halifax and then you dropped in country occupied by the Germans and you'd only done one training jump. Then you kidnapped the German scientist and drove right *into* the fortress. There wasn't much more danger you could have got into if you'd tried."

She reached for his hand across the table and took it between her palms.

"Darling, I know it sounds like the glossy cover of some cheap adventure story, but that's just the point. You simply weren't meant to live. By human standards, that is."

Silence reigned for a few moments. "Do you know what I am saying, Douglas? In my crude way I'm saying that you really have no business being here at all. That here's something incomprehensible in the fact that you *are* here. Imagine me saying this, the queen of the agnostics! I guess what I mean, in effect, is that you have survived because of divine intervention. The next question, of course, is why?"

Of course Howard had wondered about the reason for his survival, but these were random thoughts. He never allowed himself the luxury of pursuing them, bringing them to some logical conclusion. Now Sybil had done it for him and momentarily had stunned him. Eventually he tried to slip away from the causative puzzle she had placed in front of him.

"All very interesting," he said, "but I think mainly for the theologians and philosophers. For us there is a much more immediate and practical side of the problem to be resolved first, isn't there?"

She nodded. Of course he was right. In a day or two she would have finished typing the 400-page report. By the end of the week it would be on its way to Berlin.

33

A few days later, Sybil opened the door to face a gentleman of medium height in a crumpled raincoat, holding an old briefcase, overstuffed with papers. They eyed each other for a few uncomfortable moments before he spoke.

"Mrs. Howard?"

And when she nodded, he continued.

"My name is Smith. I'm with the American Army. There are a few things that we should ..."

But by that time Douglas had reached the door, opened it wider and Smith walked in, taking off his raincoat and throwing it across a nearby chair a bit too readily, thought Sybil, then entering the living room and looking around, obviously enjoying what he saw.

"Nice place. Really nice. Must be a pleasure to live here."

"It is," Howard agreed. "You say that you're with the U.S. Army. Do you have an identification of some kind?"

Smith looked at him, surprised.

"Why sure!" he reached into his pocket and brought out a laminated ID card. Howard glanced at it. The name was indeed Raymond Smith. Still, the man had a slight accent that did not fit the ID.

"But, of course, that isn't my real name,"

Smith seemed to be able to read his thoughts and to be enjoying himself immensely while doing it. "You see, I'm in Intelligence."

Sybil didn't care for the game at all. While Howard and Smith had already sat down she remained standing, eyeing the newcomer suspiciously.

"Well, Mr. Smith or whatever your name ..."

"I came to talk with you about Harry Mindon."

"Where is Harry? Has anything happened?" asked Howard.

Smith thought for a moment before answering.

"We don't know. You see, there was an automobile accident in Berlin on Xantenerstrasse last week and it was Colonel Mindon's jeep which caught fire. There *was* a body inside the jeep which was wearing his uniform, but there were also a few discrepancies. Although the jeep did catch fire, it was put out rather quickly. It really didn't burn long enough to damage the corpse beyond recognition."

"I don't understand ..."

"For the past month or so," Smith continued as if no one had spoken, "we have been watching Mindon. We thought at first he had his fingers in the black market. Almost everyone does in Berlin, but generally they try not to be overly vulgar about it. With Mindon it could have been much more than that. He had some good friends among some fairly high-ranking Russians. If you knew how isolated the Russians insist on being there you would understand how strange it all seemed."

Howard said nothing. But he strongly suspected that as of this moment the relaxed, wonderfully therapeutic mood of Cornwall had been broken.

"We have just started checking into some of the things Mindon had been involved in commander. And according to Major Mindon's report on his visit to the military hospital at Sevenoaks last fall, you were at that time near death. In the opinion of the doctors there, quoted by Mindon in his report, your coma could result *only* in death ... Do you have any idea why he would say that?"

It took a few moments for Howard to catch his breath. He and Sybil looked at each other, saying over to themselves Smith's last words to see if there possibly could have been some misunderstanding.

"No," said Howard finally. "When Harry visited me at Sevenoaks I was well on the road to recovery. I certainly was not in a coma."

"What did he say to you?"

"He said that Operation Lister was being kept a secret both by the Russians and by the West. He also said that Stanislaw Jaroscynski, who had been part of the Lister team, and a man named Jiri Palka, a member of the Czech underground who helped us, had been arrested. Or rather that they disappeared."

Smith nodded.

"So far all true."

"He also brought a letter from Palka's wife."

"Addressed to you?"

"Yes."

"What did it say?"

"It asked me to help Palka."

"Hmm," said Smith. "That one we haven't got. It wasn't in Mindon's files."

"Well, where did it come from?" asked Sybil.

"Mrs. Howard, if Mindon was in contact with the Russians he certainly had no trouble getting a letter from Palka's wife in Czechoslovakia. If it *was* written by her. But that really doesn't matter as long as your husband *believed* it was from her, does it?"

Sybil shook her head.

"Commander, what did Colonel Mindon want from you during his visit to Sevenoaks? I mean — surely he didn't come just so he could personally deliver a letter from Mrs. Palka?"

"He asked me for a detailed report on Operation Lister. Then, when it was finished, I was to get in touch with him. With him personally."

"We see it this way," said Smith after a few moments of reflection. "In saying you were near death, Mindon has written you off so far as the military is concerned. Only you yourself could reawaken our attention by your sudden reappearance, practically from the grave. You were instructed to send the report to Major Mindon personally. He would probably have asked you to come to Berlin, then simply taken you and the report through the Branderburg Gate and no one would have ever heard from you again. Except that Mindon himself had to run before the report was finished for some reason."

No one said anything for a while. They watched one of those rare winter sunsets for which photographers sometimes wait weeks. Sybil made tea and they drank it silently until Smith suddenly seemed to have thought of something important, something that should have been asked right away. He turned to Howard.

"We really aren't going to solve this puzzle here. You should come to Germany for a few days."

Sybil recoiled. She obviously still didn't trust him and Smith immediately noticed.

"Not to Berlin. To Straubing, not too far from Munich. Look, I'll work through the British Admiralty if it makes you feel any better. We will issue your orders through them. I think that we need the peace and quiet of the Bavarian countryside plus all sorts of other files to get to the bottom of this."

Sybil looked at Howard for an answer. The commander mulled it over for a while. Then he turned to Smith, asking,

"All right. When do you want us?"

Dr. Prokop Drtina, the Czechoslovak Minister of Justice, turned the piece of paper over in his hands for at least the tenth time. He read the message on it again.

> We have received word that Hana Dykova is alive in the Soviet Zone of Germany, that she is detained at a place called Schwachstein near Cottbus, and that she requests to be placed before a Czechoslovak court in order to explain her wartime activities.
>
> *Rektorys.*

Rektorys was an army captain, now attached to the Czechoslovak Military Mission in Frankfurt. Drtina knew him from wartime London, where they had both served in President Benes' exiled government. And Rektorys, of course, knew why his message should have been routed straight to the Justice Ministry, although it probably should have got there via either the Ministry of Defense or the Interior. The latter handled police matters. But both of these ministries were in the hands of the Communists. Perhaps the Foreign Affairs Ministry could have been consulted, but there the weak minister Masaryk wanted to be considered above politics and not likely to involve himself in something as controversial as this.

Because the whole Hana Dykova case was potentially explosive. Since the war it had been generally assumed that she was dead. If she really was alive and held by the Russians, then there must have been a good reason for it. Like so many others who had disappeared in the East since the war, she must have known something about the Communists that made them uncomfortable.

The last thing that the Czech and Slovak democratic parties needed right now was to make the Communists — home-grown and Russian alike — more uncomfortable. An uneasy truce reigned between them and the Marxists. The democrats were hoping it would last until the next election in which the Communists would be soundly beaten. But the country was also surrounded by Russian troops, stationed in Poland, East Germany, Hungary and Austria. They could march in and end the truce at any moment. That's why provoking them by requesting the extradition of a controversial figure like Hana Dykova could be an extremely unpopular move. It could also mean her death if she knew something the Russians didn't want her to tell. But, according to Rektorys, it was she herself who had requested her extradition.

At the same time she was one more Czech film star whose wartime activities were highly suspect. Early in the war Lida Baarova had been ordered out of Berlin by Hitler because of her sensational affair with Goebbels. Another, Adina Mandlova, was in prison, awaiting trial on charges of collaborating with the Germans. It was unlikely that Hana Dykova's case was any different and it was hardly worth upsetting the Russians because of it.

Drtina got up from his desk and walked to the window. He drew the curtains aside and looked down on the street where military uniforms were now becoming rarer, where stores once again were beginning to display something more than bare shelves and apologies, and from which the rubble

caused by bombing and street fighting had finally
been cleared. The country was slowly returning to
normal. But if it wanted to preserve its prewar
democratic traditions it had, above all, to respect
each individual's rights. There was no other way.

He returned to his desk, sighed deeply and tore
a piece of paper from a pad: *Request for an extradition*,
he wrote at the top of the page in large, firm
letters.

34

A rickety Dakota brought them to rubble-filled Munich, where they were picked up by Smith in a U.S. Army Ford. Taking them to a remote section of Straubing, he introduced them to the two servants in a comfortable house. Then he took the manuscript from Howard and for the next thirty-six hours or so left them on their own. But on their second morning he was sipping coffee from a polka dot mug and conversing with Sybil when Howard finally found his way downstairs. He got up with a smile as the commander entered, handing him back the manuscript.

"You have finished reading it already?" asked the amazed Howard.

"Not only that, commander, but we have also already made a copy. I thought we might talk a bit about it."

"Do you have any theories?" asked the commander.

"About Mindon?"

Smith scratched his head.

"Well, actually Mindon has become secondary to the whole business. It doesn't really matter if he is dead or just hiding somewhere, that's for the boys in Berlin to unravel. Here we are much more interested in what he was after. You see, he had you write out a long report on Lister just so they could see if you knew ... and if you considered it important enough to include it in your report."

"Have you come across anything that might give you a clue as to what *it* might be?" asked Howard.

Smith absentmindedly lathered some butter on a roll and topped it off with a heaped spoonful of strawberry jam.

"Mindon was absolutely right when he told you that whatever it was the Russians were after would probably seem perfectly innocuous to us. He was certainly in a position to judge. What we really need is a confirmed paranoiac to read your account, commander, and then venture an opinion. Anybody else is operating at a definite disadvantage."

Smith broke into a broad grin and Sybil found herself laughing along. She liked him better now. In his Bavarian costume and fluent German (which he used with the servants), he was certainly mysterious, but in that mystery which surrounded him there was a strong sense of purpose.

"What about Palka and Jaroscynski, Mr. Smith? Any news about them?" Howard asked.

"Just Smith is good ... No. We have checked out the story Mindon gave you and there were some fairly big holes in it. First of all, no one has seen Jaroscynski for almost a year now. That bit about him walking around Krakow seemed romantic enough, but unfortunately there was no truth to it. Palka and Jaroscynski are simply missing. Under the circumstances General Eisenhower's directive still stands — no word about Operation Lister is to leak out."

After breakfast, the work began in earnest. "What I thought we might do," Smith began, opening the folder with the copy of Howard's report in it, "is to go over the whole thing. To bring in things you might have forgotten, to enlarge things you might have only skimmed over ... For example, let's start with the moment you touched the ground at Pastviny and let's recall every single person with whom you came into contact there."

And so it went. Smith kept firing his questions at a steady, unrelenting pace. Aside from the report itself there was now a pile of notes which Smith had made and whose volume equaled the original manuscript.

Two weeks had gone by, consisting of uniformly gray cold days. Smith arrived at the house one morning, joining the Howards for breakfast again. In the middle of buttering his roll and spreading his beloved, oversweetened, German strawberry jam on it, he suddenly put his knife down. "I think I should confess: I still don't know why the Russians are so interested in keeping Operation Lister under the lid and why Harry Mindon ... well, actually I do know about that one now."

"You know that?" Howard leaned forward.

"I know that Harry Mindon was an active member of the Communist Party while studying at Cambridge during the thirties. It took us this long to get it out of the damn limeys. Apparently they don't consider it very important," Smith sputtered.

"So he has been working with the Russians all along?" asked Howard.

"So I would say that he has been working with the Russians all along," Smith agreed.

Gradually at Straubing, Howard noticed that Sybil was not feeling herself. One night, when she complained of a headache after dinner, he followed her up to the bedroom. That's where she suddenly and uncharacteristically broke down, rushing into Howard's arms and in between deep sobs letting it all out.

"I can't take it any more Douglas. At first I thought it was all so deliciously exciting — this whole Lister business and the spies and good-guy games, chasing across Europe. But I'm scared now: this merry-go-round is turning a lot faster than I bargained for. Somebody is going to get hurt ..."

It was late at night when she finally quietened down, but her sleep was not peaceful. Howard, who stayed awake most of the night thinking about Smith, the East Europeans, and Mindon, stroked her head whenever she became too disturbed.

In the morning, when Smith came to visit, Howard had decided. It was time to leave Lister, the armed forces, and the European continent behind.

Smith nodded when he was told. He lit a crumpled Camel, then commented:

"Well, of course, we were about to suggest the same thing. There is nothing more that can be done by you here. At least *we* can't think of anything."

"Can we go then?" asked the excited Sybil.

"Go where?" said Smith. "Where would you like to go?"

"Home," Howard and Sybil said simultaneously. They looked at each other, then took hold of each other's hand.

"What I mean is that I don't exactly know where your home is," confessed Smith.

"England, of c..." started Sybil, suddenly remembering that for Howard things were not that simple.

"Frankly, we would much rather see you in the other home — in Montreal," said Smith.

"Why?" asked Howard.

"Because it's farther away. And safe — from the Russians and things."

Sybil understood first. And she instantly agreed that Canada was to be their new home, that the new continent would mean a fresh start, getting lost among the North American millions, an end to Europe's war and intrigues.

"Then Montreal it is. How soon can we go?" she asked.

"Wait a minute," laughed Howard. "I don't know what I can do in Canada." The reality of leaving the Navy's womb suddenly struck him. He scarcely remembered what came before the war. It seemed like centuries ago.

Smith chuckled.

"You won't starve. You have quite a bit of money in demobilization pay coming your way, so there'll be plenty of time to look around."

"When can we go?" Sybil asked.

Smith scratched his nose.

"Well, there's this hospital ship leaving Bremerhaven the day after tomorrow, heading for New York . . ."

"But we would have to go to England first ..." Howard started to say.

"Why? Don't be silly. Someone will pack up my things in London and sell the Morris. Can I get into Canada just like that? I mean without a visa or anything."

"That's all been arranged. Your papers are waiting for you at the base," the omniscient Smith assured them. "By the way, even high-ranking heroes are to inform their commanding officers when they intend to get married to a foreign national. We have taken care of it, but for a while it looked as if you had been living in sin for the past

few months — so far as your command in London is
concerned anyway."

Again there was the railway station and again
Smith was in his green hat, this time in Munich.
Sybil would have liked to think he was at least a
little bit sorry to see them go, but his face did not
show it. The train started to move and Howard and
Sybil waved to the receding figure in the green hat
with a brush and in a loden coat with an upturned
collar. They watched until he changed into a small
dot, finally obscured by a cloud of steam.

"Funny guy, isn't he?" the young lieutenant
who accompanied them looked up from his Colli-
er's magazine.

"What do you mean?" Howard asked.

"I mean the way he dresses up, wanting to
remain the mysterious Smith at all costs. It's really
a form of escape from one's past. If you tell people
your name is Smith you have no past and all the
unpleasant things in it are automatically erased."

"Maybe it's needed for his work. Doesn't he
need to remain anonymous?" Sybil asked
innocently.

"Are you kidding? Everybody within 300 miles
of here knows who he is."

"Except us, we don't know. Tell us, lieutenant," Sybil pleaded.

"Smith is Rudolf Staubinger, formerly a
member of the Reichstag. One of the eighty-four
Social Democrats who voted against the Enabling
Act in March 1933 — the law that gave Hitler dic-
tatorial power. Staubinger was pretty outspoken
against the Führer and had to get out of Germany
fast. First he went to France, then to America. His
wife and two sons stayed behind. He tried to get
them out, tried his darndest. Seems he enlisted

every Social Democrat in Europe to help. But the
first time she tried to escape she was caught and
put into a concentration camp. That's where she
died — in Mecklenburg. Probably even before the
war started."

"How horrible," said Sybil. "What happened to
his children?"

"He has been trying to find out ever since he
returned to Germany. But I don't think he has any
idea."

The train gathered speed now, heading north
toward the sea. The compartment became quiet.
Sybil looked out the window, feeling sorry that she
had not known Smith's story before. Her attitude
would have been quite different.

35

Hana Dykova slowly started losing hope. She knew that in her weakened condition and in the unheated cell she was unlikely to survive the winter on her meagre rations. Her hair was still being cut every two weeks, but the former Wehrmacht corporal was now gone. He had been replaced by a much younger man who never made the slightest attempt to address her.

Several more times she heard the sound of gunfire in the adjacent courtyard. Perhaps the barber no longer lived and perhaps he never did manage to get the message about her out of the prison. Perhaps she was not destined to leave Schwachstein at all; her hope had been a sham.

The weather grew colder. She developed a cough and fever. She was sitting on her bunk, huddled inside her heavy overcoat and blanket (the rule about not disturbing one's bunk during the day had long ago been discarded), her mind on Douglas again, picturing him beside her in the attic of her house at Pastviny, sipping on a cup of tea and smiling, warm, tranquil, contented ...

But then she forced the image out of her mind. She knew that such emotional indulgencies dangerously sapped her meagre remaining strength. Outside it began to snow again.

The door to her cell opened. Since it was not time for a meal, bath, or the barber, it constituted a totally unexpected event that made her rise and stare wide-eyed at the soldier who entered and motioned for her to follow. She buttoned her overcoat and started down the long, stone-floored corridors behind him, to an office occupied by an obese Russian officer who actually offered her a chair, then a loaf of bread with some soup much thicker than she was used to. While she hungrily lapped up the food, he got up from behind his desk and circled her, all the time studying her with the utmost interest.

The suprising thing was that he spoke Czech, not German. She hadn't heard Czech since she had left Pastviny. It was an unexpected treat that she so much wanted to portend better times. When she finished her food she pushed the dish aside and looked up at the officer.

"I think our investigation of you here is coming to an end," he said simply with a smile. "We are now certain that you have done nothing that is punishable under Soviet Law; but of course we cannot speak for the Czechs. We will be returning you to them, you know."

She said nothing. Her heart was beating too wildly.

"There is one thing we wanted to ask you though: how good a friend of the Tiesenhausens were you?"

She thought about her answer for a moment. It could be crucial.

"I wouldn't call myself a friend at all. I knew Frau Tiesenhausen because we were neighbors."

"Hmm," the Russian acknowledged the answer. "And you had never been to visit Adam Hill during the war?"

"No. It was in the Reich. The Czechs were not allowed there without special permission."

"Have you heard any rumors about what was happening up there?"

"Yes. Most people said that Hitler was working on some sort of a secret weapon there." She tried to answer truthfully, convincingly, perhaps hoping that the officer would be disarmed by her sincerity, but also because she had little strength left to be devious.

"Did you suspect what kind of weapons they might have been?"

"Not until Commander Howard told me."

"Did he tell you anything else? About the people who may have been working on this weapon?"

"No."

Hana thought for a moment, studying the Russian's face. Then she decided to ask the next question.

"Is Commander Howard alive? Did he survive the war?"

"Perhaps ... Would like to see him when you leave here?"

Hana looked at her bony hands resting in her lap and soon she couldn't see them for the tears in her eyes.

"Oh yes, yes. I would so much like to see him," she finally managed to whisper.

Two days later the door to her cell opened unexpectedly again and the same soldier told her to gather her belongings. There wasn't much to worry about. She buttoned up her overcoat and put on her German infantry cap. She wasn't paying attention to anything else she might have left behind; her excitement was too great. And again they meandered through the corridors, but this time out into the courtyard, still sprinkled with snow and so slippery that twice she would have almost fallen had it not been for the soldier's arm extended to her in the last moment. She smiled at him, thinking the whole thing so funny, gazing at the gray buildings surrounding her on all sides and up above at the dark clouds, probably filled with more snow. But it would not snow on her, she was going home. The war had finally ended even for her.

They stopped at the small gate leading to the adjoining courtyard through which they had to pass in order to leave the castle. They waited, while on the other side a key rattled in the lock and Hana thought how ridiculous it was for the Russians to lock this entrance which no prisoner could possibly reach. Then the low gate finally opened with a squeak and she followed the soldier through it, her head bowed.

When she straightened out again on the other side she cried out. In front of her stood a group of Russians in fur hats with rifles, an officer a bit to the side. Her first impulse was to turn and run, without really knowing where. But at least two pairs of strong hands grabbed hold of her, more dragging her along the cobblestones to a chair facing the soldiers than anything else, tying her in it with a rope while she sobbed, her mind stricken with terror and the awful unfairness of it all.

As the officer shouted an order she looked up, facing eight gun barrels made of steel so cold that it made her teeth chatter. The sound of their fire was suddenly cut off and in its place came a silence the likes of which she had never imagined existed.

36

Montreal soon became for Sybil as if she had been born there. She got a job as a nurse at a veterans' hospital within hours of getting off the train from New York. She also was the one who rented an apartment in the district of Outremont with a little greenhouse on its balcony. There she immediately planted cucumbers and daisies, for different reasons her favorite plants.

At first she insisted on dragging Howard along to auctions and department store sales, looking for furniture for their apartment. Soon she realized that he didn't want to help her choose although he was quick with grateful praise whenever she made the decision. Within a month of their arrival the basic decorating was finished. They were living in a cozy two-room, red brick apartment, furnished in colonial style with some Victoriana here and there because of Sybil's nostalgia. Just about then a letter arrived from England announcing that the Morris and most of her other belongings had been sold.

Soon it was as if the old country had ceased to exist. There was still an occasional letter from Sybil's widowed father and friends, but Sybil seemed to view them as if they came from a foreign land. In amazement Howard realized that whenever they spoke about Europe she sounded as if she were describing some highly exotic wonderland.

At first things did not go as smoothly for Howard though. It took about three weeks to finish the demobilization process. When all the forms had been filled, examinations completed and interviews endured, his hand was shaken by a pompous admiral and he was free. Howard then came home, planted himself in the nearest armchair and with one leg thrown over its armrest, grandiosely announced,

"Well, Sybil, I'm proud to report that as of today I'm officially unemployed. And that in spite of the fact I'm a highly qualified resistance fighter with the added specialty of parachute jumping. I hear that in Greece, for instance, there is great need for my qualifications. Maybe I should clean out my grease gun and follow the Hellenic sun but maybe I should first study up on which side is right over there. Not that it matters much in today's world, but one still likes to die for the right cause ..."

"Shut up, darling," Sybil answered him softly. "We'll take a few minutes out tonight and every night if you want to have some time for feeling sorry for yourself. But that will have to be after working hours because there's so much to do."

She reached for her bag on a nearby chair, opened it and for a moment rummaged through it until she found the piece of paper she wanted. She handed it to Howard.

"There's an organization that's been in business for about six months now helping types like you, hoity toity officers who go to pieces when they take off their spiffy uniforms. They rehabilitate them, make them into useful members of society again."

"How did you find out about this?"

"Darling, I work at a veterans' hospital, or have you forgotten?"

"Will you come with me? Tomorrow is your day off."

Sybil swung her legs off the couch and got up.

"Not on your life," she said on her way to the kitchen, "Tomorrow is a very busy day, what with yoga in the morning and a French lesson after lunch. Besides," she turned around, "this is something that a great big beautiful hulk of a war hero like you has to do for himself. How would it look if Mother Hawthorne brought you in there, holding you by the hand?"

Three weeks later Douglas Howard was selling life insurance for Global Mutual with singular lack of success. Within two months it was clear that although he was good with figures and details, he was abominably bad in convincing people of his honesty. Henceforth he stayed in the building. From assistant office manager he rose in a year to be manager. A couple of his suggestions on how to make insurance more appealing to returning veterans marked him for early promotion.

With the purchase of an Oldsmobile and an Irish setter, Howard and Sybil slowly acquired all the trimmings of a typical suburban couple. They skied in the Laurentians and spent their vacations at a friend's cottage on Georgian Bay. Eventually they started shopping for a small house of their own and finally they started to believe that that their war-interrupted lives were taking on some stability.

Lister and its aftermath had receded to the back of their minds, although Howard still periodically wrote to Smith in Straubing, asking if there was any news about Palka and Jaroscynski. But even that ended with an official-looking letter from some U.S. Army type, who stiffly informed him that Smith had been transferred and that his letter was being forwarded to "the appropriate authority." Nothing came of it. Howard never heard from "the appropriate authority."

In the fall of 1947 Smith himself replied in a letter with a Frankfurt postmark but without a return address.

"Dear Commander and Mrs. Howard:

Sorry to be so tardy with my reply. I have been traveling and some of the things I found out on the road are of interest to you. First of all, thanks to your old friend General Bedell Smith's appointment as our ambassador to Moscow, we now have a man in Russia who is acutely interested in the whole Lister affair. His pressure on the Russians has already produced some results.

We don't know about Jaroscynski yet because things are much tighter in Poland than they are in Czechoslovakia. But Palka is back home in his beloved Orlice Mountains of Czechoslovakia. That's where I've been traveling. I saw him but unfortunately he didn't have much to say that could help us find out exactly what it was that the Russians were after. He was picked up by the Russians in 1945 and flown some place in the Ukraine, to a military camp near Kiev. There he was kept in what didn't exactly look like the worst of prisons, but he was still totally isolated until early this year. He was then suddenly packed into a truck, driven to Slovakia and released in Bratislava with a thousand-crown note in his pocket. No one interrogated him during his stay in the Ukraine. His food was fairly decent. He also received adequate medical care and his bed was reasonably soft. He never saw Jaroscynski while there.

What do I think? I think that Palka was in the Ukraine waiting to be shot. Then something happened. And here is another guess: It had something to do with Mindon who, I am certain, is now in the USSR and not in some grave in Berlin. My guess is that he managed to convince the relatively dense Russians that killing Palka and Jaroscynski would still leave you at large and that it would probably only encourage you to take some strong measures in retaliation. Something like spilling the beans, letting out everything you know about Lister.

I guess you know where all this leads: to you. I have absolutely no proof, but Mindon did try to entice you to Berlin and from there it is only a hop skip and a holler to the Russians. And I believe it is now Mindon who is calling the shots over there so far as Lister is concerned. By the way, the letter he brought you at Sevenoaks really was from Palka's wife. A man whom she considered a friend until then enticed her to write it.

I suspect we will soon know more, much more. I'll be in touch with you. In the meantime take care of yourselves.

Smith

"He tends to exaggerate a bit, doesn't he, Douglas?" asked Sybil when she read the letter.

"About what?"

"About Lister, about them wanting you, about the whole international situation. But I guess that's how they are in the U.S. Army Intelligence Corps. I hope they'll find that Jaroscynski is back in

Poland and that will put a lid on the whole thing."

"I suppose so," said Howard, returning to his book and relighting his pipe. The trouble was he was not at all sure.

37

The phone call came three days later at his office.

"Douglas Howard, is that right?" a raspy voice, switched to him by his secretary, asked.

"Yes, what can I do for you?"

"The *Commander* Douglas Howard?" the voice persisted.

"Yes, it used to be that."

"I'm a friend of a friend. Do you recall meeting a man called Smith in Germany?"

"Yes, of course, I've had a letter from his recently. Just three days ago as a matter of fact. He said there'd be new developments soon. Is that what it's all about?"

"Exactly. There is a bit more to it now. It's not just the army any more, commander. I suppose you know about the involvement of Ambassador Bedell Smith, do you?"

"I've heard about it."

"Well, there will be a conference about the whole thing in New York this weekend. I think we can finally wind it all up, but it's all still hush-hush, that's why we are getting in touch with you this way. Do you think that you could be there?"

"Certainly."

"And, er, we would appreciate if you kept this absolutely confidential. Could you tell your wife that you are going on a business trip, would that sound plausible? After you return, of course, you will be able to tell her the truth."

"Well, yes, I think so."

"Very well then. Please take the train to New York Friday night and check into the Westbriar Hotel. That's on East 50th Street, any taxi driver can take you there. At nine o'clock on Saturday morning you will receive a phone call and someone will tell you where to go. Would you like me to repeat any of it?"

"No, that's fine."

"And I am sorry, commander, that there is so much secrecy and cloak and dagger surrounding the whole thing. Believe me, it's necessary. Especially now, after what we know from Gouzenko."

"I understand. Saturday at 9 A.M. at the Westbriar on 50th Street, is that right?"

"That's right. Goodbye commander."

Watching the placid waters of the broad Hudson River out of the train window, Howard was looking forward to the explanation of the mystery which had been affecting his life for three years now. He hoped he could soon publish his story of Lister. He owed it to Hana and Tom Evans. Compared with some of the exaggerated and often ridiculous things coming out about the secret campaigns of World War II, this would be like a fresh breeze. In the end maybe it would have been a blessing that Lister had been kept secret until now. Its impact would be that much greater if it came out of the blue.

The train slid underground and in a few minutes came to a halt at Grand Central Station. He found a phone booth from which he called Sybil in Montreal to say that he had arrived safely, then hailed a taxi to take him to the Westbriar. Howard took the elevator to the cocktail lounge on the top floor where he was propositioned by a bored call girl. It made the time pass pleasantly and after two Scotches he excused himself and went up to his room to bed. It was close to midnight when he turned out the light.

He was up at seven, his usual time, and seeing that the day was turning out to be a crisp, sunny one, polished by a brisk wind, he went for a walk through the morning city. At eight he was back at the Westbriar, enjoying a plate of scrambled eggs with sausages while scanning the front page of *The New York Times*. At precisely nine, when he was back in his room, the phone rang.

"Commander Howard?" asked an indifferent voice.

"Yes."

"Will you please join us at the Burnaby? It's a restaurant on Fifth Avenue, three blocks from where you are now. You pass by St. Patrick's Cathedral and it's in the same block as Sak's Fifth Avenue, on the east side."

"I'm sure I'll find it. Will it ..."

"Fine," the voice interrupted him. "We'll expect you in about twenty minutes." There was a click and the line was dead. Howard grabbed his raincoat.

Following the east side of Fifth Avenue uptown, he paid little attention to the store windows, some of them already decorated for Christmas. He moved at a brisk pace, trying to reach the Burnaby as quickly as possible. Then a wider sidewalk indicated he was passing the cathedral and he gave it a fleeting glance. He continued uptown, past the first of the fashionable store's long series of windows and was about to pass the second when, without any reason at all — he later started to suspect that there was a divine hand in it, there was no other explanation — he glanced in the other direction. Toward the street.

He caught sight of an unusually slow-moving black limousine with its back window rolled down. And in the next moment he realized that he was looking into the barrel of a gun. He hurled himself onto the sidewalk, in the process toppling over a middle-aged lady laden with boxes who had been about to pass him. And while the terrified yelp of the lady still pierced the air, there was the sound of three muffled shots from the car, closely followed by glass shattering in the store window, then a chorus of screams from the other passers by. Within seconds, a wave of stampeding humanity, all rushing in different directions, blissfully formed an almost solid, wall of flesh between Howard and the edge of the sidewalk. The limousine speeded up, turning sharply into the traffic and, by the sound of the brakes, coming right into somebody's path. But the sound of its accelerating engine was like music to Howard's ears.

The danger had passed. He was still alive.

He had been alone with his disturbing thoughts in the glassed interrogation room for ten minutes when a heavy-set cop with a .38 under his shoulder came in, holding a manila folder. He was paying much more attention to the folder than to Howard until he found the back of the chair, pulled it away from the table and sat down in it. Only then did he look up at him.

"You're the guy they shot at?"

"Yes, my name is Douglas Howard. I am with the Globe Mutual Company and I ..."

"Yeah, yeah, I've got all that," the cop transferred his chewing gum from one corner of his mouth to the other. "The cop on the beat there wasn't asleep, you know."

"Look officer I ..."

"The name is Leibowitz, Lieutenant Leibowitz. And I don't believe any of that crap you've been dishing out to officer what's his name — Renwich out there on the sidewalk in front of Sak's. Sorry buddy."

"That's too bad," Howard visibly stiffened. "Why?"

"Because it's a typical DiStefano rub-out, that's why. Not successful, but still an attempted one. And you — a Canadian tourist — fit into it to a T."

"*What?*"

Leibowitz leaned toward him until Howard saw every detail of his brown, tobacco-stained incisors. Then the policeman more hollered than spoke:

"What do you think we are over here — a bunch of schnooks? We know what's going on. The DiStefanos have been dreaming of expanding for months now. They have Philadelphia and St. Louis already. Well, St. Louis isn't quite in the bag yet, but our people there tell us it's only a matter of days now. So now they've started putting the squeeze on the mob in Montreal, eh? Going international. How do you fit in, Howard? I don't think you're just a messenger because the DiStefanos wouldn't put on a show like this in the middle of Fifth Avenue if you were just a messenger. We're checking right now on just who the hell you are. It shouldn't take long, buddy, because from past experience we know that the Montreal cops are very cooperative."

"Look, lieutenant, I don't know what you're talking about."

That brought on an all-knowing shaking of the cop's head.

"I didn't think you would, buddy, I really didn't think you would."

"I came to New York because ..." but he decided against it at the last moment. "Because of some company business and I was shot at in front of Sak's Fifth Avenue. I don't know by whom or why."

"Where were you going when you were shot at without knowing by whom or why?" Leibowitz asked in a voice dripping with sarcasm.

"To a restaurant."

"Aah, to a restaurant. Which one?"

Howard decided to tell the truth.

"The Burnaby."

"The what? Never heard of it," said Leibowitz, swinging around and grabbing hold of a well-used Manhattan phone book. He was still leafing through it when a young man came in without knocking and handed Leibowitz a piece of paper.

"Hey Stark, ever heard of a place called the Burnaby — somewhere in the fifties on Fifth Avenue?"

Stark shook his head without even stopping on his way out.

"Well, neither have I, Howard baby. So what we have here is a Canadian hood getting mowed down by the DiStefano boys while looking for a nonexistent restaurant on Fifth Avenue."

"Now wait a minute lieutenant ..."

But Leibowitz silenced him with a motion of his hand as he read the contents of the paper Stark had handed him a few moments ago.

"All right. So maybe you're not a hood. Montreal police thinks you're a respectable businessman and a war hero to boot and your company doesn't have any known underworld connections. But something still doesn't quite fit in here."

"You're darn right it doesn't!" the angry Howard now erupted. "I've been shot at by some mob in the middle of the day on a public street and *I'm* the one that's being investigated. Don't you think it a trifle strange, lieutenant? Why don't you pull in the DiStefanos or whatever their name is and start asking them why the hell they shot at me?"

"Because," said Leibowitz after a moment of reflection and when his cigarette had been lit properly, "in New York precinct lieutenants do not pull in anyone associated with Giacomo DiStefano. Borough presidents and mayors maybe ask them a question now and then — politely, very politely — but certainly not precinct lieutenants. Not those who wish to remain precinct lieutenants — live ones, that is."

Howard was sitting in the waiting room at Grand Central Station with his suitcase beside him, watching the big clock as it neared five, the time of the departure of the Montreal train. An hour ago he wanted to take it, to get out of New York, to arrive in Montreal early next morning and forget about the whole affair. He very much wanted to return to his office, to start dictating letters on Monday as if nothing and happened. He wanted to go to the movies with Sybil Tuesday night and to resume the life he had been living for over a year now.

But he knew he couldn't. The book had not been closed on Lister, not even its New York chapter had been concluded. He could go back home, never say a word to Sybil and hope that it would go away. But chances were pretty slim that it would.

Whoever had been trying to kill him in New York could just as well do it in Montreal. Not only he but Sybil too was in danger.

Howard rose and picked up his suitcase. Outside the station he hailed a taxi. He asked to go to the Pennsylvania Station, where he would book a berth on the overnight train to Washington.

38

At the Pentagon the youngish looking captain with a crew cut, on duty in the Army Intelligence section, listened to his story, occasionally jotting down a note. It took Howard an hour to tell it. The captain closed his notebook and looked up at Howard.

"It's Sunday afternoon, commander. The worst time for this sort of thing to break. Except maybe for Christmas Day. That's why wars usually start on Sundays, when no one is around. I've reserved a room for you at the Willard. I suggest you get some rest. You'll be quite safe in Washington, especially since I'm going to get in touch with the FBI and they'll send somebody to look after you. You probably won't see him, but he'll definitely be there. At least until this whole thing gets sorted out tomorrow."

An army car drove Howard to the hotel. In its dining room over the evening meal he tried to figure out which one of the single men there was his guardian. He was unsuccessful. The place was full of businessmen who arrived in town a day early so they could get a good night's sleep before plunging into their negotiations.

Equipped with a Raymond Chandler thriller, Howard went up to his room early. At nine he called Sybil.

"Darling, where are you?" he heard her say as if from far away.

"I'm in Washington."

"Washington?"

"Yes."

"Aren't you coming home tonight, then?"

"Well, no. This darn thing is much more complicated than we thought. It requires the loosening of some American regulations. I've been selected as some sort of a moral support for the thing. But we should wind it all up tomorrow and then I'll fly up. If I can't make it, I'll call you again."

"All right. How's Washington — bureaucratic?"

"I don't know. I'll find out tomorrow."

He realized it was the first time that he had lied to Sybil and was anxious to wind up the conversation as quickly as possible. In the morning he would call the office to let them know he would not be in for a couple of days.

Soon even Raymond Chandler could not keep him awake. He switched off the light, turned over on his side and, thinking that hotel beds were really nothing like his own, he slowly drifted off to sleep.

There were three of them. An army brigadier general named Maitland and two civilians. A slightly balding fellow in an impeccably cut gray herringbone suit was introduced as an FBI agent named Collins. The other, in a properly subdued sport coat and with a pronounced chin, was from the new organization, the Central Intelligence Agency. His name was Kerry. Also present was the youngish captain Maver from the day before. He took care of the introductions when Howard arrived for the luncheon meeting at the Pentagon.

"Maybe Mr. Collins should begin. I think we should let the commander know all we have found out about yesterday," said the general, digging into his shrimp cocktail. The food had been wheeled in on a cart and arranged so that no waiter would be required. Whatever dishes needed to be distributed were taken care of by Captain Maver.

Collins coughed to clear his throat.

"Actually there isn't much that we can add at this time to what Lieutenant Leibowitz has told you yesterday. Yes, the shooting was done from the back of a Chrysler that very much resembles the one usually used by the DiStefano mob. The style of killing — on a crowded midtown street with the resultant chaos that helps the car in its getaway — has been used by the DiStefanos before. There is another similarity to other DiStefano murders. They're unique in not using automatic weapons. We have a fairly good idea as to who is their ace marksman, but that isn't important right now. We're therefore reasonably sure that the attempt on Commander Howard's life was made by the DiStefano organization."

"The question is why," interjected the general.

Kerry, the CIA man, came to life.

"Of course if the Russians for some reason — and in this case they seem to have *some* reason — if they wanted to get rid of the commander, they would hire someone to do it. There are killer specialists for Moscow just as there are for New York."

"We're actually already working on establishing that connection," said the FBI man to Kerry, "but it'll take time. The DiStefano mob is not without its informers," he added proudly.

"And you can be sure that the Russians have taken every precaution to cover their tracks. If it's important enough to kill, then it's important enough to put their best people on it. Frankly, I don't think that you'll ever be able to establish their part in it," was Kerry's way of defeating Collins.

"Yeah," sighed the general, who was now into his club sandwich with gusto, probably regretting that the iced tea was not something entirely different. "What I don't understand, commander, is how they got you down from Montreal and into exactly the spot where they wanted you. And then, of course, why they missed. Because they don't usually, do they?"

"No they don't," Collins agreed. "They sure as hell don't."

Howard didn't say anything. But in a few moments, when it became obvious he was expected to provide some thoughts on the subject, he stopped eating.

"It could have had something to do with my training. I guess my reflexes were unusually good this time. After all, it was still morning. I didn't see the man behind the gun but I did see the barrel, luckily enough, before it fired. It was fairly long, that means difficult to maneuver from the inside of a car. I can rationalize the whole thing beautifully now, but it might have been just an accident that I decided to dive toward the DiStefano car instead of away from it. To get a good shot at me on the sidewalk there so close to the car, the assassin would have had to lower his rifle to increase the angle. Chances are the roof of the car prevented him from doing that. It looks also as if they were aiming for the head. That's almost an instant kill, but the target is small.

"The other part isn't as easy to explain," Howard continued. "I was stupid. When they first called me in Montreal, they mentioned Smith all right. By now I think everyone in Europe must know that Smith is involved with Lister, particularly after his trip to Czechoslovakia. Like an idiot I told them I had had a letter from Smith that said there would be new developments soon. Then I asked them if their phone call concerned these developments. They said yes and I was convinced that they were the ones who brought up the subject of new developments in the first place."

"Smith is Major Rudolf Staubinger of the CIC, operating out of Straubing in Germany," the general explained. "He's the senior army officer on the case."

There followed a few moments of pencil tapping silence which was finally broken by Kerry.

"Commander Howard, we're very much involved with the whole Lister business at the Central Intelligence Agency. We've already eliminated lots of reasons why the Russians might not want anybody to talk about it and we're now convinced that it is because of something that went on on top of Adam Hill itself — nowhere else. Did you know that two days after the air raid Heinrich Himmler himself came to inspect the damage to Adam Hill?"

"No, I've never heard that."

"We can't tie the visit to anything specifically yet, but it does seem significant. Perhaps that's what Smith — Major Staubinger — was referring to. You see, after his visit Hitler placed Himmler in command of the German Replacement Army — the so-called Army Group Vistula. He had never held an army post before and here he was suddenly in charge of stopping Zhukov — the genius among the Russian generals."

"But all that still doesn't help the commander here, does it?" asked Maitland. "I mean he's the one they just took a pot shot at."

Again a few moments of silence which was finally broken by Maitland himself.

"Well, look, I think your personal safety is of primary importance here. We're prepared to take you and your wife to some hiding place until we have a definite word on what it is that the Russians want."

"That might be a couple of years and maybe never," Howard protested.

"I can't guarantee anything except your safety, commander."

"I would like to take some time to think it over."

"Sure. Take as long as you need. Here's my telephone number." He scribbled something on a pad in front of him then tore it off and handed it to Howard.

Collins deposited him back at the Willard. Howard lay down on his bed and lit up one of his rare cigarettes. It started to rain outside and what began as a delightful day turned into a miserable, depressing afternoon.

It had seemed a relatively easy decision at the Pentagon. Now it no longer seemed just a question of personal safety but also of the kind of life they would have to lead if they accepted the general's offer. The normalcy they had so assiduously cultivated in Montreal would be shattered. The war would never end for them. Howard was sure that placing such restraints on the lively Sybil would destroy their marriage. And it was not Sybil but he who was in danger. There was a chance that they would be safe in Canada. They had been safe there for over a year now. And whoever had attacked him had lured him to New York to do so.

He rose from the bed and threw his things into a suitcase. Downstairs, Collins was still sitting at the fountain in the coffee shop, sipping on a Coke with a twist of lemon.

"I'm going home, Mr. Collins," Howard announced simply.

"I sort of thought you would be."

"What would you do if you were in my place?" Collins swung his stool away from the fountain.

"Geez, I don't know. I'm sort of thankful that I'm not."

"If you want," Collins said, "I can take you to the airport. When is your plane leaving?"

"At six."

In the Pontiac, while rounding the Lincoln Memorial, Collins told him about the arrangements. "We sort of figured you'd be going back, so there'll be an RCMP officer waiting for you at the airport. The Mounties will take over, but they won't be able to provide total security."

"I don't really expect it."

"No. I think you understand what we're up against," Collins mumbled.

Howard called Sybil from the airport to tell her he would be arriving late and not to wait up for him. But he knew she would anyway, just as much as he knew he would have to tell her the news that very night.

The RCMP man in Montreal was Roger Langlois. He had a head full of wavy black hair that would have been the envy of any movie star. His other features, however, were definitely not handsome. Everything in his face seemed crowded as near the center as possible. There was no getting around it, Langlois was a terribly homely man. Aside from introducing himself and producing his identification card, Langlois did not say much until they were in his car on their way to Outremont.

"I think the FBI's explained what the police is able to do in protecting you?" he asked with a trace of a French accent, apparent more in rhythm and inflection than in pronunciation.

"Yes they have."

"We 'ave discussed your problem very thoroughly at 'eadquarters this afternoon. It seems there is no immediate danger to you."

"Oh? Why not?" It sounded to him a little bit like a decision reached by a group of provincial bumpkins for whom the entire affair was too complicated to make any sense.

"Please, let me explain first," Langlois pleaded with a winning smile which quickly placated Howard.

"What I mean is that there 'as been a well-planned attempt on your life two days ago which must 'ave taken weeks to organize. And the attempt was in New York, not in Montreal. Chances are, the Russians will 'ave to examine the entire thing. We're beginning to understand the Russians a little bit better, commander. All of these things are ordered from Moscow. Their people in North America are just following orders. Now a report on the failure of the attempt to kill you 'as to go to Moscow. It'll 'ave to be studied there, new proposals will be made on the basis of it. Finally one of the proposals will be selected. Orders will then go to North America and only then will a new plan be put into operation. We figure that all this will take at least a month."

"I hope to God you're right," mumbled the tired Howard. "Because I sure would like to get a good night's sleep. And I've yet to tell my wife that I'm being hunted by the Russians."

Langlois smiled and rounded the corner to Howard's street, gliding into a parking spot in front of the house with his engine turned off, lights out.

"I don't want to alert your wife as yet," he explained. "Because I'd like to give you something."

He reached into the glove compartment. Even in the dim light of the street lamp Howard saw that he brought out a shiny, snub-nosed .38 and a box of shells. He offered them to Howard.

"It's up to you if you want this. It would make us sleep a bit better if you took it. It's all arranged with the local police. They won't know anything about it and will not know as long as we authorize it. Do you want the gun?"

After a moment's reflection, Howard took the gun and the cartridges, and put them in his suitcase without a word. As he opened the door to get out, Langlois asked,

"What time do you leave for work in the morning?"

"Eight o'clock."

"And you go by car?"

"Yes."

"Then we'll go with you. You may not see us, but we'll be there."

"Fine," said Howard to Langlois already through the window of his car. He wondered how he should break the news to Sybil. As his keys made a noise inside the front door he saw the light on the staircase go on and he knew that she was on her way down.

Sybil confessed that she had suspected all along his trip had nothing to do with the U.S. government's regulations on life insurance. "But darling," she said barely containing her tears, "I thought there was another woman. Shows you how insecure I still am as your wife."

She agreed that running away and living their lives in some CIA hideout was not the answer. She didn't have to think long about that. Within an hour the explanations and discussions that Howard had dreaded so much were over. They had fallen asleep in each other's arms, thankful that they were back together, Howard promising he would never again leave her out of any decision making concerning Lister.

39

During the next few weeks Howard occasionally caught a glimpse of Langlois or other men whose faces he was now beginning to recognize. He made a determined effort to plunge himself into his work, keep to his routine. Then came the new year and the memory of that Saturday on Fifth Avenue receded still farther in his mind. Weeks before that Howard had stopped carrying his gun. It was cumbersome and weighed him down. Their life was back on its regular tracks so much that there were moments when Howard seriously considered the possibility that the DiStefanos were not after him at all, that the whole affair had been a case of mistaken identity.

But then a couple of things happened.

A letter arrived from Palka. Addressed to the Canadian High Commissioner in London, it had been mailed by someone in the American Zone of Germany, placed in a different envelope in London and forwarded to his Outremont address.

The first part was fairly routine. Palka wrote that he had been readmitted to the Czechoslovak Army with the rank of major, that he had belatedly received several decorations for wartime service and had been transferred to Prague. He was certain that it was because of the combined efforts of

Commander Howard as well as Smith whom he saw shortly after he had been released by the Russians.

But then came the second, much more disturbing part of the letter. After Smith's visit he had been called to Prague's Police Headquarters at Bartolomejska Street and questioned about what Smith said. He was told there that Smith was a fascist spy and that anyone who had any connections with him should immediately report it to the Czech authorities. Palka replied that he knew nothing about it, that he certainly would have reported Smith's presence in Czechoslovakia had he known it. That placated the police a bit. When Palka told them that he had been talking about Operation Lister with Smith, the police became very attentive and they wanted to know exactly what Smith had to say. They explained to Palka (who seemed to be an expert at playing stupid and drawing information out of the authorities) that during the war there had been widespread collaboration with the Germans at Adam Hill. They confessed that Palka himself had been under suspicion. That is why he had been taken away by the Russians. It was now clear that he had not been collaborating but until the whole business of Adam Hill was cleared up he was to keep silent. In the future he must report anything he heard about Smith or any other Westerner. Because the American imperialists and Nazi criminals are now on the same side.

It is clear to me, wrote Palka in German at the end of his letter, that I have been released for one reason only: to act as a decoy. They missed Smith because we met near the border where he crossed into Czechoslovakia, returning to Bavaria within hours and taking the

Czech authorities by surprise. But that won't happen again. They are waiting for anyone who will try to contact me. The overall situation in this country is becoming worse. The Communists now have complete control of all the security forces, of radio and the labor unions. The army is not completely on its knees yet, but it is so thoroughly infiltrated that if it were ever called upon to defend the country it would be useless.

Under the circumstances I am planning to leave, but it must be done very carefully because I want my wife and son to come West with me. But I know of no safe way. Could you help me?

Jiri Palka

On the day the letter arrived Langlois called and wanted to know what was in it. He asked for permission to come to Howard's house with one of his superiors. On the stroke of eight they came. The other man was, judging from the quality and cut of his clothes, a commissioned RCMP man. He was introduced as Superintendent Denton and listened carefully as Howard translated Palka's letter to them. There was a moment of silence when he finished. Then Denton, rubbing his chin, said slowly, "It'll be extremely difficult to bring him across. Especially after today."

"Why after today?" Sybil asked. "What's happened?"

Howard knew. He had been following the crisis in the newspapers for a week. Since its inception he had foreseen nothing but a bad end to it.

"The Communists have been preparing a government takeover in Prague for several days. Today they finally succeeded."

"Well, does that mean ..."

"That means the border is sealed. With the police in their hands, they are probably already picking up people like Palka," said Denton.

"Of course, there is an outside chance that he saw it coming. After all, the crisis in Prague has been smoldering for over a week now. Maybe he had time to make the proper arrangements and get out," suggested Howard.

"Possibly," Denton allowed. "You may be right. We'll get in touch with the Americans and the British on this and let you know."

During the lull which followed, Denton took a sip on the coffee Sybil had served him but made no attempt to rise. It was clear that Palka's letter was not the main reason why they had come. Finally Langlois spoke.

"We 'ave a request, Commander 'oward. An unusual request. It seems the other side wants to get in touch with you and negotiate. They're afraid of approaching you directly because they know that you are guarded by us. Well, not actually guarded but ..."

"I know what you mean. Who is 'they' — the Russians?"

"That's the funny thing about it," Langlois leaned forward, "because it isn't the Russians but the Poles."

"*The Poles?*" asked the surprised Sybil.

"There really isn't that much difference, ma'am. It's just that after the Gouzenko spy scandal the Russians in Ottawa have been rather reluctant to get into controversial things," Denton volunteered.

"What do they want to negotiate?" asked Howard.

"Jaroscynski. That's all they'd say," Langlois explained.

"Would you advise it?" asked Howard.

"Yes. Under certain conditions," allowed Denton.

"I don't understand. Why can't the Poles simply come to the RCMP headquarters, borrow an office and tell Douglas here whatever they want him to know?" asked the puzzled Sybil.

"I'm afraid, Mrs. Howard, that isn't the way things are done by the other side," explained Denton. "Meeting inside an RCMP office, or any other place of our designation, would imply to them that we're in charge, something they want at all costs to avoid. Besides, we could listen in on what they're saying. And even if they could make sure that we were not eavesdropping, there would still be an aura of an official meeting about the whole thing. They want us, the RCMP, to act as a matchmaker, not as the best man."

"Look, if it means that Stan Jaroscynski's life could be saved I'll even go to the Polish Embassy. They do have one in Ottawa, don't they?" Howard asked.

"I don't think that would be very wise. It would indicate a weakness on your part, something they might choose to exploit. We have a plan which we would like to suggest to you," said Denton.

"What is it?"

"Well, we thought it best if you could meet with the man out in the open. That would satisfy the neutral ground requirement. You could be watched all the time and at the same time no one would be in a position to record what is being said."

"That's fine with me. Where do you want it?"

"On Mount Royal. On Thursday. Is that all right?"

"Yes."

Denton reached to his feet and took a large

envelope out of his briefcase. He handed a large glossy picture to Howard. A wide face with a flattened nose and heavy eyebrows stared at the commander. He noted that it was not unpleasant, that the man's eyes definitely showed intelligence.

"The name is Jacek Cybulski. He's a secretary at the Polish Embassy, supposedly in charge of trade, but he also has other functions. Speaks perfect English. His father represented several Polish firms in London before the war and Mr. Cybulski went to school in England. But in September 1939 the family was caught on a visit to Warsaw and they spent the war there. The father died soon afterward but young Cybulski knew which way the wind was blowing. Our external affairs people don't think that he is a fanatic by any means and they expect him to be recalled back to Warsaw as soon as enough better indoctrinated Marxists are available for the Polish Foreign Service. For the present his government has a considerable hold on him: both his wife and son are still in Poland," Denton explained.

"And this is the man they're sending to deal with me. Isn't it a bit unusual?" asked the puzzled Howard.

"Not really," Denton continued. "After all, he's only a messenger. It's quite important that he gains your confidence. And that can't be achieved by some hardened party man. Cybulski's job will be to present to you whatever it is they have to offer in the most palatable, convincing way. He'll not be empowered to do anything but to bring back your response to those who are in a position to decide."

"Well," said Howard, rising. "Jacek Cybulski it is. Let me know what time and I'll be there."

He had put on a few pounds since Denton's picture

had been taken. But there was still an unmistakable aura of western sophistication about Jacek Cybulski. He wore a light brown camel's hair coat and a cashmere scarf which merely framed the coat's collar, leaving visible his expensive silk tie. He wore light-colored leather gloves, probably with fur inside because they appeared to be much larger than his hands. And although there was some snow on the ground, Jacek Cybulski wore no overshoes. His brown brogues had a high polish, the bottom of his gray flannels were pressed into a sharp crease.

Cybulski had the look of a wealthy man, thought Howard as he approached. There was the wide grin which spread across his face as soon as he spotted Howard — a friendly, relaxing sort of gesture that would have been a welcome beginning to any conversation. But in the last moment Howard reminded himself of what Denton had said — that Jacek Cybulski had been selected precisely because of these qualities. He was to make an impression on Westerners who were prone to judge their acquaintances on the basis of such things.

Cybulski had been leaning over a railing, looking at Montreal spread before him. Momentarily it was lit up by sharp rays of early spring sun as it managed to break through a thick layer of bulbous clouds. He took two steps toward the approaching Howard and addressed him in a loud, raspy voice:

"Commander Howard! How nice to finally meet you. You *are* the legendary hero, aren't you?"

It was said in such an endearing way that Howard couldn't help smiling.

"Mr. Cybulski? How do you do."

The Pole remained standing in his place, assessing Howard.

"It is all right to call you commander, isn't it?

Just plain Mr. is somewhat bourgeois. On the other hand, 'Comrade Howard,' you'll agree, is entirely out of place."

Howard mumbled something to the effect that to be called by his military rank was an honor, mentally noting that it was difficult to dislike the fellow.

Cybulski was still not moving from his spot.

"Commander, before we go any further, could I ask you a favor? I'm a bit embarrassed by it, but could you possibly open your overcoat and show me there is no recording apparatus underneath? Frankly, I don't think a recording machine that size could be manufactured, nevertheless I've been ordered to take the precaution."

Howard hesitated a moment, then opened his coat. But Cybulski hardly even cast a glance at it.

"Thank you. Well, now that the formalities are over with, may I offer you a cigarette?" he asked.

"No, I think I'll load up my pipe though," Howard replied. They reached the railing of the observation area and Howard placed his tobacco pouch on it. Cybulski had already taken off his gloves, inserted a cigarette into a silver holder and lighted it. He watched Howard pat his tobacco lightly in his pipe, then move his match along the edge to light it evenly.

"Fascinating. I really should try to switch. It's so much more romantic and I'm certain it's healthy as well ..."

"Mr. Cybulski," Howard interrupted, "I really haven't come here to chitchat. You see, I've never before had to bargain for a man's life like this. I'm talking about Lieutenant Stanislaw Jaroscynski, one of the great heroes of the last war."

Cybulski remained silent for a moment.

"What makes you think that he's in any sort of danger, commander?" he finally asked.

"I don't know. Just a feeling. You see, the way you go about things ..."

"You? Do you mean me personally or ..."

"I mean the Communists, Mr. Cybulski. The Russians, Bulgarians, Poles ..."

"Oh. I'm sorry to have interrupted."

"I was saying that Eastern Europe seems to be an extremely dangerous place to disappear in. And it seems to be even more dangerous for people who were involved with Operation Lister."

Cybulski thought for a moment.

"Well, you're partially right, it is a rather violent region right now but that's because of the legacy of the war, coupled with the radical socialist changes."

"About Jaroscynski ..."

"Yes. Well, he's safe. Up to the present, anyway. But you are right: his future does not seem too bright. He has been charged with treason. Just last week as a matter of fact. It took that long to sift through all the documents that had a bearing on his wartime activities."

Howard turned abruptly to Cybulski.

"What nonsense! He's a hero. A man who should be given as an example of heroism to all other Poles."

"I'm sorry, but I don't know that, commander. All I know is what he has been charged with."

Cybulski was no longer smiling.

They had reached an impasse. It was clear to Howard that Cybulski was not about to admit the falsehood of the charges. Besides, even if he did, it would have no bearing on Jaroscynski's safety.

"I suppose the charges carry a death penalty?"

Cybulski nodded without much emotion.

"All right," said Howard after a few moments. "What can I do to save him?"

Cybulski was obviously relieved that Howard didn't want to continue with the argument. He quickly took advantage of it.

"Nothing. Do exactly what you have been doing until now. Sell insurance for Global Mutual, make lots of money, have a large family and take up golf. Maybe run for a city councilman, but forget about the war, particularly about what happened in 1944. Isn't that simple? Isn't it what each one of us *wants* to do?" Cybulski smiled agreeably.

"In other words, you don't want any word about Operation Lister to leak out. Why?"

Cybulski let out a perfect smoke ring which lingered about for a few moments because of the absolute stillness of the cold air about them. They both watched it with fascination as it slowly began to disintegrate. Only then did the Pole answer.

"That really isn't all that important, is it commander?" Cybulski asked somewhat condescendingly.

"You're wrong. It's extremely important. It's part of the entire package you'll have to deliver before we make any agreement. You see, last fall I was called on the phone by someone on your side and enticed to go to New York. But you know what happened there, don't you?"

Cybulski nodded.

"I know. At that time — against my advice, I assure you — it was decided, quite stupidly, that a dead commander cannot tell stories. In East Europe the theory was that even if you have already written the story of Operation Lister down on paper, you would not be around to answer any questions. The last word would be ours, so to say. So the idea was to have you killed by a New York gangster and to smear you posthumously as a member of the underworld. At the same time a Marxist version of the entire operation would be released by someone named Alexei Tkachev, a Russian officer who had been supposedly instrumental in the destruction of Adam Hill. According to that version, your inept group of commandos had been captured by the Germans as soon as you landed and you collaborated with the Nazis from that moment on. According to Tkachev it was the Russians who penetrated Adam Hill, destroyed the BVFE operation and thereby saved the Normandy invasion."

Howard was examining the various features of the snow-sprinkled city spread in front of him while letting out thin wisps of smoke from his mouth. If Tkachev's version had become official, it would have been quite a feather in the Soviet cap. But the chances of it happening were slim. Even with everyone who was involved in Lister gone, there would still be enormous holes left in the Russian story. For Moscow to take the risk there had to be something extremely valuable behind it all.

"Why?" Howard asked. "Why go to all the trouble of inventing such a story?"

Cybulski understood instantly.

"Aah, there you have it. I told my superiors that you were quite likely to ask that question. After much haggling they empowered me to give you the answer, but only as absolutely the last resort. I could prolong this, but let's say that we have reached the last resort stage, that you refuse to go any further in the negotiations. Is that a correct assessment of the situation, commander?"

Howard nodded. Cybulski then thought for a moment as if trying to decide from which direction to approach the problem. Finally he turned to Howard, his elbows still on the railing.

"When you, Professor Tiesenhausen and Stanislaw Jaroscynski entered the Adam Hill complex — when you were actually inside the bunker — did you see any civilians there?"

"Yes, quite a few."

"Did you speak with any of them?"

"No. It wasn't exactly a social call we were making."

Cybulski smiled.

"That's funny. It's exactly what Jaroscynski said when he was asked about them. Those must have been pretty tense moments."

"Mr. Cybulski, I can't remember ever being as frightened as I was at Adam Hill."

"I can believe that."

"What about the civilians? Why are they so important?"

"Because they were not Germans, Commander. Or at least a great majority of them were not. Most were East Europeans — Poles, Czechs, Russians, Yugoslavs, Estonians — almost everybody was represented."

"So what?"

"Hmm, I forgot. You are not at home in Marxist theory and practice, are you? They were scientists — laboratory technicians, biologists, doctors and things like that. Specialists, usually recruited from concentration camps across Europe. We now know the identity of a few of them."

"I still don't understand."

"I'm coming to the difficult but key part of the problem. Among the East Europeans atop Adam Hill there were quite a few Communists — card-carrying dedicated Marxist revolutionaries."

Howard stared at Cybulski, still without much understanding. The Pole explained further.

"I'm sure there were Conservatives, Democrats, Christian Democrats and, for all I know, Jehovah's Witnesses among the rest, but that doesn't matter. The main point to remember is that there were a number of Communists among the people there. And they were working with the Nazis on a germ warfare project which, if successful, would have gone a long way toward altering the outcome of the war in favor of the Nazis. The Communists would have played a major part in this alteration. The very people whose faith and understanding of what was vital for mankind had placed them into the forefront of the struggle against fascism. Most of them had been in death camps precisely because they were Communists and willing to die for their beliefs."

A few moments of silence followed. Howard was beginning to understand.

"What happened to them?"

"That took quite some to find out. But we are fairly certain now that all of them went into the gas chambers at Auschwitz. It was ordered personally by Himmler, who came to visit the place a couple of days after the raid."

Howard was getting cold. He stomped his feet in an attempt to increase circulation. But the cold didn't seem to affect Cybulski at all.

"Why can't the story of Lister be made public without any reference to the East Europeans on Adam Hill? They weren't *that* important to it. As a matter of fact until a few moments ago I had no idea that they were even there."

"Do you realize what would happen if the story was suddenly released now, four years after it took place? There would be thousands of people digging to get at all the possible facts about it: history students, adventure story writers, journalists, military strategists, Hollywood producers and just plain nosey souls. Their first question would have to do with why it has been kept quiet so long. The truth would be bound to come out."

Howard understood perfectly. Cybulski was right. If the Marxist participation at Adam Hill was to be kept secret then the entire operation had to be kept secret. At the same time he felt a tremendous compassion for the white-coated men and women he had seen for a few moments inside the bunker. They had been given a short reprieve from death — a ray of hope that had suddenly been taken away from them with the arrival of the B-17s that morning four years ago.

A few days afterward they were herded naked into gas chambers. It must have seemed a cruel joke to them. He was revolted by the realization that anyone could condemn them, overlooking their misery, desperation and fear (how well he knew that feeling!). These people had been humans, scared and abandoned by their world in various death camps, later again on top of Adam Hill, and finally inside the Auschwitz gas chambers.

"Shall I tell you what I propose?" asked Howard after a while, his face visibly hardened.

"Please do. We thought that we might make the proposal, but it really doesn't matter who makes it."

"Very well. One: there will be no more attempts made on my life."

Cybulski laughed, but it was a bit forced.

"That goes without saying ..."

"Not only that. Should I die by some unnatural means the entire agreement is null and void."

Cybulski nodded.

"Now, I'll go straight home and I'll write a memorandum of this conversation. It'll be put away along with my report on Operation Lister. There are now several copies of the report in various places. Together with the memo they will be released to the press should anything happen either to Stan Jaroscynski or me."

"That sounds fair. By the same token, should news about the Operation leak out anywhere you'll be held responsible and we reserve the right to act accordingly."

Howard continued.

"In regard to Lieutenant Jaroscynski: I realize that you cannot allow him to leave Poland, but he will be placed under house arrest and enjoy the best possible conditions."

Cybulski started shaking his head.

"I'm afraid they'll not agree to that. Please see it from our point of view. Jaroscynski must be isolated. He cannot be allowed to meet with friends or with the public at large. Prison is the only alternative. But we agree. Under the best possible conditions."

Howard didn't say anything, but he was not fully convinced.

"It's understandable, commander, that you would like the best possible conditions for him. But remember that at present, with the treason charge over his head, Jaroscynski faces death."

"Treason!" Howard erupted.

"Look, commander, it really doesn't matter what you or I think of the charges. The point is that he is being held in a Polish prison and about to be shot. You can save his life and make prison bearable for him. But I'm afraid that you can do little else."

"Very well," said Howard after a while. "This is what I want: I want Stan Jaroscynski brought to a prison in Warsaw where he will be periodically visited by a Western diplomat who will report about his condition to me in Montreal."

"I think that can be arranged."

"But that's not all. There *are* look-alikes, you know. In addition to the diplomat's visits, I'll send a half-page letter to Jaroscynski, each month written with a different colored pen. He'll reply on the bottom half of the letter with the enclosed pen, including some detail about Operation Lister which only he could know about. This monthly pen pal business should serve to prevent you from extracting the information from Jaroscynski ahead of time, then slaughtering him."

"You don't trust us much, do you commander?"

"Fewer people in the world do every day, Mr. Cybulski," Howard commented icily.

Cybulski sighed.

"Fine then," he agreed while putting on his gloves, "I think all that can be arranged."

"Oh, there's one more thing," said Howard, emptying his pipe against the heel of his shoe. That being the prearranged signal, three men approached the pair from different directions.

"We would like you to stay with us as our guest completely incommunicado for forty-eight hours. That'll give us time to discuss the conditions among ourselves and make sure your side doesn't jump the gun and start erasing traces."

"Traces of what?" asked the uneasy Cybulski, eyeing the three RCMP men.

"We still haven't found an example of Jaroscynski's handwriting, for instance. But our friends in London are working on it day and night. In two days we should track it down if someone doesn't pull it out of the British Army files right under our noses — if you know what I mean."

"I know what you mean," Cybulski allowed.

"And don't worry, we'll let them know at your embassy in Ottawa that you are with us," said Denton, first of the three men to reach them.

"You chaps are simply marvelous. You think of everything, don't you?" smiled Cybulski. He turned up the collar of his coat and joined them on the way to the car.

40

The exhausted Howard fell asleep as soon as he went to bed, only to wake up an hour later, full of doubts. The stillness of the night and his completely altered mood only served to increase them.

The self-confidence of his dealings with Cybulski was all gone. He held out his hand. Even in the dark he could see that it was shaking. What he feared most now was that he had made the wrong decision, that he had failed those who depended on him. In horror he caught himself wondering if it would not have been better if the Poles had killed Jaroscynski. There suddenly seemed to be something dire, highly suspicious about the agreement he had made that afternoon.

They were a long way from that February day four years ago when Jaroscynski, Evans, and he sat in the darkened fuselage of the Halifax with the coast of England disappearing behind them, each one of them convinced he was going to his death and that the only important thing was to die honorably.

But, my God, what is honor?

As his hand was shaking inside the Halifax and he saw himself slowly and painfully dying under some Nazi boot, he thought he could save himself had he landed on the snowy plain, gathered his parachute, walked off to the nearest Gestapo office and offered to work with them. But he didn't. None of them did. What's more, they involved other people in their deadly game. He had lost Hana and Tom Evans. Vitek, the innkeeper, endured Gestapo torture and probable death because he couldn't do otherwise. Life after a betrayal would have been no life at all, they knew that. So they walked in fear, in terrible, mind-numbing, mortal fear.

Howard wished it was still as easy. Did Jaroscynski really want him to buy his life with the honored memories of the others? By keeping quiet? He had saved Jaroscynski's life, but what kind of a life would it be in a Polish prison?

Next to him Sybil stirred. Through her half-opened eyes she noticed he was sitting up and she reached for the cord of her nightlamp. A harsh light filled the bedroom.

"Darling what's the matter," she asked. "Can't you sleep?"

He shook his head.

"Why?"

"I've never before bought a man's life."

Sybil didn't say anything. There was nothing to say.

"I'm having a hard time coping with the times we're living in, I really am, Sybil," he confessed.

"What is it that bothers you, Doug?" she asked after a while. It was quite some time before he answered.

"There's nothing behind me to lean against. Nothing beside me to hold on to either. Smith in Germany and the mighty Pentagon in Washington have looked into it because it was, after all, an unfinished part of the war — a corner not yet tucked in. Superintendent Denton advised me to meet with Jacek Cybulski, but all that he was concerned with was my safety so that the RCMP could not be accused of providing inadequate protection for a threatened war hero. The moral content — what is right and what is wrong — that's left up to me. I find it hard to be a judge of morality. I am not equipped for it. Few soldiers are."

"So you think that according to some strange standard of morality you should have let Jaroscynski die? Is that what's bothering you Douglas?"

"Look, during the war when I was ordered to do a job — either to kill or be killed — my main concern was that all the proper precautions be taken. It was indescribably easier."

Sybil put her arm around him and smiled.

"I know it was, darling, I know it was. It's also much easier in daylight. Certainly beats three o'clock in the morning."

Howard smiled too and gave her a peck on the cheek. Then Sybil found the cord again and switched off the light. Howard's mind still swam with juxtaposed feelings, considerations and worries. But in spite of them all, within minutes he felt himself drifting off to sleep.

The man who telephoned three months later was hard to understand. His English was poor and his anxiety did not help. It was only after Howard suggested that they switch into German that things became easier. He was a salesman (or a commercial traveler, as he put it), for Czech textiles, in New York to sign some agreement on imports into the United States. He was also a friend of Jiri Palka, a good friend who was worried about what had just happened. Late in February, soon after the Communist takeover, Palka tried to cross the border into Bavaria along with several other Czech officers. During a shootout on the border two of them had been killed and Palka was one of those taken into custody. For a while his wife as well had been put into prison, but she had since been released.

Just before the commercial traveler left Czechoslovakia he was visited by Palka's wife. Actually he met her in a park near his home, but she had obviously been there waiting for him. She told him Palka had been charged with high treason. Such a charge was automatic whenever an officer tried to cross the border illegally. In the paranoid atmosphere which reigned in Prague, it was more than likely that he would be executed. Mrs. Palka had pleaded with the commercial representative to get in touch with Howard. "He is my last hope, there is no one else I know anywhere that I could turn to," he quoted her verbatim.

But when Howard asked if he had any idea how he could help, the commercial traveler's answer was negative. "I don't know anything, Mr. Howard," he almost cried into the phone, "except that Czechoslovakia has changed into hell. No one trusts anyone any more."

He was clearly glad when the conversation was over. The commercial representative had done what he had rashly promised in Prague. After he hung up Howard remained sitting by the telephone where Sybil eventually found him. He told her about the conversation and she took him by the hand and led him into the kitchen where she put the kettle on.

"Tea is the best stuff when you're trying to make an intelligent decision." She tried to divert him from his thoughts with a smile. Howard didn't even look at her.

"All right, Douglas, let's see what can be done for Palka."

"God, Sybil, I can't think of a single thing. With stable, rational countries I guess you can protest — that is if we could convince anyone on our side to file an official protest. Then there would be at least a review of the verdict. But this is Czechoslovakia we're dealing with. What I've been reading about the place during the last few weeks would make your hair stand on end. Every day they seem to be discovering another cache of arms supposedly put there by the Americans, the British, or neofascists of some kind. Their whole thrust is to get the people worked up against anything that comes from the West. Can you imagine what sort of a reception a protest or even a request that Palka's life be spared would get? It would only prove to them that he had been a part of some western plot."

Sybil stood by the stove, waiting for the water to boil.

"But you don't really know that, do you? I mean it's just something you assume would happen. Maybe the commercial traveler had been sent especially to tell you about Palka."

Howard looked at her quizzically.

"Now why on earth would they do that?"

Sybil shrugged her shoulders.

"I don't know. I don't even know if he was a commercial traveler, do I? But you always said that the basic mistake Westerners make in dealing with the East is to think that they use Western logic."

Sybil served breakfast from juice to toast and bacon without saying much more than a peremptory good morning. Howard sensed she wanted time to think and he buried himself in his newspaper. Then she sat down across from him, sipped on her tea and stared out the window. But suddenly she jumped up, shaking him by his shoulders, her face radiant with success.

"Douglas! For God's sake Douglas, I've got it! It's probably because I'm British and we're traditionally so good at this sort of thing. But why don't we play one of them against the other? I mean, what the hell, the Czechs still have a lot to learn about how things are done among the Communists, so let's teach them."

"How?"

"Is Jacek Cybulski still at the Polish Embassy?"

"So far as I know."

"So let's get in touch with him and start blackmailing."

Howard took the pipe out of his mouth and gazed at Sybil.

"Don't you see, Douglas? The Czechs are to execute Palka to keep Operation Lister out of the world's history books. Well, that's against the agreement you've made with the Poles: No killings; no subterfuge."

There was ray of hope in the whole affair suddenly. Maybe Palka had a chance after all.

"But you'll have to get mad, bloody mad, Douglas. If you come to the Poles, saying look fellas, we've made this deal and you're not very nice because your Czech comrades would like to murder Palka and then they'll say, well, we'll talk to someone in Prague — what's his name, the Party Chief?"

"Gottwald."

"Yes, Gottwald. And he'll think about it and, you see, after all, it's a sovereign country this Czechoslovakia. They can do what they want and this certainly seems to be what they want to do, isn't it? But we'll do our best and we'll call you in a couple of months ... That's no good. If, on the other hand, you say all right, I'm sick and tired of playing games with you because you foul up something awful and as far as I'm concerned the agreement is off unless you first drop all treason charges against Palka and get him to write me a letter every month with a different colored pen and, second, allow a Western diplomat to visit him to see how he is being treated.

"Unless you agree to do these things and inform me of it by next Thursday I'm going straight to Macmillan and Company and they'll be coming out with a smash hit of a best seller this very fall entitled *The Lister Report.* Take your pick, Cybulski, and make it snappy, because I'm not going to fool around with you any more!"

Howard laughed to see how quickly Sybil had adopted the North American idiom. Delivered with a British accent it was even funnier. And he had to agree that her plan for saving Palka was the only one they could come up with. He practised for a day, preparing his outburst. The following night Denton and Langlois arrived at the house to throw cold water on the plan. It simply wouldn't work, the Russians and their satellites know exactly what they're doing. They'll see through the bluster and Palka will go before a firing squad.

"And if Douglas does nothing, where will Palka go?" Sybil asked.

They allowed he'd probably die anyway.

"And if Douglas goes ahead with the plan, do you see any danger in it for anybody?" she persisted.

Denton took a deep breath and shook his head.

"And a final question: Do you have a better plan?"

Denton smiled and shook his head again. He had been caught.

"What about the official protest?" asked Howard. "Is any Allied government going to lodge a protest with the Czechs?"

"Our government isn't and neither are the British. The Americans are still considering it, but it doesn't look too hopeful."

"But isn't it at least worth trying if Palka will die anyway?" asked Sybil.

"We don't know what their plans are with Major Palka. There are some precedents where the Communists have played up a monster trial and then pardoned the defendant. It may mean a life imprisonment, but that is still a victory of sorts. If we and the Americans become actively involved, we may be handing them what to their mind is further proof of treason. In other words, we may be closing the door on possible pardon," Denton went on.

"But a direct pressure on someone like Cybulski would be entirely unofficial. It would be simply a wartime buddy speaking up, wouldn't it?" Howard suggested, looking for some response.

"That's right," Denton admitted reluctantly and Howard accepted it as a go-ahead sign.

"Where would you suggest I meet him?"

"I would suggest Ottawa," Langlois entered the conversation for the first time. "If you were really mad then you wouldn't wait for 'im to come to you, would you?"

"No, you're right, I wouldn't."

"I think that Douglas has to give the impression he has been drinking when he starts his spiel. Otherwise it wouldn't square off with the self-controlled guy that Cybulski has met before," suggested Sybil. Denton looked at her in surprise. She was right, of course, absolutely right.

"Then I'd suggest the bar at the Chateau Laurier, right across from the railway station. I've done some memorable drinking there myself," Langlois smiled.

"The trouble is that I'm not very good at holding my liquor. You see, I get rather sick," Howard confessed.

"'ow are you at 'olding ginger ale?" Langlois asked.

"Fine, I suppose."

"Then we'll arrange it so that you're served ginger ale at the bar instead of rye and ginger," Langlois explained.

Cybulski was wearing a light gray summer suit, immaculately pressed, in spite of the oppressive, humid heat which had been tormenting the capital for nearly a week. He joined Howard at the bar and immediately suspected that Howard already had done a bit of drinking. He had no idea that the red eyes were the result of a long bath in chlorinated water.

"How are you commander? Nice to see you again," he opened the conversation with a smile, extending his hand.

Howard ignored it. As he eyed the Pole he made a slight weaving motion to and fro.

"Sit down Cybulski, you bastard, so I can tell you how you've screwed me and how I'm going to screw you and your goddamn people's republic now." He nodded to the waiter who brought him an order of rye and ginger without the former, and who also supplied Cybulski with Scotch and soda.

"Haven't the arrangements been satisfactory?" asked Cybulski, somewhat reminiscent of the maitre d' at a posh hotel. "Lieutenant Jaroscynski is alive and well as your Mr. Rees saw him only two weeks ago. You've received your first letter, haven't you?"

Yes he had. A British diplomat had met with Jaroscynski, was even allowed to give him cigarettes, and in his report on the meeting indicated that Jaroscynski was healthy and in good spirits. In his letter to Howard, Stan had thanked him for saving his life and mentioned a vase of Rosenthal china which had been fastened to the dashboard of Tiesenhausen's car and which had a few small, dried alpine flowers in it. Howard was satisfied that the author of the letter was Jaroscynski.

"That's all fine. It's your comrades, the Czechs, who're playing dirty pool. They are trying to execute a man on trumped up charges. A big hero who took part in Operation Lister. The bastards."

"Who was the man?" asked Cybulski with unfeigned interest. Howard was sure that the Pole had no idea what it was all about.

"Don't play funny with me, Cybulski, you know very well who. Palka, Major Palka — a great war hero and you bastards want to shoot him."

"I don't know anything about it," Cybulski insisted.

Howard erupted with a fine spray of ginger ale which caught everybody seated within ten feet of him.

"Hah! Don't make me laugh," he said so loudly that most of the people nearby turned around. "You Commies and goddamn Marxists are all in cahoots. The great glorious revolution, that's what you're all working for, isn't it? Well, I don't give a shit what you're working for, but leave my friends alone, you hear?"

"I swear that the Polish government has nothing to do with your friend, Major Palka," Cybulski defended himself with considerable dignity. Howard ordered another drink. Then he swiveled around so that he was facing Cybulski and punctuated each sentence by poking him in the chest with his forefinger. Although it had all been pre-rehearsed, he did not expect Cybulski to accept the jabs with such docility. Howard was happy with the Pole's response. It indicated he was on the defensive.

"So listen, Mr. Commie, and listen good. Because besides being a great big war hero, Jiri Palka is my friend. I mean, if he dies I've got nothing else to live for — nothing, get me? So if you kill him, it's off, the whole damn agreement about Jaroscynski, about me keeping quiet about Lister. The whole caboodle."

Cybulski looked around him nervously. "I tell you, commander, that we know nothing about Major Palka. Czechoslovakia is a sovereign country."

"Don't start tellin' me you Poles don't know what the Russians and Czechs are doing about Lister and they don't know about you. Thass ririridiculous!"

"But we *don't* know about each other. I've never heard about Major Palka."

Howard viewed him with his eyes wide open in astonishment. "Oh, you haven't, eh? Well, I'm telling you to find out all about him pretty damn quick. Because he's important. He's what the whole goddamn agreement's all about. You're not going to kill my friend."

The commander took a deep swallow from a new glass of ginger ale. Cybulski was not drinking at all. He seemed too stunned by it all to remember the drink on the bar in front of him. Cybulski asked:

"What is it you want, commander?"

"Want? I want Palka kept alive and well, understand? Or the goddamn Operation Lister report is going to make the bestseller list in a few months. By Christmas we'll have a movie about it with John Wayne playing me."

Howard finished his glass. He felt it was time to go. There had been no slip-ups yet, but he was becoming increasingly worried that something might happen.

He slid off the seat with considerable difficulty and poked the stunned Pole in his chest for the last time.

"You've got exactly two days, my Polish buddy. Two days, that's all. If I don't hear from you by Friday then off goes the manuscript. Then comes the bestseller list."

He staggered out of the bar and up into the lobby. Once there, he looked back to see if Cybulski was following him. He didn't seem to be.

Instead of a taxi, Langlois' familiar blue Pontiac peeled off from a cluster of cars nearby and pulled alongside him. Howard climbed in and Langlois steered into the traffic on Rideau Street.

"Were you inside? I didn't notice you," said the exhausted Howard. He was dripping with sweat.

"Most of the time," answered Langlois.

"How did I do?"

"Terrific. Much better than Ray Milland in *Lost Weekend*. And he got an Oscar."

Howard grinned. He was glad it was over. Now the forty-eight-hour wait would begin. If Cybulski had swallowed the bluff, the commander might have been able to save another life.

But what if he hadn't?

Part Three:
Valery Semlyonov

41

In 1943 the Germans had shipped Valery Nikolaevich Semlyonov to Auschwitz with the hope that
within weeks he would be dead. Instead, shortly
after New Year's he found himself at Adam Hill,
warm and well fed again, convinced that some
divine power had chosen him to survive. Then
came the air raid and his escape.

He saw two springs come while he stayed at
the Svec farmhouse. At first he rarely left his
wooden cage under a pile of hay, but eventually he
started to take care of the livestock. Sometimes
at night he would venture out to gaze at the star-
studded sky. It was during those times that he felt
his destiny powerfully guided from somewhere
else. He felt certain that he was in benign hands
which, for some unknown reason, were continually
subjecting him to severe tests, and he was determined to pass every one of them.

Early in 1945 came the first signs of the
approaching end of the war. The narrow path at
the bottom of the valley was filled with never-
ending convoys of Germans in desperate flight,
heading west to give themselves up to the Americans. Then there were no more Germans. The valley remained quiet until one evening when a lone
jeep appeared with a large red star painted on its

hood. It stopped. The driver rose, scanning the countryside with a pair of binoculars.

The Svecs watched from the top of the hill as Valery ran down to the surprised Russian lieutenant, grabbed him by the shoulders, and began dancing with him around the vehicle. He had survived! He had won! The war was over!

When Valery came back up the hill, all he had to fetch was some tattered underwear and an extra shirt, all wrapped in a heavy coat made for him by Anna Svec from an old blanket. There was also a small crucifix, no bigger than a human finger, which Anna had once placed beside his cot. He felt it in his pocket as he came out of the house and looked at the two people where the main reason for his being alive.

"*Spasibo ... Dekuji*," he kept saying in both languages as he repeatedly shook her and her husband's hands. Then the tears became unmanageable and he hurried down the hill. As the jeep disappeared down the road into the woods, Valery was standing in it, waving at the two figures atop the hill.

In Zamberk the lieutenant stopped in front of the house which until a few days ago had been the Gestapo headquarters. He led Valery to the second floor, ushering him inside when asked to enter.

"Comrade Major, this is Valery Nikolaevich Semlyonov. He was taken prisoner by the Germans at Orel two years ago and —"

That's how far the lieutenant got before the chunky major more coughed then said to the lieutenant, "Get Captain Chulpenov!"

Chulpenov was much thinner. Neither the major nor the lieutenant were present in the room during the interrogation. Chulpenov's SMERSH counterintelligence epaulets signaled caution and

Valery Nikolaevich instantly decided to leave out any reference to Adam Hill while telling the story of his capture.

"Auschwitz — how did you get out of there?" asked the impatient Chulpenov brusquely.

"We were building a new barracks outside the barbed wire, Comrade Captain. I stayed behind one night. It was winter and darkness came early ..."

The SMERSH officer looked at a wall map. "It is quite a few kilometers from Auschwitz to Zamberk. Show me the route you took," he ordered.

"Forgive me, Comrade Captain," pleaded Valery Nikolaevich, "but I have no idea about any route. I didn't know where I was going except, perhaps, that I was heading south. I kept moving along because I thought that was the only way to survive. When I reached the Svec farm I had no more strength. They took me in. They were decent people and ... Can I return to my unit, Comrade Captain? Do you know where it is stationed?"

"No, you cannot go back," the officer answered without looking up. He called a name and a man entered, a private with a bayonet on his rifle.

"Escort former Lieutenant Nikolaevich Semlyonov to the prison downstairs," he ordered. "He has committed a criminal act against the state according to paragraph 58/1b."

Semlyonov had survived four years of fighting. He had, by some miracle, been snatched from Auschwitz. He had lived through the bombing of Adam Hill and been led to safety with the Svecs. He therefore believed that some power would get him through this journey with a trainload of 300 other Russian POWs to a camp somewhere in Central Asia. He was lucky to get a place near a crack in the wall of the cattle car crammed with men which stank both of their excrement and that of its former occupants.

From the very first day there were deaths. The emaciated bodies, most of them plucked right out of Nazi camps, could not stand the incessant heat, the two paper-thin slices of bread a day, and the constant jostling with other sick, stinking, thirsty bodies.

Kharkov, Saratov, Kuybishev, Ufa ... The train crossed the Urals, and it meandered through the southern steppes as if drunk, never betraying its ultimate destination. By the time they reached Tselinograd there were no more than 200 of them left, mere shadows now, barely able to move, their minds dimmed. No one talked any more.

It happened immediately after a stop at a sun-drenched hut in the middle of the Kazakh steppe. By now ten men were needed to empty the waste barrel, although the barrel itself was not nearly as full as it used to be. They descended from the car down a wide plank, upending the barrel behind the hut which served as a railway station. Afterward they washed it out with a stream of water from a pump used to refill the locomotives. Then they noticed them.

Everyone stopped, including the guard. In the dust, piled up like so much lumber, lay ten bodies, their swollen faces already covered with flies. The men stared for a few moments before they realized that the bodies were girls. Up till now Valery and the other prisoners had assumed this hell and been designed for them only. Now the universality of the suffering shocked them in a way they thought they were no longer capable of being shocked. They stood there in mute astonishment, still holding their empty barrel in the air, their thoughts away in places where such girls were alive, laughing and dreaming of a happy life yet to come.

Valery stirred with disgust. One of the flies entered a girl's nostril. He jerked his head away in a gesture shared by the whole group. Without anyone saying a word, the men started moving again. The sound of the steam released by the engine, the shouting and the usual noises of the railway station came back to them along with the grim reality of their situation.

The train was moving with its maddening rhythm across the dusty plain when Valery changed his sitting position on his coat. His buttock felt a hard object in the pocket and he reached down to pull out the crucifix. Then, without looking at it, he pushed it through the crack in front of him, giving it one final shove with his thumb which caused it to clear the crack and fall by the side of the speeding train.

There is no one, Valery Nikolaevich was now certain. Just the strong ones and the weak ones. And the strongest of the strong, like Hitler and Stalin, rule. They must kill and be killed without mercy to stay strong. The weak ones are simply killed in the process. And, because it doesn't make sense to the weak ones, they dream of God and some sort of a reward for it all. The dreams can be so fervently powerful that sometimes they even frighten some of the strong ones. But only for a while. In the end the strong ones must always win.

They slowed down to cross a small bridge. Valery Nikolaevich Semlyonov looked around him in the darkened railway car. The few living skeletons that had survived sat leaning against the sides, their heads bobbing from side to side with the rhythm of the train. No one was talking and since there was now plenty of room, no one sat near anyone else. They were isolated bodies making a long train journey toward their extinction. They were the weak ones.

He turned back to his crack. Gazing at the endless steppe for a few moments, his parched lips moved slightly. "I'm strong," he whispered.

As if to convince himself.

The Kahamir camp commander Alexander Maximovich Ripkov insisted on the proper utilization of every skill available among the prisoners. Food production in the Kahamir region, particularly on the camp farm, had risen sharply over the years, and Ripkov's good management had been noticed in Moscow. Valery Semlyonov, by now in his forties, had stopped going out with the work parties long ago. Eventually he moved from the barracks to a cubicle next to the administrative office — well heated in winter and pleasantly cooled by a fan in the summer — where he filled out government forms on an old typewriter with the faint outline of the imperial double eagle still visible on it.

There, during the winter inactivity Valery Nikolaevich conceived a plan. At the moment men had to be called out each morning at roll call to repair broken machinery, masonry workers to strengthen ruptured irrigation ditches, bricklayers to build a storage shed to be used for the northern fields. Drivers of heavy trucks were needed if fill had to be transported and carpenters for increasing space in the grain storage bins.

According to Valery's plan, men with specialized skills would henceforth be housed in certain barracks. Other barracks would have to be partitioned into sections with approximately the same number of men. The morning roll call would then no longer be concerned with individual names but with barrack numbers and section designations. The present chaos of juxtaposed names and jobs would disappear. On three pages, Valery Nikolaevich summarized his plan and its benefits, in places providing diagrams in support of his proposal.

It wasn't difficult to make sure that Valery Nikolaevich's proposal reached Alexander Maximovich Ripkov directly. At the end of the month when it was time to type out manpower reports for the ministry in Moscow, he simply enclosed his proposal among them.

Shortly after the New Year, 1952, Ripkov made one of his rare appearances in the camp office. His eyes searched through the room until they rested on Valery's gray uniform. "You Semlyonov?"

"Yes, Citizen Secretary."

Ripkov turned around and started out. When he was halfway across the room, without looking at Valery, he said, "Come with me."

The ride in Ripkov's jeep to the gate, the salute of the guard on duty, and then the continuation of it along the barely noticeable path alongside the barbed wire, seemed devoid of all reality for Valery Nikolaevich. He had not been outside the camp for almost seven years.

Ripkov's house was sparsely furnished. He pointed to an armchair and Valery, as if still in a dream, seated himself in it. He accepted a cigarette offered from a carved wooden box, then took a sip from a small glass of vodka which sent his head spinning. Finally, Ripkov gazed at Valery Nikolaevich in the same intense way he had in the camp office. "How long would it take?" he asked.

"How long would what take, Citizen Secretary?" asked the surprised Valery Nikolaevich.

"Your plan for the reorganization of the camp. How long would it take to put into effect?"

"I don't know, Citizen Ripkov. Perhaps a month, maybe more. It depends on ..."

"Come with me," Ripkov interrupted him, rising suddenly. He led the way upstairs, to a room with a dormer window, with a small table and an oil lamp on the wall. Valery remained standing on the threshold, reluctant to enter.

"Come in, come in," Ripkov invited him. This is where you will be living from now on."

But there was something disturbing about Ripkov's smile, about the way he eyed Valery as he hesitantly entered the room, in the way Ripkov slowly pushed the door shut behind him with his boot.

"Try the bed, it's very comfortable."

"Citizen Ripkov, I ..."

"No, not Citizen Ripkov any more. From now on it's Alexander Maximovich," he said, pulling him down on the bed with him.

He spoke much faster now, but also more softly. The camp commandant's hands ran along various parts of his body, gently stroking him, their faces close together as he spoke.

"It'll be different from now on, you'll see. We will work together, we will make Kahamir into something that will make everyone in Moscow sit up and take notice. Then will come the promotions, and of course you will go right up with me, alongside me. You will no longer be a prisoner but a trusted friend — an excellent friend, the other part of me, that part I have been longing for, the most important part. I will take care of you, Valery Nikolaevich, I swear that I will never leave you, never let anything happen to you, we're one now, you and I, we are one. It was meant that way. This

godforsaken place will be different now, I promise
you ..."

Valery drew away in shock. It had taken him
too long to realize what was happening and now
that he knew, he had to make a decision fast. He
stared at the heavily breathing Ripkov next to him
and he sensed that a refusal now would mean a
return to the barracks, to the work gangs and, now
that he knew about Ripkov, perhaps much worse.
There was no way out, none at all.

Valery Semlyonov swallowed a wave of revul-
sion that had engulfed him. With the utmost effort
he raised his hand and started to caress Ripkov's
stubby face.

To be effective, the reorganization had to be completed before spring planting. As a result, the usually restful winter pace had been disturbed and
there was considerable resentment on account of it,
particularly among the guards. But no more than
resentment; everyone had learned long ago that it
did not pay to come into conflict with Alexander
Maximovich Ripkov.

And now there was an added incentive. It was
announced that a member of the Central Committee, one Nikita Sergeevich Khrushchev, a Ukrainian with a special interest in the country's food
production, would be visiting Kahamir in April.

Nikita Sergeevich turned out to be much more
interested in the ways of Kahamir than anyone had
expected. The first two days he spent from dawn to
dusk in the fields, accompanied by Ripkov. He rode
alongside him in the old jeep, examined soil, talked
to workers, took great interest in the machinery,
saying little except for an occasional crude joke or
greeting. He certainly is not refined, thought Ripkov; a real peasant is this Khrushchev. But the

kind which unfortunately did not grow in great abundance on Russian soil. He was unusually shrewd, knew the land and character of the people who tilled it, also of those who controlled the tilling.

He drank a bit too much, but in the case of Nikita Sergeevich it served a purpose — after a couple of glasses of vodka he seemed to speak with increased lucidity. He left his party jargon behind and his words became as if greased to fit together better.

Khrushchev had been scheduled to leave for Alma Ata the following morning, from there to catch a plane back to Moscow, but at the last moment he extended his stay. He called Ripkov to the hotel and asked to be taken to the labor camp. There he listened to a dry recitation of statistics, interrupting now and then to ask a question for further clarification. He somberly viewed the prisoners shuffling from place to place across the camp, then gazed at the guard towers with the threatening gun barrels sticking out of them while the fur-capped guards were trying to keep warm under their canopies.

Finally he ordered his car, sent his secretary back to the hotel, and asked Ripkov to take him back to his house.

"I'm astonished at the work you have done here, at the things you have established in Kahamir, Alexander Maximovich. I've already heard about you in Moscow, of course, but I simply did not believe it. You are truly the new Soviet man, with possibilities that reach into the sky and even beyond. There is only one trouble and I'm afraid that it is a major one: we do not as yet exactly have the new man in charge of things in Moscow, do we?"

Nikita Sergeevich was intently watching Alexander Maximovich's face for any sign of disapproval, but he really didn't expect it. What he did expect from this very able, young district party leader was neutrality, a self-preserving instinct, which would make him react to the bait in some noncommittal way. Everyone sensed that the old, prewar order of things was coming to an end, but to say it meant that one was asking to be grabbed by its tentacles and squeezed to death.

"I know what you mean, Nikita Sergeevich. We too, here in the provinces, are in great need of a whiff of fresh air. Just as you must be in Moscow."

It wasn't yet an open declaration of defiance to Stalin, but it was more than Khrushchev had expected. He took another sip of his vodka and continued.

"The Man of Steel is becoming rusty in places." He laughed at his own crass humor. "And he can't be repaired any more. Replacement is the only acceptable procedure."

There was no mistaking his meaning now. Ripkov stared into Khrushchev's eyes, aware that he had been put to the supreme test. Playing it safe now and not responding might mean being forgotten at Kahamir when Stalin was gone, when his people had been replaced at the ministries. On the other hand to go with Krushchev meant taking a terrific risk. Or did it?

Alexander Maximovich stared at the obese man's shrewd eyes, at his short hands, balding head. There was more to be gained here than lost, he finally decided. "I agree. It is time we started planning what happens afterward. After he is gone."

"Exactly," the excited Nikita Sergeevich quickly replied. "And I see your Kahamir as a model, an excellent model for increasing farm production, for bringing more of our virgin lands under cultivation. The Soviet Union is not making use of its land resources. It has vast areas which would be cultivated — no, *must* be cultivated — if we are not to remain at the mercy of the imperialists for our food supply.

"Of course," said Khrushchev suddenly, "it can't be done while this country is still a big prison camp. You can't build a good, solid structure when the foundations are all rotten. Do you know how many people are in prison in the Soviet Union, Alexander Maximovich? Millions, that's how high the number goes. Into millions! For what? Are they enemies of the state? Most weren't when arrested, but they probably are by now. I don't know. And the imperialists already use it for their own propaganda. Do you know what they say? They say that Josef Vissarionovich is not better than Hitler. *Hitler!* When Stalin is gone we will have to deal with the problem and deal with it fast. But it'll not be easy, Alexander Maximovich, it'll not be easy at all."

Ripkov's eyes lit up. He pulled his chair closer and then, in the best conspiratorial style, he looked around for possible witnesses. "Would you like to meet one, Nikita Sergeevich, a prisoner?"

Khrushchev stared at Ripkov in astonishment. "You have a prisoner, a political prisoner here in your house? What is he doing here?"

"You can ask him yourself, Nikita Sergeevich," said Ripkov, already halfway up the steps. Valery Nikolaevich had heard every word from the moment the two party men entered the house. He closed the door to his room only seconds before Ripkov reached it and knocked on it. Although he shivered with excitement at the thought of meeting a

Central Committee member, he still offered a few perfunctory protests, that he was not dressed, that it wasn't proper for a political prisoner to meet a high-ranking party member. But in the end he gave in, slowly descending the well-worn wooden steps. Suddenly he found himself face-to-face with Comrade Nikita Sergeevich Khrushchev.

At first both of them found the meeting awkward. In the background Ripkov explained that Valery Nikolaevich had been responsible for the camp's reorganization plan — a huge affair which should provide for the increased production about which Nikita Sergeevich spoke a few moments before.

Khrushchev began to feel more at ease. He asked Valery to sit down, poured him a glass of vodka, then offered him a sample from a plate of meat and bread. He asked how long Valery Nikolaevich had been at Kahamir and what he was charged with. He nodded with understanding at the answer.

"There have been so many like you in the Ukraine. Some of them my good friends and I couldn't do anything, my hands were tied. They disappeared somewhere in Siberia ..." he trailed off sadly. Then, suddenly he recovered his former confident tone. "But there were others," he said, eyes blazing and his finger waving menacingly through the air, "who deserve no mercy at all. They'll stay in the camps until they rot. I mean those who helped the Germans. Those who made the artillery shells which killed our boys in the field, those who manned the machinery so the Germans could make their guns and airplanes that dropped death from the skies. There can be no mercy for them. What miserable monsters they must be, those who bought their own mean little lives with the lives of those who so gallantly defended our Motherland!"

A few moments of silence followed this outburst. Valery Nikolaevich inwardly shuddered at the frightening change in the mood of the until now jovial, plump, Central Committee member.

Then Khrushchev began asking about specific problems. Would the prisoners be willing to stay on and cultivate the land, work as free men on projects they had started? Could the party depend on them? Would at least some of them want to take some sort of revenge?

"They can be trusted, Nikita Sergeevich. But they will require proper handling before they can lead productive lives in our socialist society. The country must show them that it cares about their welfare. They will not want apologies, but a guarantee of a better future."

There was no commitment on the part of Nikita Sergeevich Khrushchev that with Stalin gone the camps would be disbanded, prisoners freed. It seemed as if Khrushchev was still undecided, as if the prospect of millions of prisoners let out to mingle with the rest of society frightened him somewhat.

The driver had been waiting outside for hours when they finally ended their talk. By that time it had become clear that Khrushchev was preparing for a power grab, that he was perhaps even involved in some plot to topple Stalin. He was too shrewd to mention anything specific. Still, as he was about to leave he grabbed the two men by their shoulders and with a friendly smile said, "You know, there's an old Cossack saying that an enemy you'll find within minutes, but it sometimes takes years to find a friend. I have made two new friends in one night, and that is a very rare thing in one's life, believe me. I'll not forget the warmth of your house, Alexander Maximovich. Nor will I forget the sincerity of your words, Valery Nikolaevich."

He turned around and a moment later he was gone. Ripkov remained deep in thought. Then, suddenly, he looked up.

"I think tonight was important, Valery Nikolaevich. Very important," he said.

Later, in bed, Valery Nikolaevich was staring at the whitewashed ceiling above him, unable to sleep.

"I'm about to join the strong ones," he whispered. "Where I rightfully belong."

42

He really didn't have to take the Czechs. They were a low-level delegation and, when you came right down to it, they weren't even his division's responsibility. Valery Nikolaevich Semlyonov was deputy chief of the West European Division of the liaison section of the Secretariat of the Central Committee of the Communist Party of the Union of Soviet Socialist Republics. The Czechs, on the other hand, fell into the East European Division — a far less important one because all the countries that figured in it were already Communist controlled. The East European Division of the liaison section was a safe, bureaucratic operation, which each year was given its quota of foreign visitors to invite and Soviet comrades to send out.

Maybe that's why Valery Nikolaevich volunteered for the assignment — it was not particularly demanding or challenging. He had just completed a six-week refresher course in Italian and didn't really have to report back to work at the Secretariat until the following Monday. But he had dropped in late on Thursday to see what mail had come in. And outside his office he had met Sineavkin from the East European Division, who told him that the Czechs were sending a low-level delegation of party school graduates who were given the trip as a reward for high grades. As usual, the security people had taken care of all the arrangements, but there was need for an official host to meet them at the airport and take them to the hotel. On an impulse Valery Nikolaevich agreed to become the host, and Sineavkin dissolved in a long, mushy speech of gratitude.

Actually it suited Valery Nikolaevich very well. His wife Nadezhda had invited some of her scientist friends to the dacha for the weekend and, as usual, they would talk business from Friday till Sunday night. It had all happened before. They simply assumed that since Valery Nikolaevich had once studied biology he was automatically one of them, but he no longer was. He had no interest in science anymore, that part of his life belonged to the past. When, seven years before, he had come to Moscow with Alexander Maximovich Ripkov at Khrushchev's invitation, the decision had to be made: was he going to a specialist in some scientific field or should he choose the party?

At Kahamir he had shown considerable skill in administration, and the party was definitely the fastest way up. Especially since Ripkov was now on Nikita Sergeevich's personal staff at the Presidium. True, his own advancement had not been as spectacular, but it had been steady. He figured that within three years he should reach the West European liaison section's chairmanship. He was now solidly among the strong ones. Alexander Maximovich Ripkov's gamble had paid off: Khrushchev had proven himself as the strongest of Stalin's heirs.

On Friday evening Valery Nikolaevich Semlyonov was seated at the Moscow airport, awaiting the Aeroflot flight from Prague bringing the Czech comrades. He felt tranquil, satisfied. The two days would be a much needed rest before a major project Valery was scheduled to tackle on Monday morning. There was now a need for a plan which would include all the possible ways in which the Soviet Party could help the growth of the Italian Communist Party. There were cultural and scientific exchanges, the Italo-Soviet Friendship Society, official visits, contacts at international conferences, and support of ancillary Italian organizations which would be of use to the Italian Communists. It was true that much of what Valery would put into his plan was already happening under the auspices of the foreign ministry, but that was just the point. There existed no comprehensive plan which would encompass all the existing contacts as well as those which, in addition, *could* be put into operation. It only stood to reason that if the plan came from the liaison section of the Central Committee Secretariat, it would be that section which would be given the authority to execute its provisions. And once that had been accomplished, it would mean another victory for the party in the never-ending struggle between it and the governmental apparatus.

Italy had been chosen by Valery Nikolaevich after a careful examination of the situation in Western Europe. Under Mussolini, the Italians had shown that they were willing to accept planned law and order if only it were presented to them in a proper way. Italy was the most promising place for West European Communism, Valery Nikolaevich concluded. He signed up for an evening course in Italian. Along with his German it would be a great asset to the liaison section.

But there was no need for foreign languages with these East Europeans, thought Valery as the small bus filled with the Czechs took them to the

hotel. The twelve graduates of the party school —
nine men and three women — all spoke impeccable
Russian. So did their leader, an old party hack
probably from before the war.

He had regarded the weekend with the Czechs
as a recreational idea. Most of them must have
been from rural areas. On the way from the airport
they gawked at the lit-up city with their mouths
open in a way that strongly reminded Valery Nikolaevich of his own arrival to attend officers' school
only three weeks before Hitler had launched his
Operation Barbarossa against the USSR. The city
was then full of uniforms and frantic activity.

But he certainly was not then staying at a posh
hotel as these comrades were. After they had
checked in at the Moskva hotel they all met again
in the restaurant downstairs for a late evening
snack. The man from the Soviet foreign ministry —
a young, eager type who probably volunteered for
this duty on Friday night — accompanied them to
the hotel and made sure that all the arrangements
were in order. Then he made his farewells because
the whole affair was, after all, the party's responsibility and tomorrow was another day for which he
had doubtless volunteered his services elsewhere.

They were ushered into a small room where
meat, cheese, beer, and brandy had been laid out.
After a few glasses which he downed with a belch,
the square-jawed security man assigned to the
group retired to a corner, placed three chairs
alongside each other, and drifted off to sleep. It
was, after all, a very low-level party group, and he
was satisfying two requirements at the same time.
One, specified by his superiors, was that he remain
with the group until they disperse. The other, his
own, that he get enough sleep at night.

While the rest of Czech group began to liven

up, Valery Nikolaevich for some reason had been accosted by the pale, sickly leader of the group named Novacek, who took great pleasure in recounting in an unusually dull way every World War II victory of the Red Army. He started with the magnificent victories at Kursk and Orel. At the sound of the last name Valery visibly flinched, interrupted in the pleasant euphoria of the week-end by the sound of the name of the city where he had been taken prisoner almost twenty years before. It brought thoughts of Auschwitz, the Svec farmhouse, the SMERSH officer, and the long, deadly journey to Kazakhstan.

Lately he had more or less succeeded in pushing all those memories from his mind. He was now much more preoccupied with thoughts of his Italian project, of his career, and a future which seemed to become brighter with each day.

The Czech's voice faded away momentarily as Valery struggled to push all the pain, death, and suffering back into his own, private Pandora's box.

"... but make no mistake Comrade Semlyonov, we will root them out, we will find them," Novacek's voice faded in again unexpectedly.

"What? Who? What are you talking about?" he asked, confused.

"Oh, I'm sorry, Comrade, I sometimes mumble and when it's in a foreign language it must be that much worse. I was speaking about the collaborators among us in Czechoslovakia. Even now, seventeen years after the war, we're still fighting them and sometimes in very high places. And not only fascists, I tell you Valery Nikolaevich, but Zionists, diversionists, and Titoists." Novacek was becoming more excited each moment. Valery remembered that the Czechs were still seriously looking for class enemies of this type. In Moscow they had already become subjects of jokes. But wasn't there still a massive statue of Stalin looming over Prague?

It was getting warmer, perhaps because of the mood of the jubilant Czechs, but probably also because of several glasses of wine Valery Semlyonov had already drunk.

"Where are you from in Czechoslovakia, Comrade Novacek? From Prague?"

"Well, now I have to live in Prague, of course. But I don't like it. Too many people, too much noise. As soon as I retire I am going back to where I was born. Back to the mountains."

"Where is that?"

"Orlice Mountains. A place called Usti nad Orlici. In northeastern Bohemia, near the Polish border."

"Oh yes," Valery tried to speak as matter of factly as possible. "Orlice Mountains — wasn't that where there was a fortress — the one that the bourgeois Benes government built against the Germans?"

"There were several. Are you thinking perhaps of Adam Hill?"

Valery nodded.

"Adam Hill. Sure. They spent millions on it, and then when the British betrayed us at Munich it wasn't used at all. But that wasn't the end of the whole thing. The Germans had been building their new rockets there near the end of the war. Naturally it was all closed off, no one got anywhere near the place. But there have been scientists and other people helping there. And do you know who they were? Czechs, I tell you. Lots of them Jews because you can always count on those whenever there is something dirty to be done, but there were Czechs who were getting paid good money building rockets for the Germans. And we don't have all those people locked up yet, not at all. I know for a fact there is a new investigation into the affair going on right now and that there are some pretty big Czech names ..."

"What was the name of that German rocket place again?" The news of the investigation of Adam Hill felt like a hot poker being inserted into the base of Valery Nikolaevich's brain. It didn't matter that the Czech comrade's facts were garbled. What mattered was the investigation. It must all be common knowledge among the higher ranks of the Czechoslovak party. Did they have a list of people who had been at Adam Hill? Were they already looking for Valery Nikolaevich Semlyonov?

Comrade Novacek must have been home asleep in his warm bed not far away, as he sat in the cattle car with the other prisoners of war. But all that had been buried, damn it. He had paid and paid and paid. When would it finally be paid for in full?

43

He remained with the group all next day, following them inside the Lenin Mausoleum, to the university, and on a long ride along the Moscow River. He didn't as yet know exactly why, but he sensed that it would be a good thing to befriend the somewhat dull-witted Czech comrade, Novacek, that it could come in handy. From what he had said it was clear that he knew nothing more about Adam Hill, that it had again become a military objective inaccessible to the public. The investigation of what happened there in wartime was a rumor, nothing more than at least a dozen stories of the same kind which were always circulating through Moscow. Without details, without reference to anything concrete. But occasionally some such rumor would be true. It simply leaked out prematurely because some investigating official or his typist got drunk and decided to unburden himself. That's what seemed to be the case here. Why bring up Adam Hill seventeen years after the war if there wasn't something to it? The rumor came from Czechoslovakia, a country he knew almost nothing about in spite of the year and a half he had spent there. What was happening there? Was it a full-blown investigation into the happenings atop Adam Hill in 1944 or was it simply someone making up stories over the fourth round of beer?

In addition to his boring ignorance, Novacek
was also incredibly conceited. Valery Nikolaevich
had soon recognized in him a type which was notor-
iously common in all the offices of his country: the
one which was incapable of anything but a slavish
devotion to the system. It had taken the place of
deity for such people because they knew that under
any other social arrangement — one which
rewarded competence instead of fanatical syco-
phancy — they would be relegated to the bottom of
the ladder. As repulsive as such types were, however, they could be very useful and the best use for
Novacek was already being developed in Valery
Nikolaevich's mind.

On Monday morning Valery went straight to
Sineavkin. Full of fake enthusiasm he reported on
his weekend with the Czechs, calling them robust,
dynamic types of which the entire socialist world
could be justly proud. "Tell me, Pyotr Ivanovich,
are they really all like that in Czechoslovakia?"
    Sineavkin was surprised by the question. The
routine coming and going of obscure delegations
had not evoked any sort of enthusiasm in his
department for quite some time.
    "Well, I ..."
    "Because with such types the future of our
entire western flank is assured. They were magnificent comrades, ready to roll up their sleeves and
get going on the big job ahead of us all. Isn't it
exciting, downright awe-inspiring?"
    "Indeed it is exciting," mumbled Sineavkin,
now completely torn away from the pile of papers
on his desk, cautiously gazing at the new Valery
Nikolaevich he had not known before.
    "I was thinking, Pyotr Ivanovich," Valery
pulled his chair around the table, closer to Sineav-

kin, "I was thinking what I wouldn't give to see
Prague with its hundred spires, the Golden City
with the Moldau flowing full of tranquility and
majesty through the middle of it ... I was thinking
that now that I have met some of them, made
friends, it would be a wonderfully rewarding
experience."

By now Sineavkin was watching Valery Nikolaevich with something approaching incredulity.

"... So I was wondering if you have a delegation of some sort going to Prague, if you need a
party man to lead them, someone who knows something about protocol and what to say and when ..."

The lathe operators had hardly disappeared into
their rooms at the Jalta Hotel in Prague to savor
their two hours of rest before the official tour
began, when Valery Nikolaevich Semlyonov was
already at the telephone. He dialled the number
Novacek had given him in Moscow immediately
after the "if you're ever in Prague, comrade"
proclamation.

The Czech comrade's voice not only did not
show any surprise, but he soon sounded as if Semlyonov had been an old friend who had been
expected in town for weeks. It was Novacek's great
conceit that was mainly responsible for his believ-
ing that there was nothing unusual about Valery
Nikolaevich seeking him out almost before putting
his suitcase down at the Jalta.

Valery had practiced enough to be able to go
through the entire procedure without having to
think too much about it. Initially there was apprehension as to whether Novacek's response would be
as expected, but that was soon gone. It was obvious
the Czech would agree to anything that was asked
of him, providing it was wrapped in the correct

package — a combination of flattery and an appeal to his sense of duty to the party.

And that was precisely what Valery had prepared for him. At the hotel lounge, after all the pleasant things were said about the beauty of Prague, about the efficiency of the hotel staff and the graciousness of the hosts, Valery Nikolaevich asked a few questions about the Czech's trip to his country a month ago, about his present work and his family. That produced a wallet-sized picture of a skeletal wife and two homely children, along with a chance for the Russian to comment favorably on them. He asked about Novacek's work at the party school and he immediately plunged into the Marxist jargon, explaining why education in ideology was the first responsibility of any truly socialist system.

Valery Nikolaevich nodded in solemn agreement. That was exactly the way he too saw it. "Ideological strength is our best weapon against the imperialists," he quoted someone somewhere, "but at the same time we must take care that the seed we plant goes into fertile soil." He now borrowed unashamedly from another faith. He was surprised how easily the detested shallow philosophizing came out of him and, judging from the expression on Novacek's face, how convincing it seemed to be.

"In Moscow you mentioned, comrade Novacek, the investigation your government was conducting into the wartime activity on Adam Hill. At a conference on state security a few weeks ago I mentioned it in passing to a fairly high official. He was very interested. Did you know that it is quite possible that there were some of our people collaborating with the Germans there? Well, not exactly *our people* in the true sense of the word — probably fascists from the Baltic Republics, Jews and Ukrainians — but nevertheless people who form the USSR. And he wanted to know details which, of course, I couldn't provide. Now, it is quite likely that the security people will ask your government for a report on the Adam Hill investigation through official channels. But all that will take time. Such things always do. If, on the other hand, I could bring back the information — providing, of course, that there were Soviet citizens involved — it would be quite something on my record. It would help my career considerably, you know how these things go, comrade Novacek. Doubtless it is the same here ..."

Valery Nikolaevich trailed off, intently studying the Czech's face. This point was crucial. If there was the slightest bit of suspicion, if he had somehow failed to fully convince the Czech that there was no other ulterior motive involved, then the reply could be devious. It could also be followed by informing the authorities.

Novacek was taken aback by the request. That much had been expected. But Valery Nikolaevich hoped that during the next few moments the Czech would recover, project the whole thing into his own career and acquiesce, fully aware of the importance of such personal initiative. On the other hand he could ...

But he didn't. An understanding smile eventually spread across the Czech's face.

"I'll ask, Valery Nikolaevich, of course I'll ask. I know exactly where to make the proper inquiries."

But even then the battle was only half won. What if Novacek really did stumble across a list of people who had been working at Adam Hill and what if — as was quite likely if such a list existed

— his name Valery Nikolaevich Semlyonov, was on it? What then? Would Novacek tell him? That was unlikely. In any case, it would help nothing. It would mean that the Czech comrades already knew. At best it would give him a few days of warning before the information reached Moscow. But what good would that do? It would only make the wait for the axe to fall that much more painful. Valery Nikolaevich's great hope was that Novacek would come back with the information that there was no list and that the investigation — if there had been an investigation at all — was nothing more than a shot in the dark. That would provide the relief Valery Nikolaevich was after. It would put an end to the nagging worry which had smoldered within him for weeks now, ever since Novacek first uttered the name of Adam Hill at the reception in Moscow.

What Novacek brought to the bar at Hotel Jalta when Valery Nikolaevich had completed the week-long tour of the country with its innumerable visits to innumerable castles, steel plants and various party headquarters, was something quite unexpected. It was neither the ardently desired relief, nor the immediate end of Valery Nikolaevich's career.

"It is a bit more complicated than I thought, comrade Semlyonov," Novacek began immediately after the waiter had taken their orders and disappeared in the smoke of the bar.

Valery Nikolaevich leaned toward him with an inquisitive expression on his face.

"In what way?" he asked, fervently hoping that his wildly beating heart and the excitement that permeated every bit of his body would somehow not show.

"Well, it seems that there are some pretty

highly placed people here involved in the Adam Hill thing," said Novacek mysteriously.

"Has there been an investigation?" Valery Nikolaevich tried to contain his excitement with all his might.

But at that point the waiter arrived with the two bottles of Pilsner Urquell, then poured them into their tall glasses with excruciating slowness. It seemed an eternity before he withdrew again.

"No comrade, there hasn't been one," the Czech began. "And there isn't likely to be one very soon either, I can assure you."

Valery Nikolaevich felt the relief sweep over him from head to toe. But there was something the homely Czech was still holding back.

Novacek took a swallow from his glass, then wiped the foam from his lips with the back of his hand. Valery waited until the maneuver had been completed.

"It's because there are some people involved who are high up. People who have the power to decide if there will be an investigation or not."

"Which people?"

"Frankly, Valery Nikolaevich, I confess that I am a little frightened of the whole thing. You know, those people involved are ruthless. They wouldn't mind at all getting rid of you and me if they found out what we are interested in. It wouldn't be the first time that people had disappeared without a trace in this country."

But Valery Nikolaevich was becoming more and more impatient.

"Which people?" he repeated his question.

Novacek looked down in his beer as if he were analysing it. He spoke only after few dramatic seconds had elapsed.

"I don't know. And as I said I don't think that I would want to know. It's just too dangerous."

"How do you know that there are highly-placed people involved?" Valery Nikolaevich persisted.

"Because they are paying someone, someone in the West, to keep quiet," Novacek explained in a loud, insistent whisper.

"Who?"

"The story is quite incredible, comrade," said Novacek, shaking his head to illustrate the point. "Because in the middle of the war Adam Hill had been infiltrated by a Canadian officer who posed as a high Nazi Party official. He was actually *inside* the fortress. He photographed what went on there and spoke with people who worked there. Unbelievable, eh? He even managed to get hold of a list of the foreigners who worked there."

Valery Nikolaevich swallowed hard.

"How do you know all that?" he asked. Suddenly he was in the middle of the holocaust on Adam Hill, again. Nineteen years had been erased. The mystery of the Wehrmacht major on his knees, probably dying, with the bombers above had been cleared up.

The smiling, satisfied face of comrade Novacek slowly came into focus again.

"There is no doubt about the authenticity of my information, comrade, no doubt at all."

"I am sorry, I didn't mean it that way," apologized Valery Nikolaevich half-heartedly.

"I know you didn't," Novacek patted him on his hand. "I have a friend in the ministry of the interior. He says it is quite possible that the list the Canadian has in his possession includes some Soviet as well as Czech and Polish citizens. Actually my guess is that there is no list. None at all.

That would be too dangerous for everyone concerned. I would say that the Canadian has long ago memorized the names."

"That's quite possible," commented Valery Nikolaevich, his mind still elsewhere.

"Then there is also something else. There is a man here in Czechoslovakia named Palka and another one in Poland. Both of them have committed treason and should have been shot long time ago. Except they haven't been. They are both friends of the Canadian who has many times tried to have them released from prison. Unsuccessfully, of course. My friend thinks there is some sort of an agreement to keep Palka and the Pole in prison but alive, and the Canadian alive but quiet."

Valery Nikolaevich took a sip from his glass without saying anything, but he was intently watched by Novacek. Finally the Czech couldn't stand it any longer.

"Well, then, wouldn't you like to know who is this Canadian that holds the key to this great mystery?"

Valery Nikolaevich's head snapped in the direction of the Czech.

"You know?"

Novacek reached into his breast pocket. With a flourish he brought out a crumpled piece of paper, folded in two. He unfolded it and placed it on the table in front of Valery Nikolaevich without a word.

The Russian glanced down. As plain as day he could see a name written by a soft pencil with a blunt end on lined paper: Douglas C. Howard, 2 Terrasse St-Jean Baptiste, Outremont, Montreal, Canada.

44

The revelation in Prague had left Valery Nikolaevich stunned. Aboard the plane back to Moscow he
sat apart from his group, his mind racing with
possible ideas as to what he should do, ideas which
he discarded almost as quickly as they were
conceived.

A recurring one was that of giving up. Of
simply walking to the security people and explaining what had happened during the war, where he
had been and what he had done. That would most
likely mean dismissal from his position and his
placement at some menial job. Nadezhda would
almost certainly leave him because his Moscow
work permit would be immediately revoked.

But that was only *most likely*. There was no
guarantee that he would not go to prison, this time
on a charge of collaborating with the Nazis. Death
was now, in 1963, almost certainly ruled out on
such a charge. But wouldn't imprisonment now he
was past fifty constitute a kind of death?

And it was the Canadian who after a few days
emerged in Valery Nikolaevich's mind as the one
who should be the center of his considerations, not
he himself. If Valery Nikolaevich surrendered to
the authorities because of something the Canadian
might or might not reveal, he would be a fool. It

would constitute his return among the weak ones.
He had fought for years to get where he was now. It
would be insane to abandon it all.

No, the key definitely was this Canadian
named Howard. Howard gradually became an
obsession with him. Valery Nikolaevich had only
seen him once for a fleeting moment nineteen years
ago, but he thought about him so often and so
intently that he started to imagine he knew what
he looked like. He saw him as a stoop-shouldered,
short man in a heavy overcoat and with an ever-
present cigar. A man with an all-knowing smirk on
his face. He suspected that he had been influenced
by the stylized, xenophobic image of Westerners as
they were shown in the Soviet press, but he didn't
care. Howard had become real for him. It was
much easier to think of him that way.

At first he had considered arranging a meeting somewhere, to talk with him and explain his
predicament. But soon he discarded the idea. Why
should he be moved by the pleas of a Soviet Communist official? And what would Valery Nikolaevich plead for? That he keep quiet? He had already
done that until now. And in the future? The Canadian's silence about Adam Hill depended on his
two friends who were in prison in Poland and Czechoslovakia. It was their well-being that bought his
silence, not some sympathy for the plight of an
obscure Russian Communist.

That is, if such sympathy could possibly be
evoked on the part of a Westerner living in an
imperialist, jungle-like world. Chances were that
the Canadian was a capitalist, hardened to suffering. A ruthless money-maker, well used to tram-
pling over human misery. If he had been an officer
during the war he must be a capitalist in peace-
time. And in that case he could hardly be expected

to harbor sympathy for a Marxist who had collaborated with the Nazis on a project which the Canadian had come to destroy.

Early in September Valery Nikolaevich became convinced that the Canadian had to die. Almost simultaneously with that decision came his promotion to the post of deputy chief of the West European division. It came as a direct result of his Italian liaison plan which he had completed only a few weeks before and which, he had heard from highly placed friends, had been extremely well received by the Secretariat. And it was as a result of this promotion that a plan for the killing of the Canadian Douglas C. Howard was hatched in his mind.

Initially, only the rough outlines of it were obvious. Italy would be the place where Howard would die because it was to Italy that Valery Nikolaevich could travel without much trouble. It would be easy to convince his superiors that the implementation of his plan would require a first-hand examination of the local conditions. Dozens such trips abroad were authorized each year and frequently for men with much lower rank than his.

The most difficult part would be to entice the Canadian to come to Italy. But even that was not hopeless. A letter from Moscow promising help from someone with an entree into the officialdom would surely not be ignored by him. It couldn't be. The problem was, of course, that he might be too suspicious to follow Valery Nikolaevich's suggestions without informing the authorities.

But that chance Valery Nikolaevich had to take. It was quite unlikely that Valery himself would have to do the killing. The Italian Party would certainly know of people who could be used for such purposes.

The travel permit came within a week with most importantly, the sum of 5,000 American dollars. This, in addition to his own personal expenses, had been authorized for people both within the Italian Party and outside of it for services rendered to the Liaison Plan.

45

Howard had called home earlier to tell Sybil he would not be back in time for dinner, to eat without him and to go off to her Gallery Auxiliary meeting. They would see each other when she returned. Lisette had left the table set for him when he arrived shortly before nine and she quickly brought in a bowl of his favorite consomme with a wedge of lemon on the side. While he was eating his soup he examined the mail. There was a Queen's University alumnae magazine, a couple of bills and a postcard from a friend who was spending his holidays at Martinique.

Then his attention was caught by a triangular stamp with unusual colors. He pulled it out from the pile and his next spoonful of soup did not reach his mouth. The letter was from the USSR. He studied the strange-shaped envelope made from inferior paper full of small particles. There was no return address. His own had been typed on a typewriter whose letter "d" seemed to be constantly jumping up. It was in German.

Dear Mr. Howard:

I am concerned about your two friends — Palka in Czechoslovakia and the Polish one. There may be a way out of prison for both of them, but it will have to be unofficial, without the authorities in any country taking part openly.

Of course, your government will have to be informed eventually, but initially I would like to meet with you privately in Rome. I will explain why Italy was chosen during our talk. For the present will you please note the following information:

On Monday, November 18 please check into the Grand Hotel Plaza, Via del Corso no. 126. We will contact you there.

There was no signature. The German was good and there were no mistakes in the typing. It struck Howard that the letter must have been written by someone with access to a typewriter with a Western alphabet, a rare thing in the Soviet Union. As a result it must have been at least semi-official. Howard reread the letter. Actually nowhere did it say that on the part of the Russians it was unofficial, just not openly official. And other things seemed to point in that direction. To mail as mysterious a letter as this from the Soviet Union to Canada must require official sanction as well.

Should he go? Was it safe? There really couldn't be much danger in going to Italy. He owed it to Jaroscynski and Palka who were still rotting in jail when most East European prisons were being emptied of political prisoners. Besides, he had not taken a vacation this year, there had been too much to do in the office. Howard was anxious to see Europe again. All reports from there indicated that the continent was back on its feet, that business was booming and that for North American tourists it was not only conveniently inexpensive but also only hours away. Europe-bound jet planes were taking off from Dorval Airport almost every hour. And he had never been to Italy.

When Sybil returned from her meeting he was all but decided. His enthusiasm proved to be contagious. After the initial doubts about an anonymous letter from Russia as the basis of an invitation, she too succumbed to the thrilling prospect of a European trip. Before the evening was over, all available atlases and maps of Europe had been hauled out. They were in the middle of planning their route.

Three weeks later, as Howard was picking up their passports, he paused a moment as he was putting them into their envelopes at the governmental office. Shouldn't he at least notify them that he was going to Italy and that he had been contacted by the Russians? But notify whom? It was more than fifteen years since he had spoken with the RCMP. True, there was still the gun way back in the drawer in his study, but it was there because the authorities had forgotten about it. Who knew where Langlois was now? And Denton must have retired years ago. He didn't feel like making a personal appearance at the headquarters, explaining his problem and then have some clerk spend hours searching for the long lost folder while he and a lieutenant sipped tepid coffee.

And what could they do then? Nothing. They would duly record the fact he was leaving and ask him to please check with them when he got back. At the most they would ask him to report to the Canadian Embassy in Rome and there the formalities would be repeated. If anyone went further and notified the Italian Police, there was a good chance that the man who wrote from Moscow would find out and never make contact. He owed it to Palka and Jaroscynski to give it a try and to do it on his own. They were in far greater danger.

The short, bald Italian who met Valery Nikolaevich Semlyonov at the Fumicino Airport showed
himself a devout Stalinist even before the end of
their ride to the apartment on Via Nomentana,
where the Italian Communist Party kept an unofficial residence for official visitors.

Before the war Luigi Paccini had been imprisoned by Mussolini, but he managed to escape
through Trieste to Yugoslavia, then on to Russia.
He had once spoken passable Russian but it was
now rusty and he was grateful to Valery Nikolaevich when he switched to Italian. In that language
he could better explain the predicament of the Italian comrades who had come so close to victory in
1948 and who had, since then, decided to play the
parliamentary game at which they could not possibly be any good. In that field the wily bourgeois
politicians were far more skilled than the impatient revolutionaries could ever be.

"It's not with the *parliamentari* that the power
lies, but with the *proletariati* comrade. I don't have
to explain that, do I?"

At first Valery Nikolaevich allowed the Italian
to ramble on. He was studying with fascination the
bustling city, its wide avenues and narrow, ancient
streets, all of them filled with cars and other signs
of prosperity about which the Russians wouldn't
even dare to dream.

It would have been better to keep quiet. But
under the first, astonishing impressions it was difficult. In the midst of another of Paccini's tirades
about the poor, oppressed masses, he interrupted
him.

"But it would seem to me, Senor Paccini, that
your main problem here in Italy is that you have
simply run out of the true *proletariati*."

There followed a stunned silence. The short

Italian turned to him with incredulity. Soon it changed to distrust.

"How do you mean that, comrade?"

Valery Nikolaevich shrugged his shoulders.

"Very simply! I don't see the clear-cut road to revolution here that was so readily visible in my country in 1917. You may have to build your own road to socialism here," he suggested casually.

Paccini's eyes were ablaze now. He was furious.

"So. Our own road. While the comrades here look up to the Soviet Union as our example, as our shining star, you think that we should develop our own road! You've seen where their own road has led the comrades in China — to revisionism and the cult of personality that looms over everyone the way Hitler's used to in German and Mussolini's here. Surely that isn't what you want?" the excited little Italian yelped.

Valery Nikolaevich started retracing his footsteps, but he could not help feeling that the damage had already been done.

"Of course not. That isn't what I mean at all, comrade. There are the basic tenets of Marxist-Leninism which must be followed. However, we must not overlook the various stages of development in which each country finds itself at the time of the revolution. Then we should pattern each revolution accordingly."

Paccini was not fully placated but they had reached the apartment house on Via Nomentana and their first conversation had ended. Their second one took place under much more relaxed circumstances inside the homey apartment that very evening. After a few preliminary questions about life in Moscow, Paccini asked about the Italian liaison plan of which he had heard vaguely already. The Russian plunged into its explanation stressing all the time that this was a Soviet-proposed contribution toward the victory of the Italian Communist Party, but that the final decision about the feasibility of the various aspects of the plan was entirely up to the local Communists, and that Moscow would follow their decisions. Neither of them really believed that the message from Moscow was entirely true, but Paccini sounded as if he was happy with it. He asked a couple of questions about the plan, then expressed his satisfaction with the fact they were not being forgotten in Moscow. He would report to his superiors about the conversation.

That gave Valery Nikolaevich his opening.

"That part of my mission here, comrade Paccini, is not secret. In fact, we feel that it is to every true socialist's advantage to know that we in Moscow are willing to help and give generously from the deep well of our experience in providing for the dictatorship of the proletariat."

Paccini looked up from his capuccino.

"Is there another part to your mission?" he asked, only slightly apprehensive.

"Yes," answered Valery Nikolaevich mysteriously. "And I'm afraid it has some aspects which are not particularly pleasant. In fact there is killing involved. The elimination of someone who has done great damage to our efforts. A German. A highly-placed Nazi criminal. A foreigner both to Italy and the Soviet Union."

That statement too had been carefully rehearsed by Valery Nikolaevich. It produced the expected initial effect: Paccini's eyes widened and he stared wordlessly at him, swallowing with his dry mouth, hoping that he had not heard right.

"My superiors feel that the Italian comrades

should in no way be involved. The matter could, of
course, be handled through our official representa-
tives here, but they are closely watched and
shouldn't be involved in things of this sort. Someone like me, on the other hand, who comes in for a
week, gets the job done and is gone before the bourgeois investigation begins, is ideal."

"But comrade," said Paccini in a way which
indicated a bit of fear as well as fascination with
the new development, "how do you mean — Italian
comrades should be in no way involved? I am a
comrade and I am involved. You have just told me
about it so I am definitely involved now."

"No, comrade Paccini, I have not told you who
this foreigner is and where and what will happen
to him. You should not know, there is no reason to.
What is required of you is the name of a man, a
thoroughly unscrupulous man who would be willing to do the work which needs to be done. A man
who is outside the party, who would do it for
money. When you give me his name your involvement in the entire affair will end. It is possible that
eventually the authorities will trace the connection
between the man and me, but by that time I will
have been long gone from your country and out of
their reach."

"The man is to commit murder?"

The tone of Paccini's voice already indicated
he had quickly gotten rid of his scruples, that he
regarded the job as part of his revolutionary
duties.

It was part of these duties to provide a murderer when needed.

46

There was no message waiting for them at the hotel. Sybil suggested that they did not spend the rest of the beautiful day indoors. They had lunch at a nearby restaurant and, armed with their cameras, they followed the broad Via del Corso to the solid and grotesquely ugly Victor Emmanuel Monument. Then they crossed along the charming Campidoglio to the Roman Forum. They took pictures of the setting sun against the Colosseum, one of them with Sybil clowning in the Emperor's box, turning her thumb down on the hapless Christians in the dirt below. They visited the Church of San Pietro in Vincoli and for a long time gazed in fascination at Michelangelo's powerful Moses, his hair in ringlets, epitomising timeless invincibility.

For dinner they stopped at a small restaurant on the Via Plebiscito, then followed the Tiber northward along its bend, toward the Vatican and Castel San Angelo. By that time the sun had disappeared. In the dusk the first shimmering lights of the Eternal City gave it an unforgettable beauty.

Sybil was enchanted. Her feet ached and she felt the time difference in the form of drowsiness, but she insisted that they stop at the hotel bar for a nightcap. When the waiter brought them their glasses of Cinzano she raised hers for a toast to the city.

"To Mr. and Mrs. Douglas C. Howard, Canadian pilgrims at the Eternal City. May all their days in this wonderful place be as pleasant as this first one."

She took a sip, then gave Douglas a playful peck on the cheek.

"Are you happy, love? I mean, is it a kind of dream vacation for you as it is for me? I don't feel at all middle aged. And all because of the agelessness of this place. Jesus Christ, Douglas, can you ever begin to imagine three thousand years?"

There was still no message waiting for them at the hotel but a few moments after they entered their room the phone rang.

"Mr. Howard?" asked a male voice in German with slightly unusual accent which Howard couldn't immediately make out.

"Welcome to Italy," the man continued when Howard introduced himself, "Do you drive?"

"Yes."

"That's good. Will you then please rent a car tomorrow morning and go to a place called Canato? It is a small town to the east of here, between L'Aquila and Teramo. Would you like a moment to write down the information?"

"Yes, thank you."

After a while the man repeated the names.

"At Canato there is a place called Albergo di Gatto — do you have that Mr. Howard? Albergo di Gatto."

"Yes, I have that down."

"Please try to be there about noon."

"Excuse me, but why can't we meet here in Rome? Wouldn't it be easier all around? You *are* in Rome now, aren't you?"

There was a slight hesitation on the part of the caller.

"Yes, I am in Rome. But we cannot meet here because I must first be sure that I am not being followed. I have been up until now. Have you told the authorities about the letter?"

"I assure you I haven't. I have followed your instructions."

Again a slight pause.

"Yes, you probably have. Foreigners from socialist countries are watched in Italy as a manner of routine."

"I am sorry you are having difficulties."

"It is a problem that can be overcome if we cooperate. Please drive to Canato tomorrow morning. We shall meet there."

"Yes."

"Goodbye Mr. Howard."

Next day was another cool and sunny one. Howard rented a Fiat 500 with a convertible roof and the little car delighted Sybil. They wound their way through the city eastward, toward the Pescara Autostrada. Finally they were out of the city center, driving beside the Campo Verano Cemetery toward the freeway.

"Aren't we just plain lucky, Douglas? I mean a day like this and we are on our way to the Gran Sasso d'Italia in a little toy car with its top down. It's heavenly, that's what it is!"

"On our way to where?"

"Gran Sasso d'Italia. The name of the whole region where Canato is. It was on the road map."

Howard smiled. It has been a long time since he had seen Sybil this happy.

The Albergo di Gatto was a cozy place, full of charming wooden decorations, deserted now in the

fall except for a solitary farmer who sat in the
alcove near the bar, drowning his troubles with one
glass of Grappa after another. He clearly wasn't
the man they wanted and he also ignored them
completely. But the owner was happy with the two
guests for lunch who were interesting foreigners to
boot — a type of guest that ventured to out-of-the-
way Canato only rarely. Starting with his special
mountain minestrone soup, he produced in rapid
succession some excellent pasta, veal a la Parmigi-
ano and home made Spumoni ice cream, serving it
all along with his private stock of wine.

Sybil was lavish in her praise of his culinary
powers and he in his turn did not stop praising the
charm of the Canadian signora. They were relaxing over a cup of espresso when the ancient wall
telephone rang and the signore answered it. Howard was certain it was for them.

"*Si* ... *si, si*," the innkeeper agreed readily into
the phone. Then he turned to the pair. "You are Mr.
Howard, *si*?"

It was the same voice as the day before. "I am
sorry but I can't lose the Italians no matter what I
do, Mr. Howard. I have had to come back to Rome."

Howard didn't hide his annoyance at the news.

"Listen, aren't you being a little bit paranoid
about the whole thing? I mean, couldn't it all be a
mistake?"

"No, it couldn't be a mistake, Mr. Howard," the
man interrupted him in precise, school-learned
German. "Being an East European I am afraid I
know a little bit more about such things than you
do."

"Fine," answered Howard in equally clipped
tone. "What do we do now?"

"Come back to your hotel and wait. How long
are you planning to stay in Italy?"

"I have reserved the whole week for Italy."

"That's good. I shall call you tomorrow."

There was a click and then even the bad connection they had was gone. Howard returned to the table, deep in thought.

"Aren't they coming?" asked the concerned Sybil.

"No."

"Well, no matter darling. It has been a very nice outing anyway. And there is still the way down."

He had been staring out of the window into the deep crevasse below but at her words he abruptly turned to her.

"*They* aren't having very nice outings! They have been in prison for almost two decades. Do you know how that must feel?"

Sybil put her head down.

"No, I don't."

Howard softened up.

"And neither do I. But God, Sybil, we must get them out. The war has been over for eighteen years and Stalin has been dead for ten of them. The whole Lister business belongs to another era."

"What did they say? On the phone I mean."

"The man said that he is still being followed by the Italians and that we should go back to Rome. He will get in touch with us tomorrow."

After warm farewells they went outside. The sun was still shining, but there were now more clouds and periodically they created shadow patches which raced across the scenery with incredible speed. Sybil watched one such shadow make its way through the valley deep below them. Then, without a word, she got into the car, fastened her safety belt, taking her last look at the hotel-restaurant behind them.

Howard pulled onto the road from the deserted
parking lot and geared down as they climbed a
small hill. From its top they started winding their
way down into the valley on curves that looked like
coiled rope.

On the second one, at about fifty kilometers
per hour, it became clear to him they had no
brakes. Several emergency measures occurred to
him when he floored the pedal whose lack of resistance indicated that there was no fluid. The first
one was to somehow maneuver the Fiat across the
road to the other side, to try to bring it to a stop
against the side of the mountain. But the side was a
series of jagged, unevenly protruding rocks. Before
the car could reach it there was also a fairly deep
ditch. At this speed, Howard judged, they would
almost certainly turn over. And they were in a
convertible.

They came to a piece of straight road with a
relatively gentle descent. He considered gearing
down and already had his hand on the gearstick
when, at the last moment, he decided against it. It
would mean getting the car out of gear without any
guarantee he could force it into a lower one. Sybil
still seemed unaware that anything unusual was
happening. The frantic, noisy maneuver would be
frightening. So would be an attempt to use the
handbrake. Besides, chances were that whoever
had tampered with the brake fluid had also discon-
nected the handbrake.

The straight stretch was coming to an end.
Howard decided to take a chance on what was
beyond.

The mistake became apparent as they entered
the curve. The road coiled back at a better than
ninety-degree angle. To negotiate it successfully
they would have to slow down to something like

walking speed. Howard initiated emergency measures. When he pulled on the handbrake there was no connection with the wheels: the handle gave way without the slightest resistance.

He caught a glimpse of Sybil's eyes — wide open with terror — as he glanced at the terrain to the right of them. It was the worst it could possibly be: a high precipice with small rocks piled up at least twenty meters below and ending in a clump of thinly planted trees.

The tortured, shearing sound of metal as he tried to gear down showed there was no hope. At the same time the centrifugal force was pushing them toward the small guard stones above the precipice, at first lightly, but with increasing vehemence as Howard used all his strength to make the little Fiat's wheels follow the contour of the road.

They hit the guard stone with their right front fender — an impact which flipped the car in the air, up and over the row of guard stones and the embankment itself, as if performing some sort of elaborate gymnastics.

That was the last thing Howard remembered. He knew nothing of leaving the car in mid-flight, of the Fiat landing at the bottom of the embankment, its force knocking down two of the smaller pines, then bursting into flames.

In the apartment on Via Nomentana the following morning, his suitcases packed, Valery Nikolaevich Semlyonov sat down at a coffee table after taking an envelope from a drawer in the living room. He took out his wallet and counted out exactly forty crisp, new American fifty-dollar bills. He placed them in the envelope and ran his tongue over its glued flap. Then he looked at his watch, rose, slipping the envelope in his coat pocket.

A few moments later he was out on the street. He walked to a corner kiosk, bought a copy of *La Prenza* and anxiously leafed through it. Deep inside the newspaper he finally found it. It was a short item from the paper's correspondent in Pescara:

> It was reported yesterday by local police that two Canadians, a man and a woman, as yet officially unidentified pending notification of the next of kin, have been killed in an automobile accident three kilometers from the town of Canato in the Gran Sasso.

Valery Nikolaevich folded the newspaper and placed it in his pocket. There was no change in the expression on his face, but inside there was jubilation. He was safely among the strong ones again.

He followed the busy street for a few blocks until he reached the Via Torlonia and he waited there. In about ten minutes an old Volkswagen stopped in front of him and its door opened toward the sidewalk. Valery Nikolaevich got in. Next to him a tall, muscular man wearing an old raincoat glanced at him before starting up the car again. Without a word he extended his hand toward Valery Nikolaevich.

The Russian placed the envelope in the hand and the man, without even looking at it, slipped it into the pocket in the door beside him. They drove for a few minutes, the Volkswagen turning right at each corner until it stopped at exactly the same spot where Valery had boarded it. He was about to get out again, but in the last moment turned toward the driver.

"Thank you, Signor Pirzo. The job was well done. The money is all there."

Pirzo looked at the Russian with considerable surprise. He was not used to being thanked for his services. But he did allow something vaguely resembling a smile to cross his face.

Two hours later Valery Nikolaevich's plane was in the air.

Heading east. Toward Moscow.

47

Douglas Howard was unconscious. He had been unconscious when they found his battered body lying face down on the embankment below a hairpin curve in the Italian mountains, when three men struggled to bring him up to the road, when they placed him in the ambulance, and when with tires screeching and its siren on full blast, the ambulance started toward a hospital in Pescara.

He was still unconscious when the doctors examined him, discovering multiple fractures of his limbs, possible internal injuries and a fractured skull along with a severe concussion. It was their opinion that the Canadian had been brought in only to die.

Next day a young official from the Canadian Consulate came in, but he did not go much farther than the entrance to the ward, watching the dying commander from a safe distance and being made intensely uncomfortable by the multiple tubes inserted in the body, by the elevating devices which kept Howard's various broken limbs off the surface of the bed. Most frightening of all was the machine which raised and lowered his chest with maddening rhythm, producing a low, hissing sound.

Later in Rome the young official completed a

report about his visit, including in it copies of various medical documents he had received in Pescara. He indicated that the injured man, now identified as Douglas C. Howard, a Montreal insurance company executive, was near death, that there was no need to correct the item in *La Prenza* that morning which reported that both the executive and his wife had died at the same time. The wife, of course, had died instantly. She had her seatbelt on and her charred remains were now at a funeral home in Pescara.

Three days later, while still unconscious, Howard was taken off the breathing apparatus. His condition had stabilized. The following day a decision was made to transfer him to a Rome hospital with better orthopedic facilities. He was transported in an ambulance while still unconscious.

In Rome Howard remained in a coma for five weeks. The first indication that he might be coming out was on Monday, November 25, as the orthopedic surgeon and one of the house doctors stood by his bed. Vaguely aware that someone was in the room and that something had caused him harm, Howard, with extreme effort, managed to partially raise his eyelids. Seeing the white coats, his sluggish mind accepted the fact that they were doctors. His lips barely moving, Howard whispered, "My wife, Sybil ..."

The house doctor gently took hold of his shoulder without saying a word and Howard then knew. He gathered all his strength in an attempt to remain conscious, to find out what had happened. He soon realized that it wasn't enough, that he was slipping back. His heavy eyelids closed again and he was falling into a big, empty space. But the fall was not entirely unpleasant.

The three men came into Howard's room a week later, when he was fully aware that his wife had died and that the American President Kennedy had been assassinated in Dallas, Texas. They took their seats in chairs which the nurse had set up. On the left was the Canadian attaché Langdon in a gray flannel suit, everything about him designed to attract the least attention. His tie was striped and thoroughly predictable, his shoes unobstrusive Oxfords and his hair combed without a strand out of place. Next to him was the American, Cardorna, in an equally gray suit, except that there was a hint of a pattern in his. And to destroy the entire serene effect, he wore a forest green vest, outsize black-rimmed glasses, a brush cut, and a pair of penny loafers.

Most interesting of them, however, was the third fellow, the Czech whose name Howard promptly forgot. Although he wore a dark suit, it was so ill-fitting as to be almost grotesque. Then there were the funny pointed shoes and a nylon shirt with a slightly yellowed collar that had gone out of style years ago. His large girth also didn't help matters. But dominating his appearance were two eyes, set deep but not too deep so that their sincerity and good humor would not be readily obvious. The myriad wrinkles radiating from their corners indicated he must have smiled a lot.

It was soon obvious that the Canadian had not much to say following the introduction. The matter seemed to have political overtones which took it beyond his training and (he felt) competence. He was plainly uncomfortable. But Cardorna was right at home. He outlined the Lister story from its beginning, relating it to Howard's experiences and leaving out any references to the East Europeans who worked on Adam Hill. He had done his homework.

"Why did you kill my wife?" Howard suddenly interrupted him, staring at the Czech.

There was a moment of stunned silence. The Czech looked at the floor without a reply and the embarrassed Canadian gazed out of the window. But the American spoke.

"We're convinced, Mr. Howard, that it was neither the Czechs nor the Poles who killed her."

"Why?"

"Because we have examined their motives from every possible angle and, frankly, we have not yet been able to find one which would make sense."

"The Communists often don't make sense, Mr. Cardorna. That shouldn't be such big news to you," said Howard, his eyes still on the Czech.

"No, I disagree. They always make sense. But sometimes one has to get out of our own framework of thinking to see it," said the American.

"If I may say a few words," the Czech suddenly came to life with excellent English. Cardorna nodded, as if officially relinquishing the floor to him.

"Commander Howard, we know all about the drained hydraulic system but in order for us to have done it, it all would have to provide some sort of an advantage for our side. It does not. The agreement has been kept for fifteen years. Pens and letters crossed the ocean while British diplomats made sure that Palka and Jaroscynski were alive and well. You have also kept your word. To this day no one knows anything about Operation Lister. What would be the purpose of trying to kill you now?"

Howard had gone over the puzzle many times

himself. The Czech was right, they had no motive.
Neither did the Poles. But the loss of Sybil, the
thought he would never again enjoy her irreverent
humor, never again feel her warm hand on his
forehead, watch a smile spread across her face the
like the opening of a gaily colored fan, that all of it
was lost, was unbearable. Even more so when the
motives for it all were so obscure.

"Maybe not the Czechs and the Poles, but what
about the Russians? Everything has always been
orchestrated from Moscow anyway," he said.

"Well, not exactly in this case," Cardorna
interjected. "At least none of our investigations
have ever uncovered the slightest bit of Soviet
intervention so far as Palka and Jaroscynski were
concerned. Oh, they were probably kept informed
as a matter of routine, but they don't seem to have
taken an active part."

"There is always the first time," said Howard
acidly. "After all, my invitation to come to Italy
was sent from Moscow."

"Yes, there is. For everything." Cardorna
agreed. But that left the conversation without any
place to go.

The Canadian coughed slightly to indicate his
discomfort. The Czech finally broke the silence.

"I think I should be the one to tell you: Lieutenant Jaroscynski is dead."

Howard didn't reply right away. It seemed
unreal, almost as a joke that the Czech would give
him the news only a moment after professing his
country's innocence.

"Well, that fits right in then ..."

"I know what you think, but it doesn't," said
Cardorna quickly. "Stanislaw Jaroscynski died of
natural causes. Of pneumonia with complications.
The Polish government even went so far as to pay

the way for an English doctor to come and examine him the night before he died. When Jaroscynski was already critical."

Another pause. The Canadian recrossed his legs without redirecting his gaze. Howard was thinking about what the American had said and for the life of him he couldn't come to any definite conclusion. It had been the biggest exertion he had been subjected to since his accident and he was tired. His head ached. Was the American right? And what difference did it make when he would never see Sybil again!

"We are genuinely sorry, commander," the Czech interrupted his thoughts.

"Sorry?" Howard shot out at him. "That's nice. You're sorry now that you have killed him. Oh, you may be right, he died of complications following pneumonia, but you have held him in prison for almost two decades now and *you* must bear the responsibility of his death. How old was he? Not yet forty and he spent most of his adult life behind bars. Because your monstrous propaganda machine wouldn't function efficiently without it. Well, it still isn't functioning too well, in spite of everything. Jaroscynski is dead and Palka is in a Czech prison and in spite of it everyone seems to be well aware that you have a rotten system."

"I accept the blame, commander," said the Czech solemnly after a while, "but things are being done to correct the wrongs of the past. Stalin is no longer our ideal. I assure you he never has been my personal one."

The Czech seemed unusually understanding as if he had expected the outburst all along. And although in some ways he reminded Howard of the Pole Cybulski during their talk at Mount Royal fifteen years before, there was one difference: the

Czech might have had reservations about the system he worked for, but it was not entirely for selfish purposes. There seemed to be no indulgence in luxury here, no manicured hands, no camel's hair coat, nor the language and mannerisms of the upper classes. Although the man had said relatively little so far, Howard couldn't help being impressed by the sincerity with which he said it.

"But all that still won't bring my wife and Stan back to life, will it?" asked Howard in a considerably more conciliatory tone.

The Czech started to look at the floor again, but then thought better of it. His head came up.

"My government has last week released Jiri Palka from prison as a good-will gesture, Mr. Howard," he said softly.

"Out of prison?" asked the incredulous Howard, staring at the Czech. The news was so unusual, so joyful, that his mind found it difficult to accept.

"Yes. He is well, living in Prague with his wife."

"Could I see him?"

"Yes, of course. If you come to Czechoslovakia ..." But the American was already beginning to raise his hand in protest.

"That wouldn't really be such a good idea. We would prefer for everybody's safety if you didn't go behind the Iron Curtain, sir."

The Czech was visibly annoyed with the Iron Curtain designation.

"He will be perfectly safe in Prague ..." he began.

"Yes. Probably. But there's still some danger."

"Could we meet somewhere else, say in Austria?" asked Howard, watching the Czech anxiously for his answer. He seemed to be mulling over the request in his mind for some time.

"I don't know," he said finally. "I'll have to ask."

48

At Wullowitz, pacing back and forth in front of the weatherbeaten building which housed the Austrian border offices, Howard thought about a lot of things. He thought about central Europe and how his fate somehow seemed tied to it, about the drastic changes in his life during the past few months, about how he would manage to cope with his desperate loneliness now that Sybil was gone. Looming behind all this were unanswered questions about Sybil's murder.

Except for the red scar still visible just below his right ear, he was fit again. He still seemed to be favoring his leg, but the Italian doctors assured him it was only temporary, that limbs which have been encased in heavy casts take some time to recover their vitality.

It was cold at Wullowitz. A light wind was up and it chased small clouds of snow in circles. But there wasn't much snow and the road was completely clear. The Czechs had chosen Wullowitz rather than more frequented crossings closer to Vienna because they wanted the meeting to attract as little attention as possible. The time for Palka's arrival had been set for 10 A.M. There were still a few minutes left. It was unlikely that the Czechs would let him cross over before the appointed time.

They liked to give the impression of being totally in charge.

A bit to the side was parked a large, blue BMW whose engine periodically started to operate the heater. Inside were three men — the ubiquitous Cardona from the U.S. Embassy in Rome, an Austrian plainclothes policeman and a Canadian diplomat. Jiri Palka was to visit Austria for eight hours. As a guarantee that he would come back, his wife and son remained behind in Prague.

Howard looked toward the Czech side where everything was still quiet. The steel barrier remained down and the guard seated next to it was immobile. He wondered what Palka looked like after all these years. In his mind there was still the picture of a tall, bewhiskered man of few words, exuding determination and dependability. Certainly a romantic figure and one that closely resembled such types as portrayed by Hollywood movies. What have the terrible contrasts of the past twenty years done to him? In a few moments they would meet, Palka just out of prison, Howard full of personal tragedy. Would they understand each other?

There was a sudden flurry of activity on the other side of the border. From a car that had just arrived in front of the Czech administration building two figures emerged. A guard with a submachine gun slung across his shoulder started a short conversation with them. One of the figures then remained behind, leaning against the official-looking car, while the other started toward the metal barrier along with the guard. The man at the barrier snapped into action, raising it quickly, standing at attention as the two men passed by him.

On the Austrian side, three doors of the BMW

flew open and the men spilled out of it, straining their eyes to identify the two figures which were now walking at a leisurely pace across the no-man's-land between the two barriers. The civilian was unmistakably Palka, his body slightly bent, but the walk still proud, confident. In a flash Howard recalled the first time he had seen him. He had arrived at Hana Dykova's house, covered with snow, and was rather roughly handled by the parachutists. But he didn't mind and eventually congratulated them on being so cautious.

Halfway between the barriers the figures paused. There was a brief exchange, then the guard turned to go back to the Czech side. Palka continued alone into Austria.

Two Austrian border guards came out and stood awaiting the Czech in the middle of the road. Howard took a few steps until he was directly behind them. Eventually Palka recognized him. He grinned. He waved.

Pausing in front of the Austrian guards, he said simply,

"*Ich bin Jiri Palka.*"

The older of the two guards stepped out of his way, indicating with his hand that the way was open, and said, "*Bitte schon. Wilkommen in Osterreich.*"

Howard and Palka now stood facing each other. The Czech's head was uncovered, his snow-white hair slightly mussed by the swirl of the wind. There were innumerable wrinkles in his face, but on the whole it conveyed a feeling of serenity, of a man who had taken careful stock of his abilities and fate, matched them against each other and found himself at peace with the result.

They remained standing there for a moment, hesitating. It was Palka who first opened his arms and they greeted each other in a warm embrace. Still without a word, Howard led Palka toward his Volkswagen, opened the door for him. Then he got in on the other side and steered the car away from the border.

"Twenty years and ten months, commander, that's how long it's been. Twenty years and ten months."

"Let's try to make it a bit sooner next time, eh?" Howard attempted a joke.

Palka smiled, opening the heavy overcoat in the warmth of the car.

"I assure you that I couldn't make it any earlier. The matter was almost entirely out of my hands," Palka continued in the same vein. "By the way, where are we going? I am told by our boys that they only give me eight hours with you. They probably feel I could be easily infected by capitalism. After all my experiences, I am highly susceptible, you know."

The Volkswagen wound its way along the road southward. Through the rear window Howard could see the trio in the BMW behind them, following them at a discreet distance.

"To Freistadt, about seventeen kilometers from here. We have a table reserved there until five o'clock this afternoon."

"Good. Freistadt, Free City. I like the sound of the name." The satisfied Palka settled himself in his seat.

Palka surprised him by how little bitterness he felt about his imprisonment. He spoke about his wife, a former university teacher, who had been employed as a waitress for years and now was a manager of a cafeteria. And about his son who only now, five years late, had been finally allowed to study. He was preparing to enter university.

"He's the son of a class enemy," said Palka with gusto cutting into a large Wienerschnitzel at a restaurant on Freistadt's roomy city square. "Unfortunately for him, he seems rather proud of it. Do you have the quaint concept of class enemies in Canada? From what I hear you don't."

"No, I'm afraid we don't. Was prison bad?" Howard asked and immediately felt embarrassed by the banality of the question. But Palka did not seem to notice.

"I suppose all prison is bad because it takes a chunk out of your life which no one can ever replace. But, compared to some of my friends who ended up in forced labor camps, mining uranium in Jachymov or rotting away at Leopoldov in Slovakia, I was lucky. I was in Prague. They had to keep me well fed, otherwise the Englishman would be angry. That was one of the hard parts, keeping track of the names of the British attachés who kept changing every few months," Palka said with a twinkle in his eye.

Suddenly he stopped eating. Placing his fork and knife on the side of plate, he looked up at Howard.

"I am very thankful to you, Douglas. What you have done for me cannot ever be repaid. I am deeply sorry about your wife. Her death seems to be the standard price nowadays one has to be prepared to pay when dealing with the Soviets. They are barbarians."

"What are you going to do now that you are out of prison?" asked Howard, partially in an attempt to change the subject.

"Whatever they let me," Palka shrugged his shoulders. "I am sure there will not be too much choice. Furtunately, I place more importance on what a man is than on what he does."

"Are you all right? I mean as far as health is concerned."

Palka finished his last piece of meat with a flourish.

"Fine. No problems."

The Czech looked at Howard.

"Have they been hunting you all this time?" he asked.

"Not all the time. On and off. Apparently they tried to get rid of us when we were in Germany in 1946. In 1947, on Fifth Avenue in New York and in broad daylight, a notorious gangster family sent their boys to gun me down. Since then it has been pretty quiet until November in Italy . . ."

Howard trailed off, the thought of Sybil producing a lump in his throat.

Palka sighed.

"Did you love Hana Dykova?"

Howard looked up in surprise.

"Yes, I think I did," he said without much hesitation.

"Of course, we all loved her. She was something so beautiful and morally sound that nowadays one seems to meet people like that only in nineteenth-century romantic novels. And you, dropping from the sky, so sure of yourself, heroic. You must have seemed perfect to her."

"Not so heroic," protested Howard. "My knees were shaking all the time."

Palka smiled.

"Aah, but you kept them from being noticed, that was important," he said.

The waiter came, with two pieces of sugar-sprinkled strudel. A moment later he came back with coffee.

Time had mellowed Palka. It had also added humor, thought Howard. Or it may be that he had been like this all along. The two occasions they had met before there had been deadly serious business to be taken care of and no time for laughter. The man's calm, when every bit of his past should have made him exactly the opposite, was remarkable. Howard found himself regretting they had only eight hours together.

Palka finished his dessert, lit a cigarette and settled himself more comfortably in his chair. This was the moment Howard had been waiting for.

"Jiri, it's so long since I talked to the Americans in Washington about Operation Lister that I thought they had lost all interest. But while I was in hospital in Rome I was told that they had created a fund for the survivors. You are mentioned to the tune of 300 dollars a month for life."

Palka's eyes widened.

"Three hundred a month? That's about 8,000 crowns! Do you know what is the average wage in Czechoslovakia?"

Howard nodded and smiled.

"I know. I looked it up. Less than two thousand."

"Well, that certainly calls for a drink," Palka said enthusiastically. He called the waiter and ordered cognac.

"The best is yet to come," said Howard. "There is also a large sum of money to be used by you, should you want to come to the West to live."

Now Palka stared at him in utter disbelief.

"You must be careful with me, Douglas. I am not used to this. For the past sixteen years good news meant nothing more than an extra blanket in January ..."

"You're entitled to 25,000 dollars. Do you think that you might ever make use of it?"

"I don't know ... Things are improving at home. Just now the man at the border actually called me mister. Not comrade, but mister. That's progress of sorts. I guess the worst is behind us now. But to go out, to leave? That's a hard decision. At the moment they are watching me and my family day and night. But even if there was a chance, I don't know if I would go. I am fifty-eight, you know. That's fairly late to start again."

"You have a point ... But the money is there. Should you want to come out, all you need to do is go to the nearest U.S. Embassy."

Palka paused a moment as the full meaning of the arrangement made its impact.

"Please tell the Americans that I am deeply grateful. That they have made my approaching old age much happier."

Howard nodded.

"Douglas," Palka asked after a while, "do you ever wonder why you are still here? I mean after Hana, Tom Evans, Vitek, your wife, and now Jaroscynski in Poland?"

"Yes, I often do."

"So do I. What answers do you come up with?"

"I usually find it hard to come up with *any* answers."

"Hmm, yet in your case I can come up with a good one. You were the leader of Operation Lister and you have written it all down. You must be here to introduce and explain your report when it finally sees the light of day."

Later in the afternoon they took a walk across the square and into town. Immersed in their thoughts they followed silently the winding, ancient streets, looking into the toy-like display windows of bakery shops and hardware stores. Finally they stood in front of a baroque church.

"Are you a Catholic?" asked Palka.

"No."

But Palka took hold of his arm.

"Let's go in and say a prayer or two anyway," he said. "It's good for cleansing even Protestant souls."

Shortly after 5 P.M. they got into Howard's Volkswagen and started northward. They spoke about Austria, about the coming winter, about Christmas only a few weeks away. But neither of them touched on the subject of their future, whether Palka was out of prison permanently now and whether there might be any more attempts on Howard's life. When they arrived at the border they stayed in the car for a while. Howard reached into his pocket and handed the Czech an envelope.

"I almost forgot: here is the first instalment of your pension money."

Palka thanked him.

"It's a good thing the comrades can't see me now, accepting tainted capitalist money," he commented.

Howard reached in the back seat and came up with several parcels.

"Here are a few presents for you and your family."

A few moments later, while approaching the lighted Austrian guardhouse, Palka said wistfully, "I am really looking forward to the time when approaching my country's border will no longer feel like approaching a gigantic prison."

Without a word they again shook hands. The Austrian guard waved Palka on and Howard watched the broad back of his blue winter overcoat recede toward the Czech side, feeling sad that his friend was once again walking out of his life. He would have been a good friend to have nearby.

Halfway into the no-man's-land Palka turned and waved.

In nearby Linz Howard returned the Volkswagen to the rental agency and got into the BMW for the ride to Vienna. The Austrian who drove and the Canadian beside him were introduced by Cardorna, who then asked how the meeting had gone. Howard replied that it had been better than expected.

Cardorna seemed disappointed that Palka had not said more about prison conditions, about fellow inmates and about the general feeling in the country.

"That wasn't exactly the main purpose of Jiri Palka's visit, Mr. Cardorna," Howard reminded him. But the American did not take it as a rebuke.

"Yes, commander, but we intelligence people never sleep," said Cardorna with mock seriousness. Even the Austrian chuckled at that one.

"He didn't have any ideas about the Italian murder?" Cardorna asked after a while. Howard shook his head.

They were on the four-lane *Autobahn* and the Austrian at the wheel increased his speed. The road was practically deserted. Cardorna made a couple of attempts to get Howard to tell more about his eight hours with the Czech, but Howard was not in a talkative mood. Palka had disturbed the placid cover which time had spread over his memories. They were now all around again, sometimes taunting, at others filling him with exhilaration and a sense of achievement. He was proud, proud to have known such men and women who ...

"Mindon, Harry Mindon," Howard mumbled, half aloud as the name came to his mind.

"What was that, commander?" Cardona turned to him.

"Harry Mindon, the British commando officer who was originally supposed to be in charge of the Lister team. He defected to the Russians in 1946. I don't know why or how, but he could very well have been behind the car accident. You see he ..."

"Sorry to disappoint you, commander, but we have already checked that one out. The British went over all their people in Russia after the Philby defection. It seems that Stalin didn't trust *any* foreigners, especially Westerners. Mindon ended his life at a forced labor camp, at Magadan on the Sea of Okhotsk, sometime in 1949."

49

Luigi Paccini finished his dinner and pushed his plate away. He rose from the table and headed through his crowded apartment to his favorite chair in the living room. After years of experience his wife realized that he was in the worst of his gloomy moods. She did not bother him, quietly going about her business of gathering the dishes from the table.

Paccini rolled himself a cigarette with tobacco he took out of the carved wooden box on the small table beside him, then lit it, taking a few quick puffs. But the cigarette did not allay his smoldering anger, the feeling that revolutionary socialism, the badly needed change for Italy, was being bypassed. That morning Paccini had read the Italian Liaison Report, authored by Comrade Valery Nikolaevich Semlyonov in Moscow.

After months of discussion, negotiations with Moscow, and subsequent inclusion of clarifications and amendments, the document had finally been translated and distributed among the most trusted Italian party members.

Paccini was one of them. The report spelled nothing but disaster. Page after page of the document advised compromise, retreat, and collaboration with forces which in their ultimate effect could not be anything but reactionary. It counseled the relaxation of tension between the Party and the Church, even cooperation with it on such things as education of youth and care of the elderly. The toning down of attacks on Italy's participation in NATO was advised and, along the same lines, the report stated that traditional ties between America and Italy were so strong that they could not in the foreseeable future be severed or even substantially weakened.

In the end the report read as if only time and not organized revolutionary effort would bring about class changes in Italy. That theory, carried to its ultimate end, would make the Communist Party superfluous. And with it Luigi Paccini. And it was Semlyonov who had created this blueprint for the destruction of the Communist Party of Italy.

Paccini heard the phone ring, then his wife answering it. A moment later she called him.

"Signor Paccini," said the caller, "this is Sister Angelica at the Sacred Heart Hospital. You see, there has been a shoot-out, no one knows why, not even the police, probably between rival gangs, who knows how these things get started, probably over a girl. That is the way it often starts, a girl who takes a liking to one of them and ..."

"Sister Angelica," Paccini interrupted her wearily, "I assure you I didn't start the quarrel."

"Oh no," the humorless Sister Angelica quickly apologized. "I didn't mean that. I didn't mean that you might have ..."

"Well, then what the hell do you mean, Sister Angelica? Why are you calling me?" Paccini bellowed angrily. He did not care much for women, least of all nuns.

A moment of stunned silence followed. Paccini

was about to put down the phone when an entirely different Sister Angelica came back on the line.

"A wounded man, signore. He's dying, will not be with us much longer. Father Campagnolo is with him now, performing the Last Rites."

"I'm truly sorry, sister, but we all have to go sometimes ..."

"He keeps asking for you. His name is Niccolo Pirzo."

In the reception hall Luigi Paccini sat down on the uncomfortable bench and stared at the crucifix directly in front of him with a badly carved suffering Jesus on it. He didn't like hospitals with their antiseptic smell and soft-stepping personnel, but most of all he disliked Catholic hospitals. Here the church had found a way to tie its boat to human suffering — a potent force. It then proceeded to use it against everything which was progressive, that sincerely wanted to alleviate human misery once and for all. He was in the midst of a careful examination of the faces of those seated around him when a white-clad nun, rosary swinging by her side, beckoned to him from the doorway.

Her face seemed hard. She certainly had no compassion for Paccini who suspected that this was Sister Angelica even before she tersely introduced herself.

"This way," she said, then made sure she remained several steps in front of him as they walked through the high-ceilinged corridor, then up two flights of steps. Finally she stopped at a high, double door, only one side of which opened.

"Signor Pirzo's Room. Please do not stay long."

Niccolo Pirzo lay on his high bed, apparently asleep.

No injury was visible but his face was ashen,

haggard. A stainless pitcher with a cup stood on the night table beside him and an oxygen tank was nearby. Otherwise the room was bare.

Paccini advanced toward the bed in short, soft steps, until he stood alongside, gazing at Pirzo's face. The stubble on his face made him look even more dismal. Pirzo must have sensed someone else's presence because he opened his eyes with a great effort to look at the intruder.

"Signor Paccini ... I must tell you something ... something I've done, something terrible ..." came from his parched lips in the form of a whisper.

"A little water please," he pleaded. Paccini poured some into a cup, then held it up to Pirzo's lips. But the wounded man was unable even to raise his head. Paccini had to help, in the end pouring some water directly into the man's half-opened mouth.

After a while Pirzo continued.

"The Russian you sent ... for whom I killed ... tried to kill the Canadian and his wife. I didn't like, didn't like at all."

"A Canadian? What Canadian?" asked the confused Paccini. "There was the Nazi — the German ..."

"No, no, signor Paccini. There was no German," whispered the dying man. "Only the Canadian and his wife. His wife was always with him ... always ... there was no chance to ... she was always with him ..."

Paccini waited for Pirzo to regain some strength, his mind meanwhile racing with questions he would like to have asked Semlyonov.

"She was so beautiful ... not young but happy, always smiling and dressed like a contessa ... bellissima"

"What was his name, the Canadian?"

"Howard, Douglas Howard from Montreal ... But he wasn't killed, he is alive."

"What about her?" asked the impatient Paccini. "What happened to her?"

Pirzo's eyes suddenly opened wide, as if with terror from the vision of hell into which he was about to descend.

"I killed her, signore ... burned to death in a car wreck ... I killed her ... I didn't want to but the Russian insisted there must be a car wreck ... that they both die."

Paccini looked around the room for a chair but there was none. His knees were shaky.

"Signor Paccini," Pirzo continued with an effort, "you must know ... the Russian is bad, a murderer ... he made me kill her ... God save my soul, Hail Mary full of grace, the Lord is with thee. Blessed art thou among women ..."

Pirzo trailed off, lapsing into unconsciousness. Paccini stood by the bed for a few moments, looking at the injured man, but his eyes were not focused. He was not thinking about him at all.

Early in the morning, after a mostly sleepless night, Paccini returned to the Sacred Heart Hospital, his mind filled with questions about the Canadians and Valery Nikolaevich Semlyonov. At the reception desk he asked to see Niccolo Pirzo.

"I am sorry, signore," the young sister on duty in the deserted reception hall smiled at him with compassion, "Signor Pirzo died during the night . . ."

50

Valery Nikolaevich Semlyonov was intrigued by
the foreign-looking envelope with an Italian stamp
and he pulled it out from the official stack of mail
that had been placed on his desk. It was addressed
to him personally. Without reaching for the letter
opener Semlyonov tore it open with his forefinger.
Then he sat down behind his desk and started to
read:

Dear Valery Nikolaevich!

Just before Pirzo died last night he told
me about the Canadian Douglas Howard. So
now I know that there was no Nazi war criminal to be executed, but someone who probably
stood in your own, personal way and who had
to be murdered as a result.

Douglas Howard is still alive. Tomorrow I
will be going to see Ambassador Sirin to tell
him about the private score you came to Italy
to settle. He will handle it from there.

I only want to add a personal note: So far
as I am concerned there never was a Communist Party member Valery Nikolaevich Semlyonov, only a common murderer by the name.

Luigi Paccini

He remained seated in the same position with
the letter in his hands long after he had finished

reading it. His mind was filled with disorganized, panicky ideas which he was doing his best to subdue. In the middle of all the chaos there suddenly appeared a light which could be showing a way out.

It was Sirin.

Ambassador Yevgeni Pavlovich Sirin wasn't in Rome where he could talk to Paccini. He had been in Moscow for a week now. Two days ago Valery had been at a meeting where Sirin said he would not be going back to Rome until tomorrow — Sunday. Since Semlyonov had heard from no one, it was likely that no one in Moscow as yet knew anything about Pirzo and the Canadian commander named Howard. Not yet, because Paccini was not likely to tell the story to some chargé d'affaires. He would wait until Monday when Sirin was back.

Valery couldn't be absolutely sure about that, of course, but it really didn't matter. He would proceed as if no one knew yet because he had nothing to lose. His back was to the wall and he had to fight. And he had until Monday to come up with a plan.

One idea he discarded right away: there was no chance of going to Rome and somehow silencing Paccini. No chance at all.

His thoughts turned in another direction. Walking into the adjoining office, he took an Aeroflot timetable from his secretary's desk. It was Saturday and well past noon now and she had gone, along with practically everyone else in the building.

At first he thought of Scandinavia. He poured over the Swedish and Finnish timetables. There were plenty of flights but he had to have a reason. Something plausible.

He leafed absentmindedly through the pages,

trying to concoct a story that would make sense.
No, it had to be more than plausible. It had to be
absolutely foolproof in order to withstand the
tough scrutiny it was likely to get.

His eyes caught sight of the word Turkey. Yes,
of course. Turkey. Ankara and Zemyatin. Zemyatin had returned to Moscow from Italy only two
months ago and spent practically the entire time in
Moscow at the foreign ministry, pulling strings
and pleading for another assignment abroad.
Then, two weeks ago, he had flown off to Ankara as
the new cultural attaché.

Valery sat back in his chair to compose himself. The next step was crucial. Absolutely everything depended on it. A few moments later he
dialed the number and a woman's voice answered.

"I am sorry to disturb you, but could I please
speak to Alexander Maximovich? It's very, very
urgent."

Even the name sounded strange. They hadn't
spoken for years.

When Ripkov heard his story he was full of
suspicion. There was also an understandable desire
on his part to stay out of the whole thing. "What
about your division chief?"

"I can't find him anywhere, Alexander
Maximovich."

(That's because he was at his dacha at
Ochotino.)

"I think you should inform the KGB. I have a
number ..."

"I know the number, Alexander Maximovich.
But if I call it then the entire affair will be out of
our hands. We are most anxious that our present
excellent relations with the Italian party not be
jeopardized in the process. Before Paccini is rendered harmless he should be talked to by someone

he knows. I am sure that the whole thing can be handled without the use of guns or fists."

"What is your plan, then?"

"Once in Ankara I will search out Paccini. The man who wrote said where he is likely to stay. I will see him and try and reason with him. I know Paccini. I have downed many a glass with him."

"Why exactly would this Paccini want to kill Zemyatin?"

"He thinks that Zemyatin was behind our Italian Liaison Report which calls for complete destalinization. Because Paccini is an unreconstructed Stalinist it cost him his job."

"I have seen the report. But I was under the impression that you were its author."

"Yes, but Paccini has no idea."

"What if you don't succeed in convincing Paccini?"

"Then the others will have to take over. But at least we will have tried."

There was a pause. Ripkov was obviously mulling it over. Finally he asked Valery if he had a valid passport, then told him to stay by the phone.

In five minutes he called again.

"At the airport ask for Captain Nikolaev. He'll get you aboard."

"And the Turks?"

"That will be a harder nut to crack. You may have to wait at the airport in Ankara before we convince them."

But it had been a pro forma question. Valery was not at all worried about the Turks. He knew that while he was on his way to the airport Ripkov would make at least one more phone call to the embassy in Ankara to find out if there really was a Zemyatin who had been in Italy. He would then probably check with Khrushchev himself, then

with his blessing call Ankara again to tell them
Semlyonov was on his way. At that point there
might be a hitch because if they located Zemyatin
right away he might manage to throw some doubt
on the affair. Then again he might not. Because
even Zemyatin knew that Paccini was a Stalinist.

In any case the next hurdle would come at the
airport, with Captain Nikolaev. But even past him
he would not be in the clear. He would still be
aboard a Soviet airliner that could be recalled to
Moscow at any time before landing.

Only on the ground in Ankara would he be
safe. One phone call from the airport and within
minutes he would be whisked off again.

To Fairfax County, where the American CIA
had its headquarters.

A few minutes after his plane touched down at
Vienna's Schwechat Airport, the dark American
headed for the nearest phone. It rang a couple of
times before there was an answer.

"Yes?"

"Commander, it's Cardorna from Rome."

"Nice to talk to you again. Are you in Vienna?"

"Just landed."

"Do you have enough time for a visit?"

"Plenty. Actually I came to see you,
commander."

"Well, then I am honored. Will you be right
over?"

"I'll try."

Less than an hour later Cardorna rang the bell
downstairs at Howard's apartment house,
announcing himself over the intercom. On the
third floor the door was already opened and there
stood Howard in his sweater and slippers, his ever-
present pipe in his mouth.

"Nice to see you again," he greeted him, then he was ushered inside the apartment. What he saw took his breath away. The place was furnished with opulent old world elegance. There were thick Persian rugs on the floors, polished mahogany furniture, and paintings in elaborate golden frames covered the walls.

"Wow! It's a regular palace. You really know how to live."

"Global Mutual is very nice to its employees — even to those executives who retire at the age of fifty-five."

"So you're retired now?"

"Theoretically. But I have been doing some consulting for the Austrian Association of Insurance Brokers. In fact, it's become so bad that they even gave me an office ... Sit down. What will you have to drink?"

Cardorna settled himself on a low coach below a large picture of an Austrian general astride a white steed.

"I suppose I shouldn't. I'm on duty, you know."

"I thought that only applied to policemen."

"Fine. You've just convinced me. Scotch and soda."

"Why Vienna?" Cardorna asked while Howard was preparing the drinks.

"Well, I didn't want to go back alone to Montreal. I guess there's much that's still European in me. It had to be a German-speaking country but not Germany because they still tend to get on my nerves with all their efficiency and didacticism. And it couldn't be Switzerland. The Swiss bore me to death."

"Has anything been happening since Canato? I mean threats and things?"

"No, thank God it's been quiet. In spite of the

dire things your people predicted when they found out that I was going to settle so close to the Iron Curtain."

Howard put down his drink and became even more serious.

"Do you know who killed her?"

Cardorna nodded.

"We're fairly sure now. The Italian police really didn't want us to tell you. They'd prefer that as few people knew as possible."

"Thank you for coming then. Was it an Italian?"

Cardorna nodded.

"Yes. A small time hood named Niccolo Pirzo. He died last week. Killed in a scuffle."

"Have the Communists killed him?"

"Doesn't look like it. Of course, we could be wrong, but it sure doesn't look like it."

"How did you trace him?"

"With the help of God, his agents here on earth anyway. We knew that five days before your wife was killed a Russian named Valery Semlyonov from the party liaison division in Moscow came to Rome. He left again the day after the accident. At the Rome airport he was picked up by a hardened Stalinist named Luigi Paccini. And this is where God comes in: Paccini had been rude to a nun at the hospital where Pirzo was dying. Sister Angelica — God forgive her — took vengeance by informing the police that a high-ranking Italian Communist Party functionary visited the decidedly low-ranking hood Pirzo on the night of Pirzo's death."

"Have you asked Paccini about it?"

Cardorna thought about his answer for a moment.

"No. That's exactly what I came to explain.

You see, at this point we're right in the thick of Italian politics."

"And the Christian Democratic government is afraid to move in on the powerful Communists, is that right?"

Cardorna looked at him, surprised.

"No, no. It's nothing like that. As a matter of fact they'd love it dearly if they could saddle the Commies with the murder of a wife of a Canadian hero. But they'd have to able to make it stick."

"Why can't they?"

Cardorna scratched his head.

"You see, Paccini's visit to the hospital was downright stupid. If a political murder has been committed and if you are a high-ranking Communist who may be implicated you simply don't go and visit the murderer in the hospital, much less sign in with the nurse at the reception desk. And Paccini knows quite a bit about surviving, became quite skilled in it during the war. Why would he now make such a stupid mistake?"

"I don't know. Why would he?"

"We don't know either. Paccini knows. But the moment the police begin asking him he'll not only clam up but start putting up every barrier against the investigation that he can think of. At the moment he has absolutely no idea that the police are on to him."

"Then there is nothing that can ..."

"Except wait. I know it must be exasperating as hell on for you. But waiting patiently and keeping an eye on Paccini is our only hope."

Howard took a deep swallow on his drink. For a moment the two of them remained silent. Then the commander spoke again.

"So many people dead. Now, a quarter of a

century after the thing. Could it be that Hitler really put a curse on us all?"

"I think the curse has been broken."

But Cardorna thought it best to quickly change the subject.

"Are you in touch with Palka, commander?"

"Yes, he writes fairly often. And now and then there's even someone going to Prague. I try always to send something but he seems to be getting along quite nicely on his pension. Except that I miss him, I'd like to talk over the war with him again — like the old geezers at the legion back home."

Cardorna glanced at the open typewriter in the corner of the room with a stack of paper alongside it, looking very much like a manuscript.

"Memoirs?" he asked. "It's about time."

The commander smiled.

"I'm afraid it's much more modest than that. I'm simply updating my report on Lister. People should know."

"They certainly should. Well," Cardorna started getting up, "I'd better be going."

"Are you going back to Rome tonight?"

"Yes. At ten."

"That's hours away. How would you like a nice, gemütlich Viennese dinner and a bottle of Gumpoldskirchner?"

"Well, I ..."

"You've already been drinking while on duty. Since all is lost anyway, you might as well make a night of it."

Cardorna grinned.

"You sure know how to lead a young, innocent civil servant astray, don't you commander?"

The man who met Howard at the airport in Cubuk was not Cardorna. He was darker, the cut of his suit was unmistakably Turkish, and when he spoke his accent further confirmed his nationality.

But he didn't speak much. After welcoming the commander and making certain that his bag was safely inside the car, he sat down behind the wheel, guiding the silent Mercedes south, toward Ankara.

Howard really didn't feel much like talking either. This was his first brush with the mysterious East, a place he had long planned to visit with Sybil. He felt another sharp twinge of pain at the thought. Such memories left behind a residue of loneliness which sometimes lasted for hours. The modern Turkey around them reflected in the wide road from the airport heavy with traffic, gave way to narrow, drab streets. They were filled with noisy humanity and redolent with exotic and sometimes not so exotic smells.

He was surprised when the car stopped in front of a nondescript building, one of hundreds in the neighborhood. Howard expected to be taken to the U.S. Embassy or some such official looking place. The driver came around to his side and held the door open for him.

"This way, sir."

They made their way to the entrance through the thick passing crowd and past a small group of gawking urchins who had assembled on the narrow sidewalk. Inside it was dark, even darker than he expected because of the sudden contrast to the bright sun outside. But Howard's companion seemed to know his way up the long staircase to the first floor. There, in a sumptuously furnished apartment with leathery furniture they were met by the smiling Cardorna, extending his hand to Howard for a warm handshake.

"We didn't have to wait long, it seems," he said by way of a greeting.

The commander was puzzled.

"What is this all about? I didn't ..."

"Sorry. I couldn't say too much over the phone. Semlyonov has defected," Cardorna explained, offering Howard a chair adjacent to a large, darkened window, too modern to be in harmony with the rest of the decor.

"Is he here?" asked Howard, sitting down.

"On the other side of this glass. Do you want to see him?"

"Not just yet. Do you know why?"

"Why he defected or why he had your wife murdered?"

"Both, I guess," said the commander thickly. He didn't like the feeling of being so close to the man who was responsible for destroying most of the happiness in his life.

"Of course, we haven't told him that we know about his involvement in the Italian murder. But we have been carefully probing his background and got a few clues. For example that he was a POW during the war. He escaped from Auschwitz and spent over a year hiding on a Czech farm about five miles from Zamberk. You know where that is?"

Howard nodded.

"Well, I'm sure you'll find it interesting. He didn't want to tell us but he really had no choice. Better we found out from him because he knew we would try to corroborate what he tells us with our people in Moscow. He also decided to tell us he was in Prague last year with a delegation of Russian lathe operators, but we knew that already from another source. That Prague trip was strange because Czechoslovakia is out of his sphere of com-

petence. In the Western European Liaison Division
of which he was deputy chief they really should
have nothing to do with Eastern Europe."

"So what do you make of it?"

Cardorna thought for a moment. Obviously he
wanted to formulate it so that it wouldn't sound too
definite.

"We suspect that he was at Adam Hill and
somehow managed to hide it from the Soviets. As a
returning POW he spent a few years in a labor
camp, then started rising in the hierarchy after
Stalin's death. Somehow, probably through the
Czechs, he found out about your involvement and
then came to the conclusion that the only way his
presence at Adam Hill could be held secret was by
eliminating you."

"Do you plan to hand him over to the Italian
police?"

"Yes. He has a bit of an overblown idea of his
importance. Expects to be taken to the U.S., to be
given a new name and eventually a motel of his
own somewhere in Ohio. But that's only for the big
guns. He had little to tell us because he was not in
intelligence. Besides, he's a murderer and we owe a
few favors to the Italians."

"Could I see him now?"

"Yes, in a moment. I would like you to listen to
his voice first and see if it was him on the phone in
Rome and Canato."

Cardorna flicked a switch on a tape recorder
behind him. A voice asked someone in German
about his experiences at the Kahamir Labour
Camp in Kazakhstan.

The reply was slow and hesitant — character-
istic of a perfectionist, anxious to avoid grammati-
cal mistakes. But already after the first few words
Howard knew.

"It's the voice from Italy. There's no doubt about it."

Cardorna nodded and turned off the machine.

"There's a chance you may have seen him too, although I doubt it. On the other hand he probably knows you quite well. He had plenty of time to study your face in the lobby of Grand Hotel Plaza."

Cardorna turned on another switch beside him and the window next to them lit up. In the corner of a medium-sized room, on a sofa with an oriental design, was a man. He wasn't wearing his shoes and beside him on the floor lay a German newspaper. He was asleep. Howard studied his large-jawed profile but came to the conclusion he had never seen the man before. He shook his head and Cardorna flicked off the switch again.

"Let's pay a social call on Comrade Valery Nikolaevich Semlyonov," he said, rising.

Outside on the landing waited the Turkish driver. It was he who unlocked the door of the adjoining apartment to let them in. When Cardorna opened the door to the living room the commander could see over his shoulder that the Russian jumped up, startled. Howard didn't understand what it was that Cardorna was saying to him in Italian, but then he heard his own name and realized he was being introduced. The Russian's eyes widened at the sound of Howard's name. At the same time he spotted the commander in the doorway.

Feeling the door closing in on him, he made an instant decision. With a muffled scream he lunged forward and succeeded in catching both of them off guard. Cardorna flew to the left under the impact of the Russian's elbow. Almost at the same moment Howard was thrown against the wall of the hall, Semlyonov hurtling past him unto the landing.

Out on the landing the Turk had the quickest responses. A moment after he hit the floor there was already a gun in his hand, but Cardorna saw it all the way from the living room. "Don't shoot. He can't get far," he yelled.

Very slowly the commander rose, supporting himself against the wall while his head was spinning. Gradually everything started to return into focus, but by the time he was stable enough to stand without support and start walking, he was alone. The sounds of the Turk and Cardorna running down the long flight of steps faded away. Reluctantly he followed them out of the apartment, down the steps and into the street.

There he paused, the midday sun temporarily blinding him. Still, he noticed that the street was now almost empty, with the stores closed, shutters over their windows. Halfway down the block a small group huddled over a body. As he came closer he first noticed the shoeless feet, then the small opening in the Russian's neck through which the bullet had entered. Finally the pool of blood underneath.

"The Uskudarian shot him," the Turkish driver muttered without any sign of emotion. "The neck. No one knows who he is, but that's how he operates."

"Does he work for the Russians?"

The Turk nodded.

"Most of the time ... I should get a blanket."

He turned around and started toward the Mercedes. Howard felt weak. As if all the nerve ends in his body had suddenly been activated. He leaned against the building and rubbed his forehead.

Cardorna was squatting by the body, examining the wound. Finally he turned to Howard.

"Damn them! We suspected they probably

knew about this place, but it really didn't matter much because with us escorting him they wouldn't have tried anything. Of course, when he came out alone ..."

Cardorna trailed off, shrugging his shoulders. The driver returned with a coarse gray blanket from the car's trunk. He spread it over Semlyonov's body and the crowd seemed relieved now that death had been obscured again. One by one they started chattering among themselves. Cardorna rose and walked over to the commander with concern on his face.

"Are you all right?" he asked.

"I would very much like a brandy . . . I'm afraid I am getting to be much too old for this sort of thing."

Cardorna smiled faintly.

"You shall have it, commander. But then we'll have to pay a visit to the local police headquarters. We have a bit of explaining to do."